SEE ME FALL

SHE SWEARS SHE'S INNOCENT. BUT WILL
ANYONE BELIEVE HER?

SUSAN WILKINS

For Sue Kenyon, who makes it all possible.

1

Emma Harris opens her eyes slowly. A chilly dawn light is filtering through the blinds. She blinks.

No! Too bright.

Her head is pounding. Did she really drink that much?

She turns her face into the pillow and something isn't right. It's squidgy with an alien smell.

Where the hell is she? Not in her own bed.

She forces her eyes fully open and looks around. In the half light, the room is grey. And big. Not the small compact bedroom in her flat. The bed is enormous too. The duvet is striped.

She sits up in a panic. The room spins. Her head is stuffed with cotton wool. The hangover from hell. Where is she? How did she get here? In a strange bed and stark naked.

Focus. Remember.

Last night. What happened? It was a big anniversary party. The best gig her company has had for ages. She used a country house hotel near Cambridge. She'd done business with them before, so they gave her a good discount. A hundred and fifty guests for a sit-down dinner. A six-piece band. The clients were a couple in their fifties. They seemed very pleased. Told her so. Everyone was having a good time.

It ended about midnight. The hotel staff were clearing up. They'd managed the whole gig just the two of them. Just her and Amber. She doesn't drink when she's working. Maybe one at the end of the evening to wind down.

So what the hell happened next? And where's Amber?

She shoves back the duvet. It's heavy and thick. Sliding her legs over the side of the bed, she sits up. That's when the pain hits her, sharp and shooting, from her groin up through her belly. Her whole pelvis feels as if it's been crushed. She reaches down and touches herself. Between her legs, there's dried blood.

You've been raped.

But she can't remember. She can't remember any of it.

She examines her body. In the half-light of the room, it's not that clear, but she has bruises on both thighs. She touches herself gently with a shaking hand. Her clitoris, her vagina, everything is sore to the touch. She shudders with horror. Her brain is screaming.

Who did this to me?

Her eyes dart around the room and she listens. Is he still here?

There's the sound of traffic. A busy road? But inside it's quiet. Eerily so. Where is he? In another room?

Glancing around, she sees a chair. And draped over the back are her clothes. It looks as if someone has picked them up and dumped them there in a heap. Her bra is on top. Under the chair, her shoes have been placed neatly side by side, as if someone has tidied up.

Her heart is pounding. This is his place. He must still be here. She jumps out of bed and grabs the bra.

Get out! Get out now! Ignore the hurt.

Panic is driving her. She puts on the bra; her hand shakes as she struggles to fasten it. She picks up her knickers and finds them ripped in half. Her dress, her beautiful green dress, is crumpled up. It's simple and elegant, just below the knee. When she's planning an event for clients, this is what they want to see. Professional but stylish.

She's shaking all over now, but manages to pull it on. She looks around. Tipped on its side in a corner, she sees her bag. She grabs it, shoves her torn knickers and tights in it, picks up her shoes and creeps towards the door. She must get out before he comes back.

The door to the room is ajar. She listens intently for any sound. Running water? Footsteps? Is he in the shower? In the kitchen?

The hall is wide and spacious. A wooden floor. The front door is a couple of metres to her left. No sign of him. She tiptoes towards the door, praying that she won't need a key to open it. But it has a simple lock that you just turn.

The blood pulses in her ears.

She shoots one look back down the hall, opens the door, steps out and eases the door shut behind her. It closes with a small click.

Where the hell am I?

Some kind of apartment block? Upmarket. A carpeted corridor. And clean. The vague odour of chemical air freshener. She has no idea what floor she's on, but there must be a lift somewhere.

The doors are all identical. Heavy, gunmetal grey. The number etched on a neat plaque beside the bell. Should she ring one of the others? Ask for help? Get them to call the police?

But they'll know him. He's a neighbour. They'll think she's just some crazy woman. This is an expensive place.

She is a crazy woman, battered and bruised, with torn knickers in her bag and her shoes in her hand. Running down the corridor.

Only now she realises there are tears streaming down her cheeks. She wipes her face with her hand.

Just get out.

At the end of the corridor, she finds the lift. Fifth floor, it says on the wall. She presses the call button. She can hear the swishing down below as the lift ascends. It's so slow! She wills it on. The doors glide open and as she steps inside; she glances back along the corridor. No sign of anyone. The doors close. She's made it. Home free.

2

When Detective Chief Superintendent Rachel Knight received the news that she had a place on the next Gold public order commanders' course run by the College of Policing, she was walking on air. Best not to show it. She didn't want to appear smug. But once she's ticked this off the list, she can apply for the Strategic Command Course. Then it will be apparent to all her colleagues, she's the one. Hard work, discipline, sacrifice. These things matter. Out of all the officers she trained with twenty years ago, many have fallen by the wayside. Some have found their niche. But she's the one who'll make it to the very top.

This thought buoys her as she walks through the corridors of the conference centre towards the dining room. She arrived late last night. Now, over breakfast, she'll get her first look at this year's cohort. Her colleagues. Her rivals. Because to be honest, however pleasant everyone is on the surface, the reality is they'll all be vying for the same jobs over the next few years. Assistant or Deputy Chief Constable first; the jobs that are a springboard to the top slots. These could crop up anywhere in the country.

'I'm not moving to bloody Wales,' said her husband, Simon. 'Or Cornwall. Some place that's fine for a holiday, but a nightmare for anything else.'

She just smiled. They'll cross that bridge when they come to it. Simon blusters, but he always gives her what she wants in the end.

In her heart, she wants the Met. Doesn't everyone. But that's a nest of vipers. Maybe one of the other large cities, Manchester or Birmingham. Her current job, heading the Major Crime Unit for Bedfordshire, Hertfordshire and Cambridgeshire, means dealing with a lot of overspill from the London area. Plenty of London villains live on her patch. Plus, if she worked in the capital, that would resolve any problems with her husband. She could commute.

She's pondering the possibilities as she walks into the large, airy dining room. Breakfast is served canteen style. She joins the short queue. The man in front turns and smiles at her.

He's tall, handsome even, mixed race. Something quite rugged and sexy about him. He gives her a warm smile.

'Here for the course?' he says.

She nods and smiles back. He's looking her up and down. They're a similar age, fortyish. She can feel the pheromone buzz. He's wearing a wedding ring, too. Does he think she's a fool? On a course, and on the lookout for a bit of extra marital fun? Does he think they won't know? That sort of behaviour gets noticed. Coppers can drink and let their hair down. She's done her fair share of that. Had the odd fling. Not that Simon knows. But now, at this level?

Her phone vibrates. She reaches into her bag, lifts it out, and looks at it.

'Excuse me,' she says. 'My daughter.'

He tilts his head; another teasing smile. He hasn't given up.

Rachel walks towards the door, as she answers the phone.

'Good morning, darling.'

'Oh God, Mum. I was praying you'd pick up. Something awful has happened and I don't know what to do and—'

'Amber, stop panicking. Slow down. Tell me what's happened.'

Accident? Car crash? Simon's dead?

All these years in the job, she's seen most kinds of horror. On the surface, she knows how to be calm and collected. But it doesn't stop you from thinking it.

She can hear the nervous breathing.

'Emma showed up about ten minutes ago, and she's in a dreadful state. I don't know what to do.'

Emma. Of course.

At the mention of her sister's name, Rachel feels a tightening in her chest. This is bloody typical. Some bloody attention-grabbing melodrama of her sister's. And it's the last thing she needs this morning.

She takes a deep breath. At least it's nothing serious. Just Emma. The priority is to calm her daughter down.

'Darling, I'm sure it's not as bad as you think. Take a breath and tell me slowly.'

'I don't know where to start. We were doing an event last night, an anniversary party…'

Here we go. When Amber went to work for her aunt's events company, it was supposed to be temporary. A way of earning a bit of money in the summer before university. But Emma being Emma, she started putting ideas into her niece's head. Cut loose. Go travelling. As a result, Amber deferred her university place. A gap year, she said. But it's turning into more than that. Now Amber has decided that perhaps she doesn't want to study Law. She needs time to explore. To discover her true purpose. More crap fed to her by Emma.

Rachel can feel her anger rising. But she can't let Amber see it. It only makes a bad situation worse.

'... we'd more or less finished,' Amber is saying. 'It was late. Emma said I could get a lift with one of the chefs who works in the kitchen there.'

'Do you know him?'

'He's fine, Mum. He lives near here with his family. So I left her there on her own, and I shouldn't have.' She sounds really upset.

'What do you mean?'

'Someone's attacked her, Mum. She's been raped. She woke up in a strange apartment, had no idea where she was. She's really upset.'

Rachel can feel her heart thumping.

Really? More like she got drunk and can't remember who she shagged.

'Amber, let me talk to her.'

'She's really upset.'

'Hand the phone over.'

There's a bit of shuffling and her sister comes on the line.

'Are you alright?' says Rachel stiffly.

'I know what you're going to say and I wasn't pissed. I was working.'

'Just tell me what happened.'

'I don't know. I can't remember. That's the scary bit.'

'Tell me what you can remember.'

'It was an event. Wrapped up about midnight. Guests

were gone. Amber got a lift. Hotel staff were clearing up. I was, I dunno, finishing up.'

'You didn't drink anything?'

'I told you. I was working.'

'I'm talking about any kind of liquid at all. If you were slipped something like GHB, it would've been in a liquid. Tastes a bit salty.'

'Oh, well, yeah. I had some sparkling water. Left over from the tables.'

'Amber says you've been raped.'

There's no reply, but she can hear her sister weeping.

Oh shit! This sounds bad.

'Listen to me, Em,' she says, softening her tone. 'Listen to me carefully. You need to go to the police and report this.'

'I don't know if I can…' She's sobbing. Gasping for air.

Rachel feels uncomfortable. And guilty.

You shouldn't assume… but when Emma's involved?

'Hey, c'mon,' she says. 'It'll be fine. We have trained officers. They deal with this all the time. I'm going to make a call. They'll come and get you. Don't wash. Don't change your clothes. Just go as you are.'

'I'm… I'm… sorry.' Her voice is tiny, and the obvious distress rips into Rachel.

She swallows hard. This is her little sister, okay, her annoying little sister. But the idea that some scumbag has targeted her sends Rachel into a different kind of rage. But she needs to be efficient. Forensic evidence, that's how these bastards get caught.

'Emma, it's not your fault. It's not. Let me speak to Amber again.'

The phone is passed back.

'Mum?' says her daughter.

'Where's your Dad?'

'Already gone to work.'

'Okay. I'm going to make a call. They'll send a squad car and one of the officers will be a specialist who deals with sexual offences. You need to follow their instructions. Answer their questions. Both you and Emma will need to be interviewed.'

'Mum, she looks to me like she should go to hospital.'

'What d'you mean?'

'She's covered in bruises. All up her arms. And she's been bleeding. Who the hell would do this to her?'

Rachel has a lump in her throat. These are the crimes she hates the most. Sexual violence against women. And for this to happen to her own sister! She's incandescent, but she needs to be calm and efficient.

'I know, darling. I'm sorry I'm not there. But the officers will take her to a special suite at the hospital. They'll assess her and get her the medical treatment she needs.'

'Okay.'

'And they'll ask you to make a statement.'

'Me? Why?'

'They'll want to know what happened and what she told you when she arrived.'

'I don't see the point of that. She needs urgent help.'

'Yes, and this is the quickest way for her to get it. But if someone's raped her, evidence must be gathered.'

'What? You think she hasn't been raped?'

'No, I'm not saying that. Listen to me darling, stop panicking. I'm going to hang up and make the calls. You sit tight. They'll be there soon.'

'Sorry. I didn't know what to do.'

Oh Amber!

'It's okay. You've done the right thing. And listen, don't let her wash or anything.'

'Okay. Are you coming home?'

'Yes, of course. I need to sort a couple of things out. I'll be back very soon. Just take care of yourself. Love you.'

'Yeah, me too.'

Amber hangs up. Rachel takes a deep breath. This is not what she needs. There won't be another course until next year. And what can she do that her specialist colleagues can't? But it's her sister.

It'll look bad. Emma needs you.

She feels an avalanche of conflicting emotions. She needs to get a grip.

But this is not the first time she's had to drop everything and rush to her sister's rescue. Emma has a talent for turning everything upside down.

She's been raped. It's not her fault.

She looks at her phone, scrolls through the numbers, and makes the call.

3

The cemetery is still shrouded in early morning mist as Dean Jessop gets out of his car. His car? It's borrowed. But he's resisted the temptation to steal one. He's only been out a week. No point in being reckless.

He did his time, kept his head down and his mouth shut. Still, five years in prison is a long time. And that's why he couldn't be there for Kelly.

He pictures his little sister. She was a good kid, and she'd understand. Wouldn't she?

He bought some flowers at a garage; a nice, fancy bouquet. They look expensive. He opens the back door of the car and gets them out.

The air is sharp and damp. He sucks down a lungful. It clears his head. Now he's here, he feels better. In control again. On top of things.

According to the old man, they got her a nice spot, up the

hill with a nice view. Craig paid for it all. They gave her a good send off.

Fucking Craig.

But he'll deal with his brother later. It's in hand. It's all in hand. He doesn't need to dwell on that now. Kelly comes first.

He takes a piece of paper out of his jacket pocket. The jacket's borrowed too. Not the designer threads he used to wear before he got put away. It's denim; dirt cheap. He looks like a van driver. But then that's what his probation officer, silly cow, wants him to be. A van driver. As if?

He opens out the paper. It's a map of the cemetery. The old man couldn't pinpoint the position of her grave, so he had to phone Craig. That was fun.

The path winds around a bit and up the hill. There are a few trees. Tall trees. Lots of graves, obviously. No one about. Fortunately.

Some headstones are really fancy. Statues. Angels. That sort of thing. They should get Kelly an angel. To watch over her. He likes this idea.

It's a fair pull up the hill. But he manages it with long, loping strides. He may be forty-two, but he's fitter than most blokes ten years younger than him. He worked out every single day of his sentence. When they wouldn't let him go to the gym, he did it in his cell. That's what kept him sane. He saw plenty lose their nut and start taking all sorts of crap. Crack, spice; spice was the worst. But it comes down to self-control. You can use drugs to give yourself a little boost; the secret is not to let them use you. That's a mug's game.

Pity he never had a chance to teach his sister how to do that.

He gets to the brow of the hill. There's a little group of trees. Her grave is third along and it is a good spot. The marble headstone says her name. *Beloved daughter, mother and sister.*

Just looking at it makes him tear up. He wipes his nose with the back of his hand. Bloody Craig could've sprung for an angel. Mean sod. But now he's out, he can rectify that.

He squats down and places the bouquet on her grave.

What do you say? He's never been good with words. They weren't that sort of family. But that doesn't mean there wasn't love. The old man was tough, but fair. They got the odd clout as kids, but only when they deserved it. He'd done some stuff in his time, the old man, but no one could accuse him of hurting his family.

Dean was seventeen when their mum died; Craig was fourteen. But Kelly was only twelve. Far too young to be losing your mum. He should've looked out for her more, paid more attention to her. The old man was broken. That's how much he loved Mum. He ended up drinking. After that, it all went shit-shaped. No one's fault, really.

He places his palm on the marble. It's icy cold. He's seen people do it on the telly. But it just feels weird.

He clears his throat and sniffs.

'Listen, Kel,' he says. 'I don't know if you can hear me. But I wanted to come clean and admit it. I let you down. I should've kept an eye on you. Trouble is, by the time I realised it was too late. You was already with that junky bastard and already pregnant.'

He pauses and glances around. Talking to a cold block of stone must look pretty strange, but there's no one to witness it.

He rocks back on his haunches as he tries to picture his sister's face. Blonde hair. Giggly.

She lost her kids. They called her an unfit mother. That was the straw that broke the camel's back, according to the old man. But it was still down to the junky bastard that they both got nicked.

Kelly should've never gone to prison. That sticks in his craw. Should never have happened. How was his precious little sister ever going to cope with that? She wasn't.

'Don't worry,' he says. 'When that junky bastard gets out, I'll be waiting for him. I promise you that. He won't get the kids back. No way.'

There's a squawk above him. He looks up. A crow has just settled on the topmost branches of a nearby tree; it's sitting there dark and regal, looking down at him. Maybe it's true. You come back as something else. Maybe it's her, come back as a bird. The thought makes him smile. He can imagine Kelly as a crow.

Standing up, he addresses the crow. 'I'd take them myself. But look at me, Kel. What do I know about kids? You know what I'm like. Let's be honest, I wouldn't do them no good. And Craig's wife is a snooty cow. I wouldn't let her near them.'

The crow is preening. A loose feather spirals down towards him. He picks it up.

'But some nice people have fostered them and they're both together. Nice people with a bit of money.' He's making this bit up, but he wants to make her feel better. 'They've got a chance of a better life. I figure that's what you'd want.'

The crow launches itself from the branch, wings gently flapping. He watches it fly away.

Then he glances around. Graveyards are weird. No one about, yet it feels as if there are loads of people watching you. Perhaps it's all these dead people? They got nothing else to do. His head's spinning.

Losing it again. No! A crow's a fucking crow.

He shakes himself. Chucks the feather away. He doesn't

believe all this woo-woo stuff. He's not stupid. When you're dead, you're dead. That's the beauty of killing someone, you know when they're gone. You see it in the eyes. Gone. You're here, still living and breathing, they're not. It's obvious.

And he'll see that look on the junky bastard's face. And Craig's. He just has to wait. But then, revenge is a game of patience. And Dean Jessop is more patient than people think; five years inside, he's had to be.

4

Emma sits in her sister's kitchen as they wait for the police to arrive. She's still shaking. But her whole body is tense with fear and shock. Rachel told her not to wash or change her clothes. Yet she longs to just stand under a hot shower and let the water wash the hurt away.

It probably won't. She's examined her arms. Bruises are already forming, as if someone has grabbed her. She's also discovered blood on the back of her head, caked in her hair. She must've fallen, but she has no memory of it. There's a small lump.

Rachel mentioned GHB, the date rape drug. Yet who? Or where? She keeps racking her brains. She has an unremitting, throbbing headache, like a bad hangover. But she never drinks when she's working. What was the last thing before she blacked out? She can't remember.

Did you invite this somehow? Put out the wrong vibe?

A random memory pops up. Her mother slapping her legs

repeatedly. The sharp sting of her mother's hand. How old was she? Not quite five? She'd been out playing and some older kids, a group of boys, had persuaded her to take off her clothes and do a dance for them, naked. She didn't mind. It was fun. The freedom. The attention. Until her mother found out. She went ballistic. She shouted: *Never never let boys think you're easy, that you're that sort of girl.* This was followed by the slapping and the pain.

Are you that sort of girl? Is that the problem?

She looks across the room at her niece. Amber has the fresh, unscathed look of the young. Bright, hopeful eyes. A ready smile. She laughs a lot. She was a happy kid. Emma enjoyed watching her grow up. No one ever hit her.

'Do you want some more water?' says Amber. 'Or a coffee? Surely that wouldn't matter.' Her beautiful face is full of concern but also uncertainty. Their roles have been brutally reversed.

Emma was the savvy aunt, the wrong side of forty, been round the block a few too many times. She was supposed to be the one to give advice and help. She was the rescuer. When Amber was a teenager and got drunk, she'd call her aunt for a lift or a cover story.

Rachel isn't the easiest parent. As a cop, she's seen too much of the nasty side of life; she expects the worst. And she has big ambitions for Amber. In Emma's view, this is a burden for any kid to carry. Do your homework, get the grades. Piano lessons after school. Endless pressure. Kids need to hang out with their friends, muck around, fool the grown-ups from time to time. But Rachel can never see that.

Simon is hard to pin down. A good dad, but evasive. Always telling stupid jokes to make people like him. He takes his lead from Rachel.

It puzzled Emma when her sister married him. Rachel

was a real looker; always turned heads. When they were young, Emma was fascinated by her big sister. And jealous. The sophistication, the make-up, the clothes. When Rachel went off to university, she let her little sister visit. Back then, Rachel had a string of boyfriends, and they were all super hot. But then she graduated, became a cop and married Simon, which made no sense to Emma. He's a man in a suit. Not sporty, not handsome. Safe maybe?

Not that Emma could claim to be an expert on marriage. Hers had gone to shit in spectacular fashion. She and Neil are still arguing, through lawyers, over the details of their divorce settlement. The greedy bugger is insisting he should have half her business. But he's been declared bankrupt. He's always been useless with money, always in debt. What he had, he spent. And for a while, it was fun. They'd travelled a lot. He built them a fantastic house. But the bank took that.

She thinks about Neil. He's pretty mad at her. Could he have attacked her? Was this payback? Was he capable of something like this? Their last mediation session at the lawyers had turned into a stand-up row. He'd called her all sorts. A spiteful, manipulative bitch. A lying cow. He was steaming. His solicitor had more or less dragged him out of the room.

People get upset with her, really upset. She seems to have that effect, although she doesn't understand why. It's one of her mother's favourite barbs. *You have a talent for upsetting people, Emma.*

As far as Emma can recall, it's the only talent her mother does think she has.

Did you upset someone? Why can't you remember?

She looks at Amber and tears well in her eyes. Since it happened, her thoughts have been so scattered. Has she already cried? She can't remember. What she did is she ran. Barefoot, out of the building.

She found herself on a busy main road on the outskirts of Cambridge. An upmarket area of new apartments with city views. She'd scrabbled in her bag. Phone. Wallet. Still there.

There was plenty of traffic crawling by but few pedestrians. An older bloke with a dog gave her a dirty look. Some loose woman wandering aimlessly and shoeless after casual sex with a bloke she met on an app? That's what he saw. She wanted to ask his help, but the judgement on his face told her what she needed to know. This is how people were going to react.

She sat on a wall and put on her shoes. She looked at her phone. Who was she going to call? Her heart was still pounding in her chest. From the fear. From the running. She changed her mind. She recognised where she was. It was on a bus route she'd often used.

She walked. It was cold and she was coatless, wearing only a dress. But she tried to seem as normal as possible. She walked to the bus stop and caught the bus out of the city centre. She got off and walked the remaining quarter mile to her sister's house. The shoes pinched, and she was shivering.

Amber had opened the front door and Emma collapsed into her arms. The relief of a kind face had overwhelmed her. But Rachel was away on a course and Simon had left for work. It was never her intention to burden her niece with this. She thought Rachel would be there.

Now Amber is scanning her. Her eyes are damp, but her jaw is set. She's holding out a quilted jacket.

'Put this on,' she says. 'To keep you warm.'

'I just want to strip off, throw everything in the bin.'

'Mum says you mustn't.'

'Yeah, I know,' says Emma. 'And I'm sorry.'

'Sorry for what?'

'Sorry for dumping all this on you. I just assumed your mum would be here.'

Emma reaches out and pulls her into a hug.

'C'mon,' she says. 'Don't be silly. You were absolutely right to come here. I'm just mad as hell at what this bastard's done to you. I could kill him, I really could. And Mum thinks the same. I know she does. This whole thing is just horrific. But they'll get him. Mum'll get him. I know that too.'

Emma forces a smile. 'But I'm supposed to be your smart, cool aunt. Not this.'

Amber just squeezes her hand.

5

The conference centre is on the outskirts of London, so it's only an hour's drive for Rachel to make it back to Cambridge. She explained the situation to the course co-ordinator. They understood. Annoying, but necessary.

As she drives up the M11, she's ticking with irritation. Unless she can get on another course soon, her application for the Strategic Command Course will be delayed another year. She tries not to think about that.

But there's one thought that keeps seeping into her mind. This is so bloody typical of her sister. When Rachel is on the up and up, along comes Emma and throws a spanner in the works.

You can't look at it like that.

If her sister has been the victim of a violent rape, of course she's sympathetic. It's terrible, obviously. And she'll make sure all the appropriate actions are taken to bring the perpetrator to justice. But even so, she can't suppress that hint of resentment against her sister.

It's been like this ever since her little sister was born. Five years in age between them, but when Emma was born, it changed everything. Their mother became ill with post-natal depression. Rachel was shifted from pillar to post. A parade of relatives took care of her. Only when her baby sister was six months old did she get to go home.

None of that was Emma's fault.

She turns into the car park outside the offices of the Major Investigations Team. Amber has texted her to let her know Emma is in the rape suite and being dealt with by specialist officers. Rachel doesn't want to disrupt that process. Best to let them get on with their jobs.

She takes the clunky lift up to the first floor offices. DCI Hepburn has received her call and he stands up as she enters his tiny office.

'Morning, Alistair,' she says, trying to keep the irritation out of her voice.

'Morning, ma'am,' he replies. 'I'm really sorry to hear about what's happened to your sister. We'll obviously—'

She cuts him short. 'Of course you will. And I have every confidence in the team. But I must remain at arm's length from this investigation.'

'I realise that.'

'My job is to comfort my sister. That's all I can do.'

'Yes, of course. Have you seen her?'

'No, not yet. I was on a course. I've just driven back. Came straight here.'

He's watching her, monitoring her reactions. Decent, efficient, he understands the politics of this. It doesn't need explaining. He's canny too, he can see how hacked off she is. They've worked together for a long time.

He smiles.

'I must be steaming, boss,' he says. 'And in your shoes, I'd be the same. We all know what you're going through.'

Hopefully not.

She dips her head and glances out of the window. 'Thank you,' she says. 'I appreciate the support. Who are you thinking of for this?'

'DS Boden. She's sharp. Doesn't miss much. She's my most reliable DS, but I'll be keeping a close handle on things as SIO.'

'Haven't you got a DI available? What's Roscoe doing?'

'Compassionate leave. His father died.'

Rachel sighs. Budget cuts have led to a dearth of experienced detectives. The team is permanently overstretched and under resourced.

She has a vague picture of Boden in her mind. Thirties. Watchful. But with a bit of a career question mark hanging over her.

'Didn't she transfer from the Met?' says Rachel. 'Got herself in some hot water. Turned into a bit of a scandal?'

'Yes, that's true. But the other way of looking at it is that she's got a lot to prove. And since she's been here, she's certainly been focused on that. Works hard. Goes the extra mile.'

Rachel sighs. 'It's your call. I don't want to interfere in any shape or form.'

'Do you want to speak to her?'

'No. I don't think that would be appropriate. But I would like to be kept up to date. I'm sure no one can object to that.'

'Of course not. I'll tell Boden to talk to the Sexual Offences Liaison Officer. And I'm confident she'll deal with your sister in the most sympathetic manner.'

Rachel looks at him, she hesitates and then she smiles.

'Have you got any sisters?' she says.

He shakes his head. 'A brother.'

'Are you the eldest?'

'Yes.'

'Then you know what it's like. And what I mean by that is Emma and I haven't always seen eye to eye. We're very different people.'

He says nothing.

'We've led very different lives. She's five years younger, childless, and about to be divorced. It's all quite messy. She has a habit of picking the wrong men. She runs an events planning company. Quite small. It struggled through lockdown and the pandemic. But she's very good at that sort of thing. Organising parties and helping people celebrate. She is a bit of a party girl. Likes to have a drink and let her hair down. That has got her into trouble in the past.'

The DCI nods his head. 'I'll brief DS Boden,' he says.

Rachel can feel the muscles in her gut tightening.

Have you said too much?

'I'm not saying that's what's happened here. I just want to offer a bit of context.'

'Of course. No problem.'

He's waiting for her to go so he can get on with his job. But go where? She feels at a loose end. She should be sitting in a seminar room getting stuck into her course. She fights her annoyance.

It's not Emma's fault.

'Right,' she says. 'Thanks Alistair. I should let you get on.'

He smiles. 'Once the SOLO has finished, it'll be you she needs, boss.'

Rachel forces a smile. But she finds that a disturbing thought.

6

DS Jo Boden stares up at the block of flats. She's flanked by DCs Mackie and Chakravorty.

'Nice gaffe,' says Mackie. 'Not your usual drug them and drag them into the ally lark, then?'

Boden glances at her junior colleague. Or rather, up at him. He towers over her; she towers over Chakravorty. Standing outside the building, they must appear like a comic trio.

In her initial interview with the Sexual Offences Liaison Officer, the victim, Emma Harris, was able to provide an address. She knew the area, could identify the building, said the flat was on the fifth floor, probably number 27. This information was relayed to Boden.

'Are you trying to be funny, Mackie?' she says.

'He's being defensive because he's a bloke,' says Chakravorty.

He gives Chakravorty a sheepish look. 'Just saying it's not what I would've expected.'

Boden has had the same thought, but she doesn't acknowledge it.

She was summoned to the DCI's office as soon as she arrived at work. He was brief. The Detective Chief Super's sister was the victim of a violent rape. She had no memory of the actual event and it looks like she could've been given GHB or Rohypnol. The problem was the former would've already cleared out of her system.

Boden hasn't spoken to Emma Harris yet. Forensic samples were still being taken, and she required some medical treatment.

However, if the perpetrator was still holed up in what they're assuming is his flat, they should be able to move on this quickly.

Boden has only met Rachel Knight a couple of times. She's in charge of the whole of MIT over the tri-force area and has a steeliness and an air of confidence about her that Boden admires. She has an impressive track record as a detective, too. But for your sister to be raped is going to be tough for anyone, let alone someone in her position. Boden can imagine that the Chief Super would like to be kicking down this particular door personally.

And for Boden, it raises ghostly memories of her own sister. But that's part of another life now. One she's had to put behind her. Leaving London and the Met was supposed to help with that. But it hasn't. It takes an act of will to force all this aside.

Focus on the job.

She glances at Chakravorty. 'Have we got a name, Prish?'

Chakravorty reads from her tablet. 'Electoral register and council tax records say the owner is Howard Sampson.'

'Let's see if he's home,' says Boden.

Mackie is already at the main entrance. He presses a couple of random buttons on the entry phone.

'Police. We need access to the building. Could you open the door, please?' He holds his warrant card against the viewfinder. The door clicks open.

Mackie walks in. Boden and Chakravorty follow.

They take the lift to the fifth floor. It's spacious. Carpeted and mirrored.

'This is pretty fancy. Bet flats here don't come cheap,' says Mackie. 'You got your mortgage yet, Skip?'

At first, she hated the fact he insisted on calling her Skip. But she's given up arguing with him about it. Now the familiarity is oddly comforting.

She gives him a wry smile. 'How's your mum?' she says. 'Chucked you out yet?'

'He keeps telling me he's handy round the house,' says Chakravorty. 'Mr DIY.'

'It's true,' says Mackie, grinning. 'Give me the right screwdriver. I can fix anything.'

Boden and Chakravorty exchange long-suffering looks.

They emerge from the lift and follow the corridor to number 27.

'Let's hope she got the number right,' says Boden. She gives Mackie the nod. He raps loudly on the door.

Nothing.

'Gone to work?' says Chakravorty.

Mackie hammers the door again. 'Police!'

The door of number 25 across the hallway opens. A small man with round glasses, about seventy years old, peers out at them. He has the look of an owl.

'Are you looking for Howard?' he says in a plummy voice. 'Is something amiss?'

'Do you know if he's usually at home at this time, sir?' says Boden, showing him her warrant card.

The little man has a professorial air. Wayward wisps of hair around a bald tonsure.

'Well, he's an accountant. But all this working at home nowadays. No one keeps regular hours, do they?'

'Have you seen him this morning?' says Boden.

The owl shakes his head. 'We're neighbourly. But we don't spy on each other, officer. It's not that sort of place.'

'Thank you for your help, sir,' says Boden. She smiles at him and waits until he disappears back inside his flat.

Turning to the others, she sighs. 'We're going to need a warrant to break the door down. Prish, you get some uniforms to secure the premises. Scott, while she does that, you guard the door in case he is in there and thinks he can make a break for it. I'll get the warrant.'

It takes Boden the best part of an hour to return to the office, get the warrant signed by the boss and then approved by a magistrate. When she returns, Mackie and Chakravorty are sitting outside in their car. Two squad cars are parked up in front of them. A curious female neighbour is peering out of a downstairs window in the block. Mackie is munching his way through a burger.

'Where's the coffee?' he says.

She frowns at him and turns to Chakravorty. 'Any movement?'

'If he's there, he's quiet as a mouse. We've got uniforms on the door and covering the fire escape at the back.'

'Okay,' says Boden. 'We'll go in and secure the flat. Then see if we can track him down.'

Chakravorty gets out of the car and waves to the officers in one of the squad cars. They get out too; one of them opens the back and lifts out a metal door ram. They all follow

Boden into the building. Mackie brings up the rear, gulping down the last mouthful of burger and wiping his mouth with his hand.

The five of them fit in the lift. 'I don't reckon he's here,' says Boden. 'But it's the alleged scene of a rape, so we'll secure it for evidence.'

'I've alerted forensics,' says Chakravorty. 'They're sending a team over.'

They step out of the lift on the fifth floor. Boden leads the way. An officer stands, arms folded, outside the door to number 27.

'Any sounds?' she says.

He shakes his head.

She signals the uniforms. One of them steps forward and swings the ram at the door. It cracks at the second blow and Mackie pushes it open.

'Police!' he shouts. 'Are you at home, Mr Sampson?' He steps inside. Boden follows.

She glances around. Everything feels very still. There's a central hallway. Prints on the walls, furniture that might be classed as antique. As they move into the flat, she notices a faint smell; dry and rusty.

She's peering into the bedroom on the right, a king-sized bed with rumpled sheets, when she hears Mackie's voice. Loud and urgent.

'Down here Jo! Kitchen.'

Boden hurries down the hall in the direction of his voice.

Mackie is standing in the doorway.

In the middle of the kitchen floor there's the body of a man, middle-aged, wearing only boxer shorts. His throat has been cut and a large puddle of congealed blood surrounds his head.

The smell. Of course.

Boden sighs. 'Right,' she says. 'Not quite what I was expecting.'

7

Emma Harris walks across the hospital car park to her sister's car. She feels exposed and raw. The officers were kind. She couldn't fault them.

The rape suite was a private room, all pastel shades, a bit like an upmarket dentist. There were two of them, both female, one stout and matronly, the other young and nervous. Possibly a trainee. They explained the process for taking forensic samples. In the end, it was no worse than a trip to the gynaecologist. The worst had already happened.

A doctor came and checked her over. She was young, but matter-of-fact. They'd do a test for HIV and various STDs. There was no serious internal damage, although she'd bled a bit. The bruises should fade. The cut on her head was cleaned. It didn't need stitching. They offered her paracetamol. Photos were taken. Reports would be written. Emma got through it in a daze. It all seemed to happen around her.

Rachel walks beside her. 'Are you alright?' she says.

Emma glances at her sister.

Rachel has the grace to shrug. 'You know what I mean,' she says.

'Everyone's been very kind,' Emma says. 'I can't fault the process, if that's what you're asking.'

The reality is the specialist officers were the easiest to deal with. It's just everyone else who's embarrassed and awkward.

Especially Rachel.

Rachel clicks the key fob to unlock the car. Amber hovers behind. 'You sit in the front, Emma,' she says.

Emma looks at the car; plush, expensive, shiny paintwork, and leather seats. Jag? Merc? Some such?

'New car?' she says.

'Oh, you know what Simon's like,' says her sister. 'He's obsessed with anything on four wheels, and always finding deals.'

They all get in. Emma settles in the soft dark leather, which envelopes her in luxury. It smells of new car.

Rachel backs out of her slot. She drives with confidence, but in Emma's view, a bit too fast. Somewhere back during her meteoric rise through the ranks, she did advanced driving courses. Emma has the sense that there's still a part of Rachel that would prefer to be screaming through the streets, lights flashing and siren blaring.

They turn out of the car park and onto the main road.

'I thought we'd go back to ours, so we can look after you,' says Rachel.

'I appreciate the thought,' says Emma. 'But I'd rather go home. Have a bath, a change of clothes.'

And a stiff drink or two.

But she doesn't say that.

'You can have a bath at ours,' says her sister. 'And we'll

go round to your flat and get whatever you need. I've called Simon. Told him to come home.'

'Why?' says Emma. 'I'm not a bloody invalid.'

Rachel is doing her usual thing. Taking control. Which Emma hates.

'Emma, you're in shock. I just want—'

'Yeah, I get that. And I'm grateful for all you've done this morning. But I've got a business to run, calls to make.'

'I can do that,' says Amber.

Emma tries to suppress her irritation. She turns round in her seat to glance at her niece. 'You've been brilliant. And I really appreciate it. But I want to be on my own. Just, kind of, y'know… calm myself down.'

Amber smiles, reaches over and squeezes her shoulder.

'Okay,' says Rachel. 'No one's trying to railroad you. We're only trying to help. Have you got the heating on in your flat?'

'It's on a timer. But I can override it.'

Emma knows what her sister thinks about her new flat. She made her views very clear when Emma moved in.

'My God, Emma,' she said. 'It's damp, it's pokey. You can't live here.'

What Rachel didn't seem to realise was that in the messy fallout from her divorce, she couldn't afford to live anywhere else.

Neil's construction business turned out to be a house of cards, and it all came crashing down overnight. He was loaded in debt, maxed out on his credit cards; none of which he'd communicated to Emma. Not that they were talking much by then. The bank foreclosed on their house.

With the aid of a lawyer, Emma was able to protect her own business from his creditors. He was now living with his mother.

They travel on in silence for a couple of miles. Emma feels lightheaded. Maybe that is the shock. She notices her sister glancing at her.

'Have you got food in?' Rachel says. 'Something light and nutritious is what you want.'

Rachel means well. But her concern is always edged with something else. Disapproval? It's there, in her tone of voice.

'I'm not hungry,' says Emma.

'What about for later on?'

'I've got stuff in the freezer.'

She has no idea what she does have. Her kitchen comprises a compact run of cabinets on the edge of the open plan sitting room. The freezer compartment at the top of the fridge is tiny. But the fridge does contain half a bottle of vodka. That much she remembers.

They turn into her street. It's tree-lined and still elegant; big, older Victorian detached houses. But on closer inspection, they've all been converted to multiple occupancy, houses divided into three or four flats, as evidenced by several dustbins outside each property.

Rachel pulls up at the curb.

'Well,' she says. 'You will call me if you need anything.'

Emma nods. Then a thought occurs to her.

'You didn't come back from your course because of me, did you?' she says.

'It doesn't matter,' says Rachel.

From the look on her sister's face, it's clear it does.

'I'm sorry,' says Emma.

Rachel reaches over and squeezes her hand. 'I was concerned about you, obviously. And I've got some very good detectives from my unit looking into this. We will get this monster and the evidence to convict, I promise you.'

'Thank you,' whispers Emma. A sense of shame is enveloping her. She just wants to get out and run.

She opens the car door and steps out onto the pavement. After the warmth of the interior, the cold strikes her. The police bagged all her clothes and her shoes. They gave her a tracksuit to wear, fleecy but thin. It looks like something they give prisoners to wear.

She shuts the car door and waves. She just needs to get inside and hide.

8

Rachel accelerates up the street. Her daughter has joined her in the front seat.

Why the hell did Emma have to say something snippy about the car? It's not that new, and she's definitely seen it before. And why won't she accept help?

Dial down the annoyance. This is no one's fault. Just bad timing.

Amber is scanning her. 'I'm sorry I called you,' she says. 'I should've handled it myself.'

Rachel frowns. 'Don't be silly, darling. How could you not call me? You did the right thing. It's fine.'

'Except you look pissed off.'

How can she explain to her daughter the little worm of irritation and doubt that burrows through her brain whenever anything happens concerning her sister?

She sighs. 'I'm just upset that some scumbag has raped my sister.'

'I really don't think it was her fault.'

Rachel glances at her daughter. She's not a kid anymore; she's smart and she reads people.

'Good God, Amber. No one's saying it is. Sounds like she was drugged with GHB. What time did you leave this event?'

'I'm not that sure.'

'You must have some idea?'

'Mum, you're talking like a cop. I didn't know what to do. When I opened the front door, she was in such a state. Just a thin dress. Her hands were blue. She was freezing.'

Amber has tears rolling down her face. Rachel feels awful. She is behaving like a cop. She's seen loads of rape victims, but her daughter hasn't. And what's worse, she knows most of them won't get justice or anything like it. But feelings get in the way of helping people.

She sighs and reaches out for her daughter's hand. 'Sorry,' she whispers. 'You're right. I sound like a cop. Default setting, I guess. Let's get home. Make a nice cup of coffee and process this. Something horrific has happened to Emma, it's bound to impact all of us. We just have different ways of showing it.'

'I think I'm being weak, crying all over the place like this. Nothing happened to me,' says Amber.

'Hey, there's nothing wrong with crying about it. You love your aunt, of course you do. You're going to feel upset and angry, and all sorts of things. I feel that too. But it's the job; I have a different way of dealing with these things.'

'None of it makes sense to me.'

'Course it doesn't. It's senseless violence.'

'What I mean is how she even got targeted. It was a family party. A wedding anniversary. No one was drunk. We know the hotel; we've done a couple of weddings there before. Emma gets on with the manager. She was still around when I left. Staff were clearing up. I just don't get it.'

Rachel gives her child a side-long glance. The earnestness and hurt in her face is heart wrenching. She wants to wash it all away. But she can't.

The problem is there's a reckless and impulsive side to Emma. Fortunately, Amber's never witnessed that.

'We will interview everyone,' says Rachel. 'There'll probably be CCTV at the venue. There're all kinds of video footage out there nowadays. We'll get to the bottom of this. I promise.'

Amber turns to smile at her. She wipes her face with the back of the hand.

'I worry I got it wrong and let you down,' she says. There's a tremor in her voice.

'Absolutely not,' says Rachel. 'You never let me down. Ever. You did exactly the right thing.'

They drive on in a companionable silence, heading south out of the city. The short drive to Great Shelford is uneventful. It's a pretty village and the comfortable upmarket setting has always appealed to Rachel. They bought before property values got silly. A neighbour further down the lane recently sold for two and a half million, which made Simon smug.

Rachel turns into the drive. Her husband's old Porsche Boxster is already there.

Using her key, Rachel lets them into the house. It's detached, originally late Victorian with an Arts and Crafts influence. Rachel loved the exposed timbers and tall gables on sight. It needed work and modernisation. But the result is a subtle blend of old and new, which pleases her every time she walks through the door.

'Right, coffee!' she announces. 'And something to eat. I ended up missing breakfast.'

At the sound of her voice, Simon Knight emerges from the study. He's in a business suit, opening some mail with a silver letter opener.

'Where's the fire?' he says. 'Your text said come home urgently.'

Rachel throws her bag on the hall table and heads for the kitchen. 'Last night, Emma was attacked and raped,' she says.

'Oh my God, how awful? Is she alright?' He follows her into the kitchen.

'Not really. She's in shock. She can't remember how any of it happened. I tried to bring her back here so we could take care of her, but she insisted on going back to that scabby little flat of hers. I didn't want to argue with her.'

He shakes his head in disbelief. 'Poor old Em. How did it happen?'

'Not sure yet.'

'She wasn't, y'know, going on the apps again?'

Rachel gives her husband a filthy look. She's aware of their daughter watching them. 'Simon, she was at work. Doing an event. If you recall, Amber was working with her too last night. This happened after Amber left.'

'Oh, I see.' He hesitates, then he adds, 'What about your course?'

'I called Mum,' says Amber.

'Obviously I had to come home,' says Rachel. 'Emma turned up here. You'd gone to work.'

'Gym, actually. Before work. I'd booked a session with the trainer.'

Simon is older than her, pushing fifty. She suspects he still smokes, although he denies it. And he drinks too much. She doesn't mind his paunch; he does.

'Whatever,' she says. 'Anyway, you weren't here. So I came back.'

He turns to Amber. 'Did you try to call me?'

She nods. 'You weren't picking up, so I tried Mum.'

'Trainer insists the phone is off. Sorry, sweetheart.'

Rachel looks at her husband and her daughter. This has thrown all of them. They stand in their large, airy kitchen; they've all had their days disrupted by Emma, who's not even there. No one is saying what they're thinking.

Amber shrugs and scans her parents. 'I'm going to take a shower,' she says.

'Good idea, darling,' says Rachel.

Simon watches their daughter disappear down the hall; he turns to his wife. 'Bloody hell, Rachel. You know what Emma's like with her hook-ups. Who says she didn't finish work and send Amber home because she'd taken a fancy to some hunky-looking waiter?'

'Sssh! She'll hear you.'

He lowers his voice to a whisper. 'All I'm saying is your sister's got form.'

Rachel goes to the kitchen door and closes it.

'I haven't had a chance to talk to her on her own. Amber was there.'

'What about that time, when she was still with Neil, and they'd had some bust up, she went out on a complete bender, and she woke up in a hotel in Birmingham? She couldn't remember then how she got there.'

'This sounds different. She is hurt.'

'She puts herself in risky situations. You know she does. Feels ashamed. And then lies about it.'

He's got a point.

'I just don't know,' she says with a huff. 'I've driven fifty miles to get back here. Haven't eaten. Haven't even had a bloody cup of coffee.' The tears come from nowhere. She can't stop them.

'Come here,' he says, pulling her into his arms. 'This is not your fault.' He rocks her and kisses her hair.

The relief of him. Always solid and dependable.

She nuzzles his chest. 'I know that,' she says. 'It's bloody Emma. Always bloody Emma.'

9

Boden stands in front of DCI Hepburn's desk. He has his arms folded and what can only be described as a peeved look on his face.

'Have we got an ID for the body?' he says.

'Not yet. We know who owns the flat. But there wasn't anything apparent to say it was him. I didn't want to dig around too much. But CSI have just gone in.'

'No. Best to leave it to them. Slashed throat, you say? Expertly done?'

'Not really. Looks like they had a couple of goes.'

'Signs of a struggle?'

'Yeah. Broken glass on the kitchen floor. Wine glass, I think.'

'Murder weapon still at the scene?'

'Not that I could see, boss.'

Hepburn stands up and slots his hands in his trouser pockets.

'So we've got an allegation of rape and now we've got a murder at the same location of an unidentified male. What are we looking at here? Are they connected?'

'I spoke to the SOLOs. Emma Harris was subjected to some degree of violence,' says Boden.

'Okay. Let's say they are connected. She knows him. Rough sex, which still could've been non-consensual. He hurt her. She was upset. He went into the kitchen. She came at him with a knife, took him by surprise?'

'That's a possibility, boss. But why report it? That doesn't make sense. You think she'd run, pretend she was never there?'

'Her sister's a cop. Perhaps she's smarter than that. Whether it's a casual hook-up or she knows him, she'll realise the flat is going to be full of her DNA, plus phone records and CCTV could place her there. So she's just going to give us a different version. He raped her. She was defending herself.'

'Or she didn't do it?' says Boden.

'Or she didn't do it,' he says, sighing.

'What do you want me to do? Shall I bring her in?'

Hepburn paces. 'She's still a rape victim and should be treated as such. But we have to question her about this body.'

Boden hesitates, then she says, 'I appreciate it's a difficult situation, boss.'

'You're talking about Rachel Knight? You do nothing differently to what you'd normally do, Jo. Let's be clear about that. And I know Rachel; she wouldn't want or expect anything else.'

Is he being disingenuous? She can take a guess what he's really thinking. The politics of this; it could all get messy very quickly. And Knight is his boss.

'What I meant,' she says, 'is this is a rape victim who

could also be a murder suspect. Do we regard one offence as more important than the other?'

He gives her a sullen look and huffs.

He is thinking about the politics. He has to.

The investigation is going to be complicated enough without the Detective Chief Super's personal connection. If her sister is in the frame for murder, Knight will have to step down as head of MIT. For Hepburn, the whole thing is a hot potato.

Boden waits.

Hepburn sighs. 'Listen Jo, early start for the team. Coffee and a bacon roll before you move on?'

Boden smiles. 'Good idea.'

He's looking for some breathing space. Understandably.

'In the meantime, talk more to the SOLOs. Get their take on Emma Harris. Plus, we'll also need all the forensic evidence they've gathered.'

'Right.'

As Boden walks back across the office, she can hear Hepburn on the phone. He's asking for an appointment with the ACC. So he's going up the chain of command. He's got no choice. This has to be done by the book in order to protect all concerned.'

Mackie is leaning on his desk, scrolling on his phone. Chakravorty is staring at her computer screen. Boden joins them.

'Bet you made his day,' says Mackie jovially.

'Yep,' says Boden.

'I'm in the CCTV system,' says Chakravorty. 'The apartment block is near a main road. Nearest camera is at a junction about a hundred metres away.'

'Does Hepburn think she did it?' says Mackie. 'Let's face it, she must've.'

'Let's keep an open mind and follow the evidence,' says Boden. 'Before we talk to her, let's see if there's any evidence of when she actually left the building. Was it this morning, as she said in her interview?'

'If she killed him last night, why didn't she get out then?' says Chakravorty.

'Exactly,' says Boden. 'And I'd say that body's been there since last night. Post mortem'll tell us. But let's assume it has for now.'

'What do you reckon Knight'll do?' says Mackie.

'Nothing, if she's got any sense,' says Boden.

Although that seems unlikely.

'It's not her fault though, is it? You can't pick your relatives,' says Chakravorty.

'Who wants to go down the cafe and get bacon rolls?' says Boden.

'Always happy to volunteer for that, Skip,' says Mackie, jumping to attention.

'I was hoping you would,' says Boden.

Hepburn needs time to consider how he's going to handle this. But he's put Boden on point, so she does too. Getting heavy with the Detective Chief Super's sister won't enhance anyone's career prospects.

10

Emma Harris is soaking in the bath; the water is as hot as she can bear and the tub filled to the brim. As she moves, it slops onto the floor. She doesn't care.

She's rested a large tumbler of vodka and ice on the wash-basin. On an empty stomach, probably not a good idea, but she doesn't care about that either. Her body is sore and her mind is numb. She can't seem to wrangle her thoughts into any sort of order. She has a deep, pulsing headache.

What the hell happened?

Nothing makes sense.

The shutters in her brain have come down. She was at the hotel, checking around, making sure everything was sorted out after the event. Then wham, she wakes up in a strange place and someone else's bed with a thumping headache. And she can't explain it.

Where's her car? She owns an ancient Nissan that she

bought for cash. She used it to drive to the hotel. It must still be there.

It's November. She had a coat. Where's that?

Her handbag was with her. It contained her phone and wallet. But she also had a backpack with files. Details of the clients and their requirements for the event. Menus. Confidential business information. She wouldn't have just abandoned it.

Nothing makes sense.

Rachel mentioned the date rape drug, GHB. But if that's the explanation, how was it administered? She did drink some mineral water from the bottles placed on the tables. But if one of those had been tampered with, was she even the intended victim? Or was it a random, opportunistic attack?

It makes no sense.

This was a family party. A wedding anniversary. She remembers arriving in the late afternoon to set up, talking to the hotel manager, Val. They know each other; they've done business before. It's always been friendly. If someone drugged Emma and carried her out of there, where was Val?

Her brain is crawling with questions for which she has no answers. But her priority is to get clean. She scrubs herself with a sponge and shower gel.

This is the first time she's used the tub as a bath; normally she showers. And it's not a full length. In order to immerse her shoulders and torso, her knees have to be folded up. The shower curtain hangs limply over the sides of the bath. The shower fitment drips.

She wonders how her life has come to this. She's the wrong side of forty, living alone in a rental flat, childless, and with an ex-husband who hates her and is trying to squeeze every penny he can out of her. Is it just bad luck?

Be honest. You're a fuck-up.

She had the same opportunities as her sister; more Rachel would argue. So how has she made such a mess of things?

Too lazy, that's what Mum says.

Lockdown and the pandemic brought her business to a standstill. No one needed an events planner. But she is getting back on track. The clients are rolling in and she's paying off her debts. She does most of the work herself, with the support of her niece Amber. For everything else, she uses freelance contractors. But she has a roster of regulars: a florist, a car hire service, several caterers.

Amber started to help her out in the school holidays. They'd always got on. Amber is such an open, bouncy girl; a real people person, unlike her mother. The summer between school and uni, Emma offered her a proper job.

That upset Rachel big time.

Emma smiles at the thought. Rachel had her daughter's career all planned out, and she blames Emma for leading Amber astray. But this is so unfair. Amber's just fed up with studying, fed up with exams, and isn't even sure she wants to be a lawyer. She needs time out, and a chance to work out who she is and what she wants.

She wants to be more like her aunt. Cut loose. Have adventures. She's told Emma as much, and of course it's flattering.

Soaking in the warm water helps. Emma lets her mind drift. She's always tried to follow her heart.

She dropped out of uni after the first year. The course was boring. She met a German boy in the holidays, fell madly in love and followed him to Thailand. They travelled together for six months. It was a great adventure. She learned loads more about the world than a degree in sociology would've taught her. He dumped her in New Zealand for another German; Emma subsequently heard that they'd married, settled in Munich and had two kids.

When she got back to the UK, she got a job in a bar, and that started her off in the hospitality industry.

The big mistake was marrying Neil. They went out on a casual basis for several years. It was an open relationship which suited them both. Great sex, no hassles.

Neil was a builder; a big, hunky bloke who loved to joke around. They laughed a lot together. Nothing was ever serious. Neil had his mates, his nights out, and no desire to settle down. It suited Emma at the time. She had other relationships. Quite a few. But she kept circling back to Neil.

She thinks about her ex. Is it conceivable he could be behind this? The last time they met in a lawyer's office, it ended badly. He did threaten her. But it was in the heat of the moment, surely? He had a temper which he found hard to control. But he'd never been violent towards her, and she was married to him for ten years. When they rowed, he'd storm off. Go to his mum's. Sometimes for days.

Could this be Neil wanting to frighten her, teach her a lesson? Undermine her confidence? He knows her pattern of work, her car. He could easily have followed her. Borrowed a fancy apartment from one of his golf club buddies.

It's a horrible thought, but there's an eerie logic to it.

The water in the tub is cooling, and the more she thinks about it, the more it makes sense. It's been stalemate between them for months. Neil wants to break her. Get her to agree to his demands. He's a determined little sod when it suits him.

It's horrible, but it makes sense.

He did this to her. She can feel it. He's strong, used to pick her up with ease; light as a feather, he used to joke.

Somehow he got someone to slip the GHB into her drink, then he came in, scooped her up, into the back of his pickup and they were away.

She's crying now. Sobbing in dry gulps.

This was Neil. He did this to her. She's convinced of it.

11

Dean is still getting used to driving again. On the way back from the cemetery, he put his foot down, had a little burn. The wheels are borrowed. A brand new Toyota four-by-four. Black, shiny, tinted windows. Neat. It belongs to an old mate, a lad he's known since school days. They started together as runners for Dean's dad when they were thirteen. Liam's done well for himself and avoided the law. Dean doesn't mind that. He's not envious. Liam's solid, one of the few people he can still rely on.

A proper mate.

He offered Dean the car for as long as he needed it. The main reason Dean accepted was so he could drive up to Craig's door in it.

After the cemetery, he stopped off, got a coffee and a pastie. He wandered round the shopping mall for a bit. He needed time to wind down. If only his sister could've been with him. They'd have had a right laugh. He could've bought her something nice, and maybe a toy for each of the kids. But he's been robbed of all that.

Life's so fucking unfair.

But he's made amends to Kelly. Now he needs to settle with his brother.

Craig has built himself a ranch style house out in the countryside. It's got land and stables. The snooty wife, Kate, rides horses. They've got two kids, both girls. He forgets their names. Just little clones of Kate.

Dean drives up to the electric gates. Big, solid steel bars. High fence, cameras all round the perimeter of the property. Craig takes his security seriously. He may want the world to see him as a legitimate businessman now, but there are still plenty of people who know he's a drug dealer.

There's a fancy intercom on the wall beside the gate. You have to look straight at it, so it can see your face. Dean presses it and smiles. The gates click and swing open. He drives up the sweeping drive to the front of the house. By the time he reaches the front door, Craig is outside on the doorstep, wreathed in smiles, waiting to greet him.

But Dean takes his time. He leaves the tatty denim jacket in the car. The black T-shirt shows off his torso and pecs to advantage. Craig is shorter than him and younger, but he's a mess. Saggy gut, loose shirt, trackie pants and flip-flops.

'Come here, you bastard!' says Craig, laughing and pulling him into a hug. 'What took you so fucking long? How long you been out? A week? You couldn't find the address?'

'Just needed to adjust and spend a bit of time with the old man,' says Dean.

Craig frowns and shakes his head. 'Yeah, I get over as much as I can. But it's a sad sight, like he's a ghost of the bloke he used to be. Breaks my heart, I can tell you.'

Dean just nods. A massive stroke has put the old man in a wheelchair. He lives in a care home, paid for by Craig.

'I appreciate what you done for him, Craig.'

'Well, he's the old man, isn't he? How's he doing with the physio?'

'He walked a step or two with his wheels. But I can see the frustration in him.'

Craig beams. 'He must be so made up to see you, though. You coming out; he's really been looking forward to it. We all have.'

Dean meets his brother's gaze.

You wouldn't if you knew what's coming.

Craig shepherds him into the house. The hall is massive. Dean's no expert, but the decor looks tastefully posh. It's not overblown, with gold chandeliers and that sort of thing. There's no whiff of gangster about it. It looks like the kind of house a banker might live in. Everything cool and expensive. Dean suspects that's down to Kate.

She emerges from a side room and she's all smiles too. She's a classy looking woman, Dean'll give her that. There's nothing trashy about her. She's never plastered in make-up and she never walks around with her tits in your face.

'My goodness, Dean,' she says. 'You are looking so fit.'

She reaches up and gives him a peck on the cheek. She smells of something exotic and expensive. Dean finds her proximity arouses him. He remembers when Craig first met her. He went to college to do some stupid business studies course, and she was in his class. Her parents had money and didn't like their daughter hooking up with a kid like Craig. Dean wonders what happened to them. Has Craig got them banged up in a care home somewhere too?

Kate pats him on the chest. Her nails are long and perfect. 'You need to get this husband of mine in the gym with you and knock a few pounds off him. Too many business lunches.'

Craig chuckles. She's teasing him, but he doesn't seem to mind. He gives her a gooey-eyed look.

Dean can't imagine feeling like that about a woman. He's happy enough to shag them, but he's never let one get under his skin like that. No way.

'I thought we'd have a spot of lunch beside the pool,' says Kate. 'But don't worry. I know you two have got a lot of catching up to do. Once we've eaten, I'll leave you in peace.

The pool turns out to be covered and located in a huge hangar at the back of the house. It's warm in there, like a hot house, and there are random palm trees in pots and a spa area.

The three of them sit at a glass table and a black girl in an apron serves them. Dean has had to put up with prison stodge, but he can still appreciate good food when he tastes it. It's all very fresh and beautifully presented. A prawn linguine with salad. Craig pours from an expensive looking bottle of white wine.

'How are the girls?' says Dean. He knows how to make conversation. He's not a peasant.

'You won't believe how they've grown,' says Craig, scrolling on his phone for a picture. 'Ariella's just sixteen. And she's a complete head-turner, just like her mother.'

He shows Dean a photo of a bright-eyed blonde. She does indeed resemble Kate.

'But she's far cleverer than me,' says her mother. 'We're hoping she'll go to Oxford.'

'Marry herself a real toff,' adds Craig proudly. 'Think how useful that could be.' He winks.

He shows Dean a second shot of a little kid on a pony. 'Imogen's twelve,' he says. 'But y'know what? She's sharp as a tack. I reckon she might outstrip her sister one day.'

'They look like terrific kids,' says Dean equably. 'You're lucky to have them.'

'It's not too late for you, mate,' says Craig. 'Find yourself a nice girl, settle down. Kids give your life a different perspective.'

Smug bastard.

'You know Kelly's two have been fostered,' says Dean.

'Yeah, I heard. That was a bad business.' Craig frowns and sips his wine.

He might not want to talk about Kelly, but he's not going to get a choice.

'If I'd been out, I'd've done something about that junky bastard,' says Dean. He fixes his brother with a hard stare.

Kate shifts in her chair and stares down at her plate.

'Trust me, Dean,' says Craig. 'I tried. Kelly was impossible to deal with. I'm sure Dad would tell you that if he could.'

Dean takes a deep breath. He has to keep his temper here. He's been thinking about having this conversation for too long. Ever since they called him into the Governor's office and gave him the news about his sister.

'What's the word shrinks use?' he says. 'An intervention? Isn't that what you're supposed to do?'

'I offered to pay for rehab. She didn't want to know.'

Dean slaps the table with his palm. 'If you'd nailed that junky bastard's feet to the floor, then she'd've gone, wouldn't she?'

Kate stands up abruptly. 'I've got some calls to make,' she says. 'I'll leave you to it.'

Dean looks up and gives her his best smile. 'Nice lunch, Kate. Thank you.'

'You're welcome,' she says and scurries away.

Craig shakes his head and sighs.

'Listen,' he says. 'If you want to know, I wish I'd done exactly that. But I doubt it would've worked. She didn't want to get better. She just wanted her next fix. The kids were going hungry—'

'That wasn't her fault.'

'Alright, have it your own way. You didn't see her. But I'm telling you, Dean, you'd've been as frustrated as me. I mean, c'mon, she was my sister too. And as kids, I spent far more time with her than you did. You were always out with your mates.'

Dean can feel his heart thumping. The truth is he should've been there. He looks at Craig. He's always been a player, as far back as Dean can remember. But he's the little brother, two steps behind Dean his whole life. Now he's over-taken him. Runs the whole show. And that niggles.

This place. The money. It's all wrong.

The two men look at one another. Dean doesn't trust himself to speak. It's taking all his willpower not to cry.

Craig stands up and grins. 'You know what?' he says. 'Let's get you a proper set of wheels.'

'No need. Liam's loaning me the Toyota for as long as I want.'

'It's a piece of crap. A teenage drug dealer's car. Except Liam's not a bloody teenager, is he?' Craig laughs. 'You ever drive an Aston Martin?'

Dean shakes his head.

'Then it's time you did, son. Come with me.'

Dean follows his brother out of the enormous pool house into the yard at the back. He knows what his brother's up to. Craig's trying to buy him off, which is fine. For now. And anyway, he does quite fancy an Aston Martin.

12

Tuesday, 12.20pm

Emma is shivering. She's wrapped in a towel and has her phone to her ear. It rings, then goes to voicemail for the third time. She circles the coffee table in her small sitting room, leaving damp footprints on the carpet. She's impatient. Val must be busy. This time she opts to leave a message.

'Val, it's Emma Harris. Sorry to hassle you, but I really need to talk to you about last night. Could you call me back? Thanks.'

She goes into the bedroom, drops the phone on the bed and dries herself. Her hair is damp and stringy. She's shampooed twice, but it still feels dirty. She should blow dry it, but her thoughts are scattered. It's hard to concentrate on anything for long.

Urgently. You should've said urgently. Sod it!

She opens the wardrobe. What she needs is something clean and cosy to wear. There's a mirror on the back of the door. She catches her reflection. She doesn't want to stop and look, but she can't help it.

There are bruises on both forearms and one on her shin. It's as if she's been dragged and her limbs have knocked into things. She counts five marks of varying sizes. The one on the shin is the most painful. If that had happened when she was conscious, she would've felt it.

Neil? Could he have done this?

That doesn't seem possible. Yet he is the obvious suspect. She gets out fresh underwear and a thick pair of walking socks. She puts these on quickly, followed by a T-shirt, trackie bottoms and an old cashmere cardigan.

The flat is always on the coolish side. Poor insulation, badly fitting windows and radiators which take ages to heat up. Red hot or tepid, they have no settings in between.

Her phone vibrates. Val. She grabs it.

'Hey, Val,' she says. 'Thanks for calling back.'

'Yeah, sorry, I was in a meeting. And it could be something of interest to you. Our regional manager is thinking about putting on a wedding fayre. Our big ballroom would be perfect—'

'Val, can I stop you there? Sorry. I need to ask you a couple of things about last night.'

'Oh, okay. I thought it was a good evening. Were there any problems?'

Emma is at a loss. Where to begin?

'Is my car still there?'

'Your car? Hang on, let me look out of the window.'

'It's a sort of rusty orange colour. A Nissan.'

'Oh, yeah. I think I can see it right at the end of the car park. Did you take a cab home?'

'I don't know.' She hesitates. Just say it. 'Val, I was attacked.'

'Oh my God! Where? Not here, at the hotel?'

'I don't know. I can't remember.'

'Oh, that's awful. Are you alright? Who attacked you?'

'I don't know. Well, there's someone I suspect, but... I need to talk to the police about that.'

'The police are involved? God, I hope it's not one of our staff.'

Emma senses a defensive reaction. They don't know each other that well. Is Val worried the hotel might be blamed?

'Val, I'm not blaming the hotel for any of this. I'm trying to work out what happened to me. I ended up in some strange flat. I don't know how I got there. And... I'd been raped.'

She's said it. Out loud to a person who's neither the police nor family. She realises the hand holding the phone is shaking.

She'll think I'm a slag.

'Oh my God, Emma. That's just horrible. Obviously, if there's anything I can do to help.'

Concentrate.

'The last thing I can remember is all the guests had left. Staff were clearing the tables. My assistant, Amber, went home. But I stayed to make sure everything was done. When did you last see me?'

She can imagine Val, behind the desk in her rather smart office. They've had coffee there together on several occasions, from a silver pot poured by a waiter, when Emma was there to discuss an event.

'Umm, let me think,' says Val. 'You were doing something with the floral decorations, I think?'

The flowers! The colours flood into her mind. Russet hues, a late autumn arrangement. The clients loved them.

'Yes! I remember that. The ones left over we donate to the

hospice. The guy was supposed to come and collect them this morning.'

'He must've done. Because they're gone.'

'What about after that?'

'I went back to my office to finish up. Handed over to the night manager. And I went home. I think you were still in the ballroom.'

The night manager!

Emma realises she's clutching at every piece of information as if it's a nugget of gold.

'Who's the night manager?' she says.

'We've got three. But I'm afraid he's gone home.' She's sounding defensive again. Perhaps she's feeling badgered.

'Okay, thanks Val.'

'Hang on, a minute.' A muffled sound as a hand goes over the phone. Then she says, 'Have you lost a backpack? Black with a red strip?'

'Yes. It's got files inside.'

'The gardener found it this morning in the flower bed below the ballroom terrace. I'll keep it for you.'

'Thanks.'

'And seriously, if there's anything else. And we're happy to help the police.'

'Thanks, Val. And look, I'm sorry about all this.'

'Don't be. It's not your fault. I just feel guilty that I went home. But I'm sure that if any of the staff had seen anything happening…'

'I know. I'll collect my backpack when I come for the car. Maybe later today. I'm not sure.'

'Take care of yourself, Emma.'

'I will.'

Emma hangs up and slumps down on the bed. Is that what Neil did with her backpack? Tossed it into a flowerbed?

It still doesn't make sense.

The police gave her water to rehydrate her and a rather murky mug of tea. But she should eat something, she knows that. The queasiness hasn't gone away. She took a couple of mouthfuls of vodka when she was in the bath, but it burned her gullet. She needs food.

Her sister's voice, lecturing her, echoes in her head.

Something light and nutritious.

Why wouldn't she let Rachel play Florence Nightingale? The problem is, every time she walks into her sister's lovely home, she feels a failure. And she didn't need the additional burden of that today.

She wanders into the main room and opens one of the kitchen cupboards. There's muesli. In the fridge, she finds yogurt and blueberries. In the freezer compartment, there are a couple of ready meals and a pizza. She opts for the muesli.

Dipping her finger in the yogurt, she tastes it. Past its sell-by date, but it's okay.

She's just settled on the sofa with a bowl of fruit, yogurt and muesli when the doorbell rings. It's tempting to ignore it. Who would be calling round anyway in the middle of the day? Probably a delivery for one of the other flats. But the ringing is persistent.

She goes to the ansaphone on the wall by the door and presses to speak. 'Yeah?'

The crackling reply is hard to decipher. Like most things in the flat, it's a piece of crap. 'DS... Bod... can we....'

'Sorry. Are you the police?'

'Ye....'

Emma presses the button to release the door.

Should she tell them about Neil? She can't decide.

She can hear footsteps on the stairs. According to Rachel, detectives come in pairs. Opening the door, she waits.

Two women. Both younger than her. Rachel's lot? They could be.

The taller of the two holds out her warrant card. 'I'm DS Boden,' she says. 'This is my colleague, DC Chakravorty.'

'Come in,' says Emma. 'I'm attempting to eat something, though I don't much feel like it.'

The two officers follow her into the flat. They bring with them an air of tension.

'You've had a very difficult experience,' says Boden. 'I appreciate that.'

Emma shrugs. 'It is what it is.'

What a stupid thing to say? What does that even mean?

The cop is watching her, assessing her.

'The address you gave my colleagues,' she says, 'the place where you woke up this morning, are you certain you got it right?'

Emma holds out her left forearm. There's an ugly bruise forming close to the wrist, but above that there's still a faint ink stain.

'I've had a bath and I scrubbed it,' says Emma. 'But as soon as I got out of there, I wrote the flat number, 27, and the fifth floor, on my arm. So I'd get it right. Your colleagues took a picture. That's definitely where I was.'

The cop nods. 'Okay,' she says. 'I just needed to be absolutely sure.'

'So you can nick him, yeah I get that.'

The other cop is shifting from foot to foot. But the one who's done all the talking is staring at her.

This isn't good.

'Well,' says the cop. 'We went round there, gained access and in the kitchen we found the body of a man and we believe he's been murdered.'

Murdered?

'What?' says Emma.

'In view of that,' says Boden, 'I'm arresting you for murder.'

'What are you talking about? I haven't killed anyone. I was raped.'

'The reason we're doing this,' says the cop, 'is so we can gather evidence and question you in order to effectively investigate this serious crime.'

This is nonsense. It's a mistake. They went to the wrong flat.

'I'm now going to caution you. You do not have to say anything. But it may harm your defence if you do not mention when questioned something you later rely on in court. Anything you do say may be given in evidence. Do you understand the caution?'

'Well, who the hell is he?' says Emma.

'Do you know who he is, Emma?' says the other cop.

'Of course I bloody don't. I woke up in a strange place. I figured I'd been raped and I got out as fast as I could.'

'Where exactly did you wake up?' says Boden.

'In a bed. I guess it was the bedroom. I got my stuff and I got out.'

The tears are coming. She can't stop them. This is totally crazy. She's being accused of murder.

Don't panic. It's a mistake. Idiots went to the wrong flat.

'Look,' she says. 'This is ridiculous. I didn't kill anyone. And certainly not some bloke in a strange flat, where I've never been before. I was raped! And you're accusing me of murder! I wanna call my sister. She'll put you bloody straight. I'm the victim here.'

'I can understand why you're upset, Emma—'

'Don't fucking patronise me. Just call my sister. She'll have your fucking job for this.'

'You need to come with us. So we can sort this out,' says the cop.

Emma glares at her. 'Fuck you! Just call my sister.'

13

Rachel finds it hard to sit still. Inactivity has never suited her. So she walked the half-mile to the shop in the village and bought eggs and fresh bagels for what will now be brunch. The exercise helped release some of her pent-up tension. She's at the hob, stirring the scrambled eggs as her daughter toasts the bagels, when her phone rings. It's the Assistant Chief Constable. Amber takes over and Rachel walks towards the study to take the call.

The conversation is brief. He delivers the facts. A dead body has been found in the flat where the alleged rape took place. It looks like murder. His throat was slashed. Emma has been arrested.

Arrested? WTF?

This stops Rachel in her tracks halfway down the hall. She's speechless. What the hell has Emma got herself into?

He doesn't give her any time to process this. He ploughs

straight on. 'Obviously this impacts on your position as head of MIT,' he says.

Emma arrested? When?

'Yes, sir. I appreciate that,' she says, on auto-pilot. This is too shocking. And also absurd. She needs time to think. And she needs to speak to her sister.

'Alistair Hepburn is SIO and I have every confidence that he'll run the investigation properly.'

Oh shit! They think she murdered her attacker? Is there evidence?

'I gather you were supposed to be on a course,' says the ACC. He's such a pompous git, hiding behind formality, because this is awkward.

'I came back because of my sister,' she says calmly.

'Well, it's up to you. They may let you pick it up tomorrow, but you may not want to.'

Really? On a Gold Commander's course with a sister under arrest for murder? How will that work? Stupid prick.

'Umm, well no. Probably not,' she says.

'I didn't think you would. So you can be transferred to other duties for the duration of the investigation. We'll sort something out and get back to you.' His tone is brisk. She has an avalanche of questions, but it's clear he's desperate to wrap this up.

'Thank you,' she says.

'I'll be asking Graham Carter to step up as head of MIT temporarily.'

'A good choice, sir.'

He'll be over the fucking moon. He's been snapping at her heels ever since she got the job.

'And Rachel, if you need me, I'm here. Okay?'

'Yes, of course. And I appreciate that.'

He hangs up, leaving her stunned.

Simon puts his head round the kitchen door.

'Do you want to eat these scrambled eggs before they turn to leather?' he says.

'They found a body in the flat. Emma's been arrested for murder.'

'What? Jesus wept! Murder?'

Rachel's arms hang loosely at her sides.

'Who did she murder?' says Simon.

'I've no idea. The bloke whose flat she was in?'

Rachel notices Amber standing behind her father. She has a look of horror on her face as she pushes past him.

'Emma wouldn't murder anyone,' she says. 'She couldn't. It's ridiculous.'

It is ridiculous.

Rachel shakes her head. 'They wouldn't have arrested her without a reason.'

'Well, what reason?'

'I don't know.' In her head she's calculating. Why didn't Alistair call her and tell her himself? Because he wasn't allowed to? They've cut her out of the loop with surgical precision. How can she get to talk to Emma?

You can't.

'Well, what could've happened?' says Amber. 'Maybe it was a fight? She ended up killing her rapist? I mean, that's self-defence, surely?'

'But she says she can't remember anything.'

'You think she's lying?'

'I don't know.'

'Well, what are we going to do?'

'Amber, enough with the questions,' Rachel snaps. 'I need to think. Let's eat.'

'Eat!' exclaims Amber. 'Emma's been arrested and you want to eat?'

'Your mother's right,' says Simon. 'There's no point in panicking. Let's just eat these bloody bagels.'

'No!' says Amber. 'We must find her a lawyer or something. I'm going online to look.'

She rushes past Rachel and runs upstairs. Rachel watches her go. She can't worry about that at the moment.

She follows Simon into the kitchen.

Her husband is watching her, hands on hips. 'I just don't know what to say. Even on the scale of Emma fuck-ups—'

'Yes,' she says. 'Alright. We don't all need to go into a tailspin. It's bad.'

'Do you really think she's capable of murder?'

'Simon, I don't know. Until I can get some details…'

In the right circumstances, anyone is capable of murder.

He frowns. 'Yep, you're right,' he says.'Shall I make you a fresh coffee?'

She nods and plonks down on a stool. He picks up the frying pan and peers at the scrambled eggs.

'Just bagels then?' he says, dumping the eggs into food waste bin.

Rachel is replaying the course of events in her mind from her daughter's phone call. Emma had turned up at the house. It was early. She probably assumed Rachel would still be at home. Was it her intention to confess what she'd done to Rachel? Perhaps it was. Some casual hook-up had turned nasty. He forced her into stuff she didn't want to do, she defended herself. That seems the most plausible scenario.

'What are you thinking?' says Simon. 'Do you think she did it?'

'If I was SIO, that would be my working hypothesis until I found evidence to the contrary.'

'Yes, but you're not SIO and this is Emma.'

Rachel raises her eyebrows. 'Who we both know is prone

to risky sexual encounters with men she doesn't know.'

'You said she was insisting she woke up, had no idea where she was and no memory of what had happened,' says Simon.

'That could be true, or it could just be her cover story. What if she came round looking for help? If I'd been here, she might've told me what had happened. I reckon she was too ashamed to tell Amber. So she lied, spontaneously, and now has to maintain the lie.'

He huffs. 'Yeah well, sounds like the sort of thing she might do.'

Rachel shakes her head wearily. 'The first thing they'll do is try to connect her with the murder victim. Does she know him? Is he on her phone? Did she meet him on a dating app? Or does he work at the hotel? Then there's forensic evidence. Is her DNA on him or vice versa?'

'What are you going to do?'

'They won't let me anywhere near her.' Rachel picks up her phone. 'And Amber's right about one thing. She needs a lawyer.'

'You got someone in mind?'

Rachel scrolls through her address book. 'Charlotte Rogers.'

'Blimey, that'll cost. Who's going to pay for that?'

'I expect we are. Emma's living from hand to mouth and she's already paying a divorce lawyer.'

'I'm just saying it's a bit of a financial commitment when we don't even know the facts.'

'Simon, she'll be questioned in some depth and she needs a lawyer there to guide her. And she needs it now.'

'Okay.' He raises his palms. 'But didn't you fall out with Charlotte because she jumped ship, left the CPS and joined a criminal defence firm?'

'Yes, which is why she's the right person for this. She was one of the best prosecutors we had. And for the record, I haven't fallen out with her. In her shoes I'd've done the same. She was pushing sixty and overworked. They offered her a partnership, triple her salary, and time off to lecture in criminology at the university. I don't blame her for wanting an easier life.'

'Will she even take the case?'

Rachel shrugs. 'I can only ask.'

She dials the number and waits. Her husband is looking glum. The reality is her old friend and mentor is expensive, but he can afford it. And Emma is going to need someone exceptional.

You get the justice you can afford. She's resisted that notion her entire career, but it contains more than a grain of truth.

'Detective Chief Superintendent!' says Rogers in her gravelly, upper class voice. 'This is an unexpected pleasure. I thought I'd been deleted from your Christmas card list.' There's more than a hint of mockery.

'Well, you have caused us a little bit of grief in the last year,' says Rachel. 'But I don't take it personally.'

'Three one to us. Isn't that the score?'

She would mention that.

Rachel takes a deep breath. 'I need a favour, Charlotte.'

'Then let me buy you lunch on my very generous expense account, and you can tell me all about it.'

'I'm afraid it's rather more urgent than that. My sister's been arrested for murder.'

'Oh I see. Oh dear. That's rather awkward for you.'

Rachel has to smile to herself. Trust Charlotte to hit the nail on the head.

14

Boden sits in the back of the police car with Emma Harris as Chakravorty drives. The decision not to bring Mackie or uniformed back up was hers; part of striking the delicate balance between acknowledging that Harris could be both victim and perpetrator. It also seemed unlikely that she'd make a run for it.

They'd drunk their coffees and eaten the bacon rolls at their desks, following the boss's suggestion. Hepburn disappeared for about twenty minutes. When he returned, he gave her the nod. Senior management had been alerted. But Boden knew she was the one at the sharp end of this, and the one Rachel Knight would probably blame if her sister was mistreated.

She glances across at Emma Harris. Her initial shock and anger has turned to sullen compliance. She looks pale and detached and is staring out of the window. Perhaps she's still expecting Rachel Knight to sweep in and rescue her from all this. She doesn't understand the rigidity of the system. This has to be done by the book.

They drive in silence. Traffic is heavy and progress is slow. A persistent drizzle is making things worse. The wiper blades squeak back and forth across the windscreen.

After about ten minutes, Emma turns to her and says. 'Why don't you believe me? I just woke up. Had no idea where I was or how I ended up there. I really can't remember what happened. Rachel says someone probably drugged me with GHB.'

There's a sincerity in her voice. But also a tremor of fear. She's adjusting to the seriousness of her situation. Boden has seen this enough times to know how it goes. The truth leaks out in the cracks between the words; nervous gestures, body language, the amount of eye contact, a suspect's whole demeanour. Being arrested for murder unnerves most people; of course it does, that's normal.

But Emma's reaction was clean: an outburst of anger, followed by confusion and disbelief. It didn't feel to Boden that she was expecting it, which means she's an excellent liar, or she's telling the truth.

Boden watches. Harris's hands are tightly clasped in her lap. Now she's in shock.

This doesn't look like the precursor to a he-raped-me-and-I-had to-defend-myself defence. On the other hand, if she continues to plead total ignorance, it puts the onus on the police to prove she did it. A sympathetic jury could well buy this. *I admit I was there, but it just wasn't me.* It could be a clever ploy; just front it out.

Boden continues to turn it all over in her mind. Could Harris have spent the whole night in the flat with the body of the man she'd just killed? You'd need nerves of steel to manage that and a good deal of calculation. Most people would flee. Was someone else involved? Much will turn on whether there's CCTV evidence to show what time she left the building.

Emma Harris is staring at her; a mixture of bewilderment and resentment. Boden would love to take this opportunity to question her, but she knows the rules.

'Why can't you understand what I'm saying?' Emma blurts.

'Emma,' says Boden gently. 'We're not allowed to question you until you've had legal advice.'

'I don't need bloody legal advice. I'm telling you what happened. I've got nothing to hide. After the event I was at the hotel clearing up. I run an events planning company. I phoned Val, the manager, this morning. She said she saw me sorting out the flower arrangements.'

This all comes out in an anxious torrent. Boden gets out her notebook. All she can do is write down what's said.

Emma has tears in her eyes.

'I was scared. I realised I'd been raped. I just got up and I ran. I mean, what would you do? What would any woman do? And I was raped. I'm not lying about that.' She's staring right at Boden and waiting for a response.

Not lying about that? She's making a distinction.

Perhaps, in her own mind, the rape justifies her subsequent actions? It was self-defence. If she thinks she had no choice, a lie backed by the firm belief that she was right could make total denial a winning strategy.

'Come on, what would you do if it happened to you?' she says.

'I'm afraid I can't give you an answer,' says Boden. 'I know this seems like a very formal process, but that's to protect you.'

'That's just bullshit.'

'I realise it must feel like that.'

Emma is maintaining eye contact, but her chin trembles as she suppresses the tears. The moment is full of emotional charge. Boden wants to reach out and clutch her hand. That's the normal reaction, but it wouldn't be appropriate. She softens her gaze. This has to remain professional. But how professional is the Detective Chief Super going to feel? Not very is Boden's guess.

Boden catches Chakravorty's gaze in the rearview mirror.

Prish thinks the same. As a woman, how can you detach?

Emma wipes her nose with the back of her hand. Boden reaches in her bag, pulls out a tissue and hands it to her.

'Thank you,' Emma says. They travel the rest of the journey in silence.

When they get to the office, as Emma gets out of the car, she turns to Boden and says defiantly, 'So aren't you even going to tell me who I'm being charged with murdering? Surely I have a right to be told who I'm supposed to have killed.'

'You haven't been charged,' says Boden. 'You've been arrested and cautioned because we want to question you about this body we found.'

'That just sounds like nit-picking.'

'Yeah, I know. The law is complicated and you need a lawyer with you when you're questioned. We would certainly advise it.'

'But how do I arrange that?'

'We have a duty solicitor. Or you can phone a lawyer of your choice.'

'I don't know any lawyers. Except my niece was supposed to be going to uni this year to study law.' She smiles sadly. This thought seems to upset her. Her chin trembles again.

Boden escorts her into the building. Chakravorty follows. They exchange covert looks.

'Once you've been booked in, my colleague DC Chakravorty is going to take you to the interview room,' says Boden. 'Shall I call the duty solicitor?'

Chakravorty has Emma's phone in an evidence pouch. Emma watches her hand it over to Boden. She huffs and says, 'Yeah, I suppose so.'

Then she glances around nervously. Expecting to see her sister, perhaps?

'Can we get you a coffee or some water?' says Chakravorty.

'Just water,' says Emma.

'It's this way,' says Chakravorty.

Boden watches them disappear down the corridor. She takes the lift to the office.

She heads straight for the analysts' corner. Mackie is standing behind one of the analyst's chairs. The screens are full of CCTV images.

'What have you got?' says Boden.

'There's a security camera in the lobby of the building, but it's bust. CCTV from the nearest external camera isn't that helpful. It doesn't cover the entrance. We're going down the street in either direction to see if we can pick her up anywhere.'

'Posh apartment block? Doesn't it have cameras in the lift?' says Boden.

Mackie sighs. 'Yep. Left-hand lift works, right-hand one doesn't.'

'Let me guess, she's not on the one that works?'

'Correct,' says Mackie. 'Boss wants a word.'

Boden holds up the evidence pouch. 'This is her phone. Can you get it to digital forensics?'

Mackie takes it.

Boden heads for Hepburn's office. He waves her in.

He steeples his fingers. 'First impressions?' he says.

'She's upset and angry. Insists she's no idea what happened or where she was. I don't think she's about to argue she was defending herself.'

Not directly.

Hepburn sighs. 'Okay,' he says. 'Well, I've just received a call from Phillips, Courtney, & Cole. They're sending someone over to represent Emma Harris.'

'She didn't call them. She's opted for the duty solicitor.'

'I should imagine Rachel Knight called them. They're the top criminal defence firm in Cambridge. Very sharp. Very expensive. Their main office is in London. We've tangled with them a couple of times.'

Boden sighs. 'She's quick off the mark. How does she even know we've brought Emma in?'

'The ACC will have told her,' says Hepburn. 'She wants to protect her sister. So she's going for the heavy hitters.'

Boden says nothing, but she's glad.

Too many rapists get away with it. So if she turned on him and slit his throat, who could blame her?

'Means we need to be on our A game,' says Hepburn.

Boden nods. 'Well, we're still trying to find some CCTV that confirms when Harris actually left the building. Last night or this morning, as she says. So if we need to wait until her brief shows up, that'll help.'

'Her phone?'

'It's gone in.'

'Okay,' says Hepburn.

Boden turns to leave. She gets to the door when Hepburn says, 'I'm going to ask the question I always tell my officers not to ask. What's your gut reaction?'

Boden faces him. He must be feeling the pressure if he's prepared to lay this one on her. Hepburn is a stickler for never jumping to conclusions and just following the evidence.

How well does he know Rachel Knight? Are they buddies? As an outsider from the Met, Boden has only a sketchy view of the history and the office politics of the place. This may be why Hepburn wants her at the front of this. Everyone knows she's an outsider.

Even so, don't put your foot in this trap.

She shrugs. 'Not sure, boss.'

'The I-can't-remember story. Do you buy it? Balance of probabilities?'

Boden ponders for a moment.

'Hard to say. Maybe. But I'll be happier when we've got some concrete evidence of when she left that apartment block.'

She heads back across the office. Mackie is perched on his desk. 'What did he say?'

'We've got a bit of time while we wait for her brief to rock up. So if you could double down on that CCTV?'

'I'm on it.' He gets up.

'Scott,' she says. 'You've been here a while, haven't you?'

He turns back to face her. 'Man and boy,' he says. 'Started in uniform when I was nineteen.'

'How well do Hepburn and Knight know each other?'

He folds his arm and smiles. Although he's a big, tough looking bloke, Mackie loves nothing better than to gossip. Boden has noticed this before, and it's useful.

'Well,' he says, in a confiding tone. 'He's been following her up the ladder for years. When she had his job, he was her DI. I don't know if they go to each other's houses and have barbecues.' He muses. 'But she's quite a looker for her age, so I don't know if they've ever, y'know…' He adds a suggestive whistle.

Boden sighs inwardly. Is this just the ingrained, institutional sexism of place or a hint of something deeper? In which case, she needs to watch her step.

But she gives him a warning glance. 'For her age? You're a cheeky sod, aren't you?'

There's something relentlessly family man about Hepburn. He doesn't seem the type to have shagged his boss. But you never know.

Mackie grins. 'Just doing my best to keep you amused, Skip.'

And he does amuse her, although she'd never admit it. She already senses that this investigation is going to be far from straightforward. She's walking on eggshells. So a bit of levity is welcome.

'Find me some bloody CCTV,' she says.

He gives her a mock salute.

15

Emma sits alone for what seems like ages. They've taken more forensic samples. Scraped under her fingernails, taken some clippings of her hair. This time, it feels more of a violation. She's also been photographed, fingerprinted and another DNA swab taken. They took her clothes even though she explained she put them all on after she got home and had a bath.

Where the hell is Rachel?

Her officers would get the bottom of this. That was her sister's promise.

The door opens and a rather stout woman with an unruly mop of grey hair rolls in. She looks like a harassed primary school teacher.

'Morning!' she says in a plummy voice. Then she peers at her tiny wrist watch. 'Or is it afternoon? Anyway, I'm Charlotte Rogers.'

Emma stares at her blankly.

'Your lawyer,' she adds.

'Oh,' says Emma. 'You're the duty solicitor.'

Rogers chuckles, a low rumbling sound. 'My dear girl, the duty solicitor is younger than my dog. I have been engaged by your sister to represent you.'

Engaged?

'Oh. I need to talk to Rachel. I was hoping she'd be here.'

'Emma, you've been arrested. She can't be here. That's why she's sent me.'

'Oh.'

Emma watches the lawyer as she lowers herself into a chair, pulls a small recorder out of her briefcase, and places it on the table between them.

'I'm going to record our conversation because no one in my office can read my handwriting. However, it is totally confidential. But if you did it, don't tell me. I don't need to know that.'

'If you mean did I murder anyone, I didn't.'

'Well, that's a good start.'

She clicks the recorder on, pulls out a yellow legal pad and an expensive-looking fountain pen.

'These notes are for me. Do you know the person whose flat you were in?'

'No. It was a strange place, a strange bed. I just woke up and wondered where the hell I was. But I've been thinking who might want to do something horrible like this to me. And I wondered about my ex-husband. Well, we're not actually divorced yet, because the creep's been trying to take me to the cleaners for the last six months.'

'Name of the creep?'

'Neil. Neil Bryant. He's a builder, well was until he went

broke. He hangs out with all these rich fuckwits at the golf club. So perhaps that's who the flat could belong to.'

Charlotte is writing on the pad in a spidery hand. 'A rich golf club fuckwit,' she says as she writes. 'So what are you saying? You think your husband planned this as some sort of revenge attack and borrowed this apartment to carry out his plan?'

'It's possible.'

'Has he been violent towards you before?'

'Well, no. But he's got a temper. And things between us have got pretty bad.'

'Children involved?'

'No, it's basically about money.'

'The root of all evil, some would say,' says the lawyer with a tepid smile. 'Okay, you woke up in a strange place. Then what did you do?'

Emma repeats the story. The realisation she'd been raped. Panicking and getting out of there.

'How did you get to your sister's house?' says Rogers. 'Because doesn't she live out of town a bit?'

'I took the bus,' says Emma. 'I discovered this morning that my car is still at the hotel.'

'Ah,' says Rogers with a smile. 'We do love buses. What number bus and roughly what time?'

'It was a twelve. I couldn't say exactly when. Maybe seven thirty?'

'Close enough,' says Rogers, making a note. 'Buses have cameras. So you were in a stranger's apartment and you left as soon as you woke up and headed straight for your sister's house to obtain her help because you'd been raped.'

'She wasn't there. She was on a course. But my niece called her and she contacted some specialist officers and they took me to the rape suite at the hospital.'

Rogers nods. Her smile is benign, the eyes are a pale straw colour and surrounded by crinkly lines.

'Well,' she says. 'If they can't connect you to the body in the flat, and you have no idea who he is, presumably it's a he, then I don't think they've got a case. So you're going to have a few uncomfortable hours answering questions. They'll want to keep you here until they get the results of the forensic tests.'

'I've been raped, but I've got to sit here for hours in this box until they sort this out?'

It's just wrong. You're the victim.

She's close to tears again.

Rogers reaches across the table and pats her hand.

'That's about the size of it, yes. I'm going to talk to them. They're obliged to disclose enough information about the offence so I can advise you appropriately. So I'm hoping they might tell us the identity of the victim if they know it.'

'How long will it will take?'

'If they think it's murder, they'll have fast tracked the forensics. But here's what I'm wondering. You mentioned your ex, Neil. You suggested he might want to harm you? I don't suppose there's any chance the dead body could be him, is there?'

Those pale eyes are boring straight into her. She feels uncomfortable.

'I've told you, I've no idea who it is.'

'Well, have a little think about that. Because if we find out it's Neil, there's a very clear connection between you and him. And that could be a trifle awkward, couldn't it?' She stands up. 'I'll get them to bring you some tea.'

Could it be Neil?

As the lawyer disappears out of the door, Emma realises

that by mentioning her suspicions about Neil, she's dug herself into a hole.

The lawyer has jumped to the conclusion that if it is him, then Emma killed him.

16

Tuesday, 2.15pm

Rachel is at a loose end. She has no choice but to hang about and wait for the ACC to find her something trivial and meaningless to do. And that could take a couple of days. The idea of Graham Carter moving into her office is obsessing her. Her weaselly subordinate will certainly make the most of his moment. She also has to wait for Charlotte Rogers to see Emma and find out what's actually going on.

Charlotte agreed to represent her sister and to do it personally, as a favour to Rachel. That, at least, is gratifying. Although, as she had to explain to Simon, it wouldn't cost any less.

Simon has gone off to what he described as an important client meeting. Sometimes she wonders what he gets up to. A client meeting could easily take place in the bar at the golf club. But charming the clients and getting new business is a major part of his job, and he's extremely good at it. He has an air of amiability that most people respond to. It puts them at ease. He's great at telling jokes, even if they're sometimes quite lewd. But he tailors them to the company.

Coming home to him, after a day of dealing with sometimes horrible and upsetting situations, has always been a relief. He knows how to put it all into perspective and cheer her up. A glass of wine, a shoulder massage; he makes her feel looked after. She wishes he was here now.

For want of something better to do, she makes more coffee. Amber has not emerged from her room. Rachel pours two mugs and takes them upstairs. At least this enforced downtime gives her a chance to make peace with her daughter.

She understands Amber's reaction. Her daughter is feeling powerless and frustrated. But Rachel can't help thinking that if she was at university now, where she should be, getting on with her life instead of wasting time working for Emma, she wouldn't be tangled up in any of this.

She taps on Amber's door and goes in. Amber is scrolling on the net and gives her a baleful glance.

'I've found two local firms,' says Amber. 'And—'

'Darling, it's sorted.' She offers Amber a mug. Amber takes it.

'What do you mean?' she says.

'I've hired Charlotte Rogers.'

'Who's she?'

'Trust me, she's what Emma needs.'

'How do you know?'

'I worked with her when she was with the CPS. She taught me exactly what is needed to bring a case to trial and win it.'

'How does that help, Emma?'

'Charlotte's now a defence lawyer. But she's played both sides of the fence, so she knows the system inside out.'

'Oh.' Amber looks weary and deflated.

Rachel perches on her daughter's bed. 'Drink your coffee. If anyone can get Emma off the hook, trust me, it's Charlotte.'

Amber glares at her like a pouty teenager. 'Mum! You talk as if she's guilty. You really think Emma would kill someone? That's just nuts.'

'No, I'm not jumping to any conclusions. But Amber, listen to me—'

Wrong tone of voice.

Too late. Amber jumps on it. 'No. This is totally unfair on Emma. If she says she doesn't remember, then she's telling the truth. She was raped, but everyone's treating her like a criminal. She's not a criminal. The whole thing is outrageous.'

Let her rant and get it out of her system.

Rachel sips her coffee and shrugs. To tell Amber she's being naïve would be counter-productive.

But her silence seems to irritate her daughter more.

'Why do you always want to believe the worst of Emma?' she says.

'Darling, that's absurd.'

'Is it?'

'Amber, I've known your aunt a lot longer than you. And she is capable of being economical with the truth.'

'That doesn't make her a murderer!'

'Let's look at this all with a bit more of a critical eye. Because that's what my colleagues will do. Why did she send you off home before her? She usually drives you home herself, especially after an evening event. So why didn't she?'

'I got a lift; it was no big deal.'

'Okay, let's say she had a thing going on with someone at the hotel, or even one of the guests at the event?'

'She wouldn't. That would be unprofessional.'

'Or she had plans to meet someone. So she sent you home.'

'She didn't send me. I was tired. She was taking care of me, which, actually, is rather nice.'

This comes out more like an accusation than a statement, which riles Rachel.

'The fact of the matter is this. Your aunt is coming out of a bad relationship with a bloke she should never have married. She uses dating apps for casual hook-ups.'

'What's wrong with that? Loads of people do it. It doesn't mean she was asking to be raped.'

'I hope you don't do it. Because as I've told you before–'

'Yeah, Mum, you don't need to repeat the lecture. But you're a cop and I don't want to think like you or see the world like you. You look at everyone with suspicion. There are plenty of blokes online who are just nice, ordinary guys. You have to use your judgement. I know how to use online dating responsibly, and so does Emma. Women are entitled to be sexual beings in their own right.'

'Amber, you're nineteen. When you've had a bit more experience—'

'Exactly, I'm not a child. And y'know the great thing about Emma? She realises that, even if you don't.'

'I'm not trying to pick a fight with you.'

'No. You just think you're right about everything. Well, I'll tell you this. You're wrong about this. Emma is not capable of killing anyone. I'm not being naïve. I know her and I believe her. She may not be as emotionally constipated as you, but she's a good person.'

Emotionally constipated? That sounds like one of Emma's lines.

Mother and daughter sit for a moment in hostile silence.

Rachel takes a breath. She's received plenty of abuse and anger in her life; water off a duck's back, it comes with the job. But she's never been talked to like this by her own child.

'Well,' she says stiffly. 'I'm sorry you think this way.'

'It's not me you should apologise to, is it?' snaps Amber.

Rachel stands up and stalks out of the room. She feels stung. But somewhere inside her head, a spiteful little voice whispers: it's not all bad. This is where Amber gets to learn a few home truths about her precious Emma.

As she walks down the stairs, her phone vibrates.

Charlotte Rogers.

She answers. 'Charlotte,' she says brightly. 'Have you seen her?'

'I have. And we need to talk.'

17

Tuesday, 2.45pm

It's Dean's third visit to his dad in the care home, and the thing that hits you as soon as the door opens is the smell. It's an odd mixture of shit, piss and death. And you can't just walk in. You have to be buzzed in and sign the visitors' book. It's fair enough, keep the old folks safe. But Dean knows how this must feel to the old man. He did two pretty hefty stretches inside; to end up locked up again and for the rest of his life, must be galling.

Dean makes a point of parking the Aston right outside the front entrance where everyone can see it. Make the bozos who run this place realise who he is. Doesn't matter where you are, in a pub, a hotel, or even a grotty care home, if they think you've got money, you get treated differently.

All the care staff wear pale pink scrubs, which is fine on the girls. But it makes the big black lad who looks after the old man into a right sissy. Why can't he have blue? Dean's asked him that. Company policy was the answer. But Dean gets on with him. His name's Jay, built like a tank. He must do some serious work in the gym and Dean respects that. And he's patient with the old man; lifting him and hauling him around, but in a gentle way.

The first time he visited, the day he got out, Dean spoke to the manager, a lady called Sharon. Fat, middle-aged, she looked the sort who'd worked hard her whole life and got bugger all to show for it. The estate where Dean grew up was full of women like Sharon, bloated, stressed and old before their time. If you play by the so-called rules, and don't grab what's rightfully yours, this is how you end up, wiping other people's arses.

But Sharon was bright and breezy as a talk show host. It made little sense to Dean. 'Your dad's done well since he's been here,' she said. 'When they come to us straight from hospital, we try to get them moving and interested in life again. We have a lot of stroke survivors and rehabilitation is what we focus on. They don't just sit around.'

Dean finds the old man in the main lounge where they're all sitting around in a circle like zombies staring at the massive TV. But the sound is turned low so no one can follow what's going on. This is the sight that tears him up, seeing the old man slumped in his wheelchair like a sack of potatoes, watching daytime TV with a bunch of old biddies.

No way you wanna end up like this. Better to top yourself first.

He strolls across the room, and can't help feeling the pleasure in his own strength and agility. Makes you appreciate what you've got, that's for sure. Some of the old biddies glance at him. One gives him a toothless smile.

The old man is dozing. Dean squats down beside the chair and touches his knee.

'Alright, Dad,' he says softly. 'It's just me.'

The old man opens his eyes and blinks a couple of times. Then some sort of recognition dawns and he grunts. A low, guttural sound, like an animal at bay.

'Yeah, it's Dean,' Dean says with a smile. 'How you doing?'

The old man says nothing; he just looks blankly at his son.

Dean stands up, slots his hands in his pockets and looks around. He feels awkward. What's he supposed to do? He feels like kicking the crap out of something or someone.

Jay appears, carrying a tray of plastic cups. He smiles at Dean.

'Alright, mate,' he says. It feels as if he's laughing at Dean, mocking his weakness. Dean would love to take him on, slug it out. Then they'd see who was the better man. But he just nods.

'How is he today?' he manages to say.

Jay puts the tray on a table. 'Yeah, he's had a busy morning,' says Jay. 'Haven't you, Jimmy? Walked a few steps with the frame.'

The old man gazes up at Jay and his expression softens. He doesn't look at Dean like that. It's as if he thinks Jay is his son, not Dean.

This gives Dean a hollow feeling inside. How is this fair? Hasn't he been a good son? His whole life, he's followed the old man's lead, looked up to him, respected his authority. Went to jail, served his sentence, didn't grass, because he knew that's what the old man expected. He's never let him down.

He notices Jay staring at him with pity in his eyes.

Fuck him!

'Hey,' says Jay. 'Why don't you help him with his afternoon cuppa? He loves his tea.'

Jay is holding up a plastic sippy cup, the sort used to feed a baby.

'Isn't that your bloody job?' says Dean. 'Or don't we pay you enough?'

Jay shrugs.

Dean walks off. He has to or else there'd be trouble. He could take Jay, no problem. He's had fights with bigger bastards than that inside and come out on top. He strides down the corridor. But there's no way out; just a fire door. He considers kicking it open, then he hears a voice behind him.

'You alright, Dean?' It's her, fat Sharon.

He turns on his heel to face her. He paints on a smile.

'Yeah, I'm just, y'know…'

He wipes his nose with the back of his fist.

'I know it's awful for you seeing your dad like this,' she says. 'I can see he was a powerful man once, big and strong like you.'

Dean nods. He can feel the tears welling up. 'He was like a rock,' he mutters.

'You have to say to yourself, that man is still there inside somewhere. He hears you.'

'You reckon? He looks at me like he don't know me.'

'Just chat to him, like you would've before. Tell him what you're doing. Just because it's hard for him to respond doesn't mean he isn't listening. I've worked with a lot of stroke survivors, and Jimmy's sharp. He watches. He knows what's going on. And with the physio, he tries. He's got a strong will.'

Dean nods. Grits his teeth. He remembers his dad running the doors on half the clubs in north London. He must've had a dozen blokes working for him and no one would've dared cross him. Then some stupid, coked-up punter tried it on and ended up in the gutter with a cracked skull. Paralysed from the neck down. Turned out to have posh parents and they were out for revenge. Isn't everyone? Too many witnesses. Some kept their mouths shut. But the old man still went down. That was the beginning of the end.

'I'll leave you to it,' says fat Sharon. 'But I'm in my office if you want to talk.'

'Cheers,' says Dean.

When he returns to the main lounge, the old man is finishing his tea. He clutches the sippy cup, but Jay has to steady his hand and guide it to his mouth.

Dean walks over. He meets Jay's eye.

'Sorry, mate,' he says. 'Bit, y'know…'

'No problem,' says Jay with a smile.

'I've got a new car. Can I take him out and show him?'

'Yeah, of course,' says Jay. 'You don't need to ask permission.'

Dean nods. Jay shows him how to take the brake off the wheelchair, and he pushes the old man out and down the corridor to the main door. He keys in the security code and wheels him out into the car park.

The Aston Martin sits there, grey and gleaming. Dean sets the brake on the wheelchair.

'Have a look at this, Dad,' he says. 'That slimy little fucker thinks he can buy me off with a fucking sports car. Well, he's got another think coming, hasn't he?'

He watches his father's face; the eyes have the same blank, faraway stare but there's the ghost of a smile.

The old man knows! Course he does. And he wants what's right too.

This realisation fills Dean with excitement. The two of them back in charge. It's what the old man wants too. It's obvious. In reality, it would be Dean running things, but that's a detail. He'll always give the old man the respect that's due, which is more than Craig does.

He squats down in front of his father and places his palms on the old man's knees. Through the trackie bottoms, he can feel bones and wasted muscles.

'Listen, Dad. I know you can understand me. I've had a lot of time to think about this and I've made a plan. I'm the eldest. You and me, we built this firm, fought hard for our turf. He just went to fucking college. But now I'm out and I'm taking back what's mine. He thinks he can grab it all and you and me and Kelly, what do we get? He was never there for Kel when she needed him. But then neither was I. And I blame myself for that.'

The old man's chin wobbles. He's trying to speak. 'Sh… sh.. e…' he takes a laboured breath. The frustration in him is palpable.

'You mean Kelly, Dad? You talking about Kelly?'

He nods. His chin dips to his chest.

'Ain't your fault, Dad. Craig should've dealt with that junky bastard, then she never would've ended up in jail. She weren't cut out for that. She couldn't hack it. There are people to blame for this. But not you.'

The old man huffs, then he shakes his head wearily. The effort of trying to speak has drained him.

'And there's going to be a reckoning. I promise you that. I'm gonna get you out of here. Craig should never've done this to you.'

The old man's eyes are watery and grey, but now he's looking straight at Dean. His lips are tight and pursed. He's frowning.

He understands. They're on the same page.

Dean squeezes his boney hand. 'Don't get mad, get even.

95

Inn't that what you always taught us? Now I know you're with me. That makes all the difference.'

18

Rachel meets Charlotte at a coffee shop in the centre of town. It's a cavernous place, stripped back to the raw brickwork with exposed pipes crisscrossing the vaulted ceiling. Because of its proximity to the courts, a number of lawyers use it. It has plenty of secluded corners ideal for private conversations.

She's the first to arrive.

Charlotte comes bustling in wreathed in scarves against the November chill.

'Thank you for this,' she says breathlessly. 'I thought it best we convene off the premises, so to speak. But this will have to be brief.'

'How is Emma?'

'She's bearing up. I've forestalled your colleagues, but they want to press ahead with the interview.'

'I can imagine.'

Charlotte plonks down on a chair. 'So, I've had a brief word with the SIO about disclosure. He can't tell me the identity of the murder victim yet. He was prepared to say that they're assuming murder because his throat was slashed.'

Rachel imagines her sister with a knife in her hand.

Is she capable of such a savage act? If this guy had just raped her? Maybe.

'Well,' says Rachel. 'I think Alistair's being straight with you. They may think they know who it is, but need to confirm it.'

'What's your theory?' says Charlotte. 'Because I'm sure you've got one.'

Rachel sighs. 'I'm just guessing. A casual hook-up that went bad. She needed to defend herself.'

'Then why is she lying about it?'

'I'm not really sure. I'd like to think that if I'd been at home, she would've come clean to me. But perhaps I'm fooling myself. We've never been that close. And Emma's evasive. She'll always go for the easy option.'

'No love lost between you, then?'

This throws Rachel.

Is she that transparent?

'I wouldn't say that. She's my sister. I care about her, of course I do.'

'But you disapprove of her?'

Rachel sighs. 'No, I'd never judge her. But we're very different. She's always been a bit reckless. She says I'm emotionally constipated. I believe that's the phrase. She's the party girl; life should be fun, or else what's the point? That's her attitude. I'm pretty sure she uses dating apps for casual hook-ups. She drinks a lot. I'm not saying it's a problem. But on a night out, I've seen her get pissed and pick up a man in a bar.'

Charlotte is surveying her with a beady eye. 'Some people would regard that as normal behaviour,' she says.

'I'm not criticising her. But I don't think she's a very good judge of character when it comes to men. She's currently going through a very acrimonious divorce.'

'Yes,' says Charlotte, 'she mentioned her ex to me. She thinks he could've targeted her as a sort of revenge attack. Do you think that's possible?'

'Wow. That's out of left field.'

'It is. What do you make of it?'

'My sister can be obtuse. A kind of admission? He raped her, she killed him? But how did she end up in this strange apartment? Because Neil is broke; he lives with his mother.'

'Emma reckons he might've borrowed this apartment from some golf club buddy.'

An outlandish idea, but it makes sense.

Rachel huffs. 'I wouldn't put anything past him. Their relationship has always been stormy.'

Charlotte folds her chubby, bejewelled fingers and says, 'I'm just trying to get ahead of the curve here—'

'Oh, I'm with you,' says Rachel. 'Hepburn will know who owns the flat. That's easy to establish. But if he can't match that with his victim, that explains the reticence. And what if it's Neil?'

'Exactly.'

Rachel's thoughts are racing ahead. She could find out if he's alive. The team doesn't yet know of his existence, so how can it be construed as interfering? She'd just be eliminating a suspicion her sister has raised privately with her lawyer.

'I could find out,' she says.

'That would help. And until we know the identity of the victim and whether they can connect Emma to him in terms of the physical evidence, I'm tempted to shut this down. Advise her to say no comment.'

'Makes her look guilty.'

'It's strategic until we know what we're dealing with. She's a rape victim and should be treated as such. I don't think she should be subjected to questioning in these circumstances. She provided the information that led the police to search these premises. Why would she do that if she knew there to be a body there?'

'It's a forceful argument,' says Rachel.

'Well, we'll go with it for now.'

'I'll see if I can locate Neil.'

19

Emma stares at the cheese sandwich on the table in front of her. She drank the tea, but the sandwich was a bridge too far.

The lawyer sent by her sister has a flippant manner, which makes Emma feel like a criminal. Or maybe it's just the fact that she's sitting here and waiting in this little box of a room. There are cameras mounted in all the corners. Discrete, but obvious. Rachel once explained the system to her: interviews are filmed and recorded. The live feed can be watched by all the detectives on their computers. So although she's sitting there alone, she's being watched. Some copper is sitting at his desk, munching his own disgusting sandwich and watching her. Every belch or fart or sigh or tear is being monitored by someone she'll never meet.

The young officer who brought her here was kind but matter-of-fact. She didn't seem old enough to be a cop, which must prove difficult for her. She was also small; a petite

Asian girl. Why would she want to do a job like this, in an organisation like this?

When her sister joined the police, it made no sense to Emma. Rachel had a degree in history and had always talked about becoming a teacher. Then she went to some careers advice thing and got brainwashed. She'd been assaulted, spat at, and told by their mother that it wasn't a suitable job for an educated woman like her. Jill Harris has always been a complete snob.

But Rachel, being Rachel, had persevered and thrived. Emma admired her for that, her capacity to just dig her heels in and get what she wanted. Over the years, it had exhausted Emma just watching her. After she had Amber, she took the minimum maternity leave, employed a nanny, and got back to work. This produced another shrewish outburst from their mother.

Emma knows what her sister thinks of her, that she's lazy and spoilt and has terrible taste in men, all of which is probably true. Marrying Neil was definitely a mistake, and to be fair to Rachel, she tried to tell her that. Emma thought it would settle things down with Neil. They'd start a family and he'd change.

People don't change fundamentally. That's what Rachel had said. The cynicism of a cop, Emma thought.

Turns out she was right. She often is.

But the babies didn't come and pretty soon Neil was out with the lads every weekend and screwing around. She wanted them to have tests and fertility treatment. He said it wasn't him firing blanks and they couldn't afford it. Emma started the events planning business to distract herself.

The door opens and the lawyer comes in.

'Right,' she says brightly. 'Oh, didn't you like your sandwich?'

'Not hungry,' says Emma.

'Okay, now, when the officers question you, I think it might be best at the moment for you to simply say no comment. Until we know who they think you've killed.'

'Why?'

'Because it's up to them to connect you to this person. If they can't, then they must release you. I've told them, you're a rape victim, and they shouldn't be treating you like this.'

'No, they shouldn't. But I've already told them, I just don't remember what happened and how I got there. If I say no comment, doesn't that make it look like I've got something to hide?'

'In these circumstances, saying as little as possible will put you in a stronger position. We do this until they tell us what the evidence against you is. This is standard practice, Emma. They'll expect it. And it's my professional advice to you.'

What if it is Neil? But how?

'Okay,' says Emma.

The lawyer goes to the door and opens it. The two officers who brought her in are standing outside. They come in and sit down.

The Asian girl smiles at her. 'Didn't you like the sandwich?' she says. 'Can we get you something else?'

Emma shakes her head.

The other one glances at the lawyer.

'If you're ready, we'll get started,' she says.

'We're ready,' says the lawyer.

They say their names, Boden and Chakravorty, a DS and a DC. Boden repeats the caution and asks if she understands.

She mumbles yes. Her brain is zoning out.

Get through this. Do what the lawyer says and they'll have to let you go home.

'Okay,' says Boden with a smile. 'You told us earlier about how you recorded the address of the place where you woke up. Could you just confirm what you said before?'

This throws Emma. She glances at her lawyer.

'Yeah, well, what I told you was right,' she says. 'But I don't want to say anymore now.'

Boden looks at her notes. 'You wrote the number of the flat and the floor on your arm so you'd get it right?'

'Sergeant,' says the lawyer. 'We don't dispute that the flat you visited was the one my client directed you to.'

'Okay,' says Boden. 'Do you know whose flat you were in?'

'No. I told them. The rape officers or whatever they're called. I had no idea where I was. I got up, grabbed my clothes and ran.'

Why are they asking all this? They've got it on video.

'Did you look round the flat at all before you left?'

'No, I told you. I ran.'

'You didn't go into the kitchen?'

'No.' She glances at the lawyer, who's sitting there, hands folded.

'We've confirmed that the body in the flat is, in fact, the owner of the flat,' says Boden.

It's not Neil!

Emma wonders if the relief shows on her face. She feels the lawyer sitting next to her exhale.

Now they'll have to let her go.

'The flat belongs to Howard Sampson,' says Boden. 'Do you know him?'

Emma feels giddy. She hears the words, but they make no sense.

Howard?

'What?' she says. 'I was at Howard's place?'

Why on earth…?

'Do you know him?' says Boden.

'Can I stop you there, Sergeant?' says the lawyer. 'I need to talk to my client.'

This washes over Emma. 'Well, yes… but…'

The DS is staring straight at her. The look is both neutral and unrelenting. Emma's seen her sister do this.

'I don't get it. The dead person is Howard?' says Emma. 'That just makes no sense.'

'But you do know him?' says the cop.

'I think we should stop,' says the lawyer again.

But Emma's not listening. Her thoughts are in a spin.

How did you end up in Howard's flat?

'Yeah, sort of,' she says. 'But not well. He's my brother-in-law's business partner. They run an accountancy firm together.'

Divorced, balding, a bit smug. He tried to chat her up last Christmas at a drinks party at her sister's. He had bad breath.

'Your brother-in-law?' says Boden.

'Simon Knight. He's married to my sister, Rachel Knight.'

Boden doesn't move. She seems to take a moment to absorb this. The DC raises her eyebrows.

Emma is shaky and confused. 'Are you saying Howard Sampson attacked me? That I'm being accused of killing Howard Sampson?'

'Did you kill him, Emma?'

'Right,' says the lawyer. 'I really do insist that we stop here so I can consult my client.'

'Okay,' says Boden, standing up.

Emma puts her face in her hands.

20

Rachel stares up at the small Victorian terraced house. She's rung the ineffective doorbell several times and hammered with her fist. The curtains are drawn both upstairs and downstairs. Next door's dog is barking fit to bust.

It doesn't look as if anyone's home. She tries to recall what she can about Neil's mother. In her mind's eye, she can picture a small nervous-looking woman; she attended her son's wedding to Emma in a rather odd mauve fascinator, which fell off and was blown away by the wind. Simon had gallantly retrieved it for her.

But she's probably at work. Is she a nurse? Rachel can't remember. She glances at her phone. The three calls to her brother-in-law's number have gone straight to voice mail. This is not looking good.

Could he have drugged and raped Emma in some act of spiteful vengeance? It's possible.

She gives the front door one last hammering for good

measure. Then she hears a noise, some shuffling, and it opens a crack. A face peers out at her, bleary-eyed.

'What the fuck?' he mutters.

It's Neil, looking annoyed, but alive.

'I've been trying to phone you,' says Rachel.

He opens the door wide. He's wearing boxer shorts, a vest, and seems to have just woken up.

'What d'you want?' he says. 'Has that bitch sent you round to hassle me?'

'Can we talk inside?' says Rachel.

He shrugs and steps back from the door. She follows him into the house. The narrow hallway contains a bicycle and several pairs of shoes. He leads her into the gloomy front room; as she enters he pulls the curtains back letting in a grey dismal light. He turns to face her, hands on hips. He's a large, muscular individual. His unshaven face looks haggard, and there are deep bags under his eyes. He's younger than Emma by a couple of years, but the booze, the partying and, Rachel suspects, the drugs, have taken their toll.

He farts loudly and makes no apology; he just stares at her.

'Emma's been raped,' she says.

He blinks a couple of times, frowns. 'What?' he says. For a brief moment, a look of horror and concern crosses his face, then it returns to neutral.

'Well, if she will shag anything with a dick,' he says, sourly.

'As far as we can tell,' says Rachel, 'she was working, clearing up after an event. Someone drugged her, probably with GHB, and abducted her. You wouldn't know anything about that, would you?'

His jaw slackens and he shakes his head in disbelief.

'What?' he says. 'You think…'

'I'm just wondering,' says Rachel. 'Because we can take your phone, we can track your movements over the last twenty-four hours, and if you have anything at all to do with this, we will find out.'

'You're a piece of work, Rachel. You know that? Sanctimonious and self-righteous. You think you know me and you can walk in here and accuse me?'

You're crossing the line. Rein this in.

'I'm not accusing anyone. My sister's been raped. I intend to find the perpetrator and bring him to justice.'

He smirks. 'The perpetrator? Is that what I look like to you? That's your judgement, is it?' He holds out his large, calloused palms. 'Because I'm a brickie? Because it's never suited your fucking dignity that your sister married a working class bloke, not some slimy accountant like your old man.'

She stares up at him. He's big and indignant, but there's nothing threatening in his stance. She's found out what she needed to know and it's time to get out of there.

'This is pointless,' she says.

He huffs. She turns and heads for the front door.

As she opens it, he stands in the hall behind her.

'Tell Emma,' he says, 'that I'm sorry to hear what's happened to her. And I hope she's alright.'

Rachel gives him a curt nod and steps out into the street. She heads for her car, which she's had to park round the corner.

As she walks, her phone buzzes.

Charlotte Rogers.

She answers as she continues to walk. 'Charlotte,' she says. 'It's not him. Neil Bryant is alive, kicking and spitting his usual venom.'

'Howard Sampson,' says Charlotte.

'What?' says Rachel.

'Your colleagues have confirmed that the flat belongs to Howard Sampson and the body found in the kitchen is, in fact, him.'

Howard? That's impossible.

Rachel stops beside her car. She clicks the key fob without thinking.

Emma and Howard?

It takes a moment for this to sink in. And the implications. Her sister was having an affair with her husband's business partner? No wonder she's been trying to lie her way out of this. But how long had this secret affair been going on?

Rachel leans on the car. It's a gut punch.

'I imagine this is quite a shock for you,' says Charlotte.

'Yes.'

'Well, I thought you'd want to hear it from me. I'll give you time to digest.'

'Thank you,' says Rachel, hanging up.

She looks up and down the street; everything looks normal. But for her it isn't.

Emma was having an affair with Howard?

It certainly feels like the sort of thing Emma would've done just to spite her.

21

Tuesday, 3.45pm

Emma is shaky and light-headed. She's been left alone again. The fact that Howard was Simon's business partner seemed to be news to the cops. They've scurried off.

The lawyer had looked her up and down. Then she said, 'I'll leave you to gather your thoughts.'

Gather your thoughts?

She has no idea what to think. Over the years, she's met Howard a handful of times, mostly social occasions. She didn't know where he lived. Why would she?

His wife left him, possibly a year ago; Emma can't remember. He was a weird guy; nerdy and awkward. They had no kids. Rachel hated the wife.

No surprise there.

If her sister doesn't like someone, she's not that good at covering it up.

Emma thinks about Howard. He had the air of a sad divorcee in desperate need of a shag. She'd tried to be kind.

Could he have kidnapped her and taken her to his flat? It seems ridiculous. Yet the cops say that's where she was.

The door opens and the lawyer returns.

'Well,' she says. 'We may have a few issues here.'

'Have you spoken to Rachel?' says Emma.

'Yes. I called her.'

'What did she say?'

'She seemed surprised about you and Howard.'

'There is no me and Howard.'

'Okay.' The lawyer takes out her yellow pad. 'You didn't know that you'd woken up in his flat.'

'No. I've no idea where he lives. Why would I?'

'You've not been having a sexual relationship with him?'

'No! I bloody well haven't. The last time I saw him was probably last Christmas.'

The lawyer is staring at her pad and writing.

'Okay,' she says.

'This is some kind of surreal nightmare,' says Emma.

'Surreal how?'

'I don't… it makes no sense. How did I end up in Howard's flat?'

The lawyer is scanning her. Emma can see the shrewdness in those pale eyes. She's trying to decide if Emma's lying.

Emma meets her gaze. 'Listen,' she says. 'I'm not a stupid woman, despite what my sister might tell you. If I'd been sleeping with Howard Sampson, and we'd had a row or a fight and I'd killed him, don't you think I would've acted differently?'

'People do strange things when they're in shock.'

'Maybe. But if it was supposed to be a secret affair, the obvious thing to do would be to run away and hide, wouldn't it? Not go voluntarily to the police so they could collect forensic evidence.'

The lawyer nods. 'True.'

Emma meets her gaze. She's got to make this woman understand and listen to her. 'I reckon what most people would do, if they'd done something terrible like that, is go home, clean themselves up, get rid of their clothes, try to pretend they were never there.'

The lawyer nods. 'Or they might feel so awful that they'd want to confess. Many people find the burden of a killing committed in the heat of the moment too heavy to bear. So, if such a person had a police officer for a sister, they might go to her house intending to tell her.'

'Is that what my sister thinks? I went round there to tell her, but when I found she wasn't at home, I bottled out?'

'I'm saying that's another scenario.'

Emma sighs. 'I don't know what to say.'

'My best professional advice at this stage is for you to say nothing. You were in Howard's flat. That is not disputed. But it's up to the police to produce forensic evidence that proves the two of you had physical contact.'

'But what if he kidnapped me somehow and took me there and raped me? Then there will be some evidence, won't there?'

'They'll be looking into that. They'll try to track his movements. Look at any vehicles he had access to. Phone records, CCTV. Any footage they can find from the hotel, who've probably got their own security system.'

'How long's all that going to take?'

'A while.'

Emma's heart sinks. When will this nightmare end?

'And you want me to just sit here and say no comment?'

'That would be my advice.'

'And who's paying for your advice? Rachel?'

The lawyer's lip curls into a cynical smile. 'You're my

client, Emma. And it's my duty to serve your best interests. You have to trust me on that.'

'You realise Rachel resents me, don't you? She thinks I persuaded Amber to take a gap year and stay working for me. But Amber made up her own mind. I've only ever been a sounding board for her. I've never told her what to do.'

'You need to separate out all the strands of this in your mind. Your sister is thinking like a police officer, she can't help that.'

'She's not thinking like a sister, though, is she?'

'If she wanted to see you go to prison, she wouldn't have hired me. In terms of the legal representation available to you in your current situation, I'm the expensive rottweiler. And my aim is to get you out of here as quickly as possible. So, I intend to keep up pressure on the police to release you on bail. They may not be willing to do that yet. But if you aren't willing to talk to them, and we make that clear, then there's no advantage to keeping you here.'

Emma nods. 'I see. I guess that makes sense.'

'If you don't feel able to trust me on a personal level, then consider this. I have a reputation to maintain.'

'I'm not saying I don't trust you. I just… I don't know…'

'You've been raped. You're upset and confused. You are a victim, and I'll do my level best to ensure that the police treat you as such. Just sit tight, Emma, you will get through this.

As the lawyer gets up, she pats Emma on the shoulder.

'Thank you,' says Emma.

'I know the tea's awful. But drink it or some water and stay hydrated.'

'Yes,' says Emma. She watches the lawyer disappear. She looks up at the cameras. They're supposed to switch them off when she's speaking privately to her lawyer. But who knows? Who knows anything? She feels wretched and powerless.

22

Tuesday, 3.50pm

Rachel decides not to call her husband straight away. Breaking this to him on the phone seems cruel, and anyway, she needs time to process it all.

She gets into her car, the car that her dear sister was so sniffy about only this morning, and drives home. She thinks about Simon and the effect this devastating news will have on him. He and Howard went to school together. Howard was the best man at their wedding. Many people found him a little strange, but he was just shy. Simon insisted he wasn't autistic. He was an introvert and a financial wizard, and the bottom line was he'd made her husband a lot of money. Simon was the front man who charmed the clients and brought in the business. Howard remained closeted in his office, crunching the numbers.

As she drives up to the house, Rachel sees with some relief that her husband is already home. His Boxster is parked in its usual slot on the right-hand side of the drive.

Does he know?

It seems unlikely that Hepburn's team will have got to him yet. According to Charlotte, they only found out Howard was Simon's business partner from Emma. But Rachel can't focus on that aspect of the problem right now. She learnt long ago that keeping control of a volatile and fast-moving situation depended on being methodical and not panicking.

Breaking the news to her husband is top of the agenda. But, as soon as she lets herself into the house, she's confronted by Amber coming down the stairs.

'Mum, there's something I need to tell you,' says her daughter in a melodramatic tone.

She raises her palm. 'Fine,' she says. 'But bear with me darling, I just need to speak to your father first.'

'So, what I think about all this doesn't matter?'

'That's not what I said.'

Amber has a stubborn expression; she's not about to be put off.

'I've decided,' she says solemnly, 'that when Emma is released, I should go and stay with her in her flat to support her.'

'Okay? Is that it?'

Amber glares at her. 'Yes,' she says.

'Where's your dad?'

'I don't know.'

Rachel finds her husband in the kitchen, with his phone to his ear, as he scoops beans into the hopper on the coffee machine.

He's chuckling. '…. yeah, and I agree. But fifty quid says I'm right. Money where your mouth is, mate.'

He notices Rachel, gives her a smile, and raises his index finger. He doesn't know.

She watches him winding up the call. Who's he's talking

to? Some crony. Simon is sociable in ways that make no sense to Rachel. He has loads of friends. He loves company and parties. She supposes he's the extrovert to her introvert; if you even believe in these rigid categories.

As she waits for him to finish his call, she paces to manage her irritation. But she must consider him. He doesn't know it, but his world, his business, is about to be turned upside down. She must break this terrible news to him like a wife, not a cop.

It doesn't help that Amber has followed her into the kitchen and is getting a carton of juice from the fridge.

Her daughter gives her a baleful glance. Rachel ignores it.

She thinks about her sister. It beggars belief that Emma would just lie to her about this and expect to get away with it. Barefaced lies. She must realise it would come out. How could it not?

And Howard. What the hell happened? A fight? Did Emma kill him? Is she capable of that?

How can you think that about your own sister?

Simon hangs up the phone. He's still chuckling. He looks from his wife to his daughter.

'Okay,' he says. 'You two shouldn't fall out over this. We all want to help Emma, but we've got different ways of going about it.' This is so typical of him. Always the peacemaker.

It's why you love him.

'We're not going to fall out,' says Rachel.

Amber says nothing. She pours juice into a glass.

Rachel moves across the kitchen towards her husband. 'I need to tell you something, Si,' she says.

He gives her a quizzical look. She only calls him Si in their more intimate moments.

She's seen plenty of dead bodies, including murder

victims. But this is personal, and the tears well up. The idea of Howard with his throat slashed. She swallows hard.

'Oh my darling,' she says. 'I'm sorry to say that Howard is dead.'

He frowns. 'What? What do you mean?'

'Howard is dead,' she repeats. 'It looks like he was killed.'

'Killed how? A road accident?'

'Killed as in murder.'

She watches him flinch. The colour drains from his face.

Behind her, Amber puts her glass down with a snap. 'Oh my God,' she says.

Simon shakes his head. The shock immobilises him. It doesn't compute; his brain won't accept it. Rachel has seen this look on so many strangers' faces. But this is her husband. For a frozen moment, they both just stand there. Then he says, 'Who would murder Howard? Was he mugged?'

Rachel is rarely at a loss for words, but at this moment she is. She scans him. His face is full of confusion and hurt. He turns away. She puts her palm on his back.

She realises there's no easy way to do this. He sinks on to a stool, leans on the kitchen counter and puts his face in his hands.

She waits. This is his friend of over thirty years. His business partner. A man he sees and talks to everyday.

She rubs his shoulder.

'I'm sorry to say it gets worse.'

'Worse how?' he wipes his nose with the back of his hand.

'Emma's involved.'

'Emma?'

'The address where she said she was raped turned out to

be Howard's flat. The body they found in the kitchen has been identified as his body.'

His face scrunches, his eyes brim with tears. He claps his hand over his mouth. The sound that percolates through is a howl of despair.

He looks at her, but through her; his eyes are wild with pain.

She tries to put her arms round him, but he pushes her away.

She and Amber exchange looks.

Finally, he speaks. 'What? What are you saying?' he mutters. 'He raped her and she killed him? He wouldn't have raped her. That's not possible.'

'Let's not jump to any conclusions. There are a lot of things we don't know here.'

'But that's what you thought before. Emma hooked-up with some guy. He raped her, she killed him.'

'Obviously, she knows Howard. So I don't know what was going on.'

'I bloody-well know he didn't rape her,' says Simon vehemently.

Rachel glances at their daughter. Amber is frowning, as if she's trying to get her head round this.

'Have you talked to Emma?' she says.

'Charlotte told me this on the phone. Just that they've identified the body, and it's Howard.'

'But what does Emma say? She didn't even know where she was.'

'Amber, all I know is what you know,' says Rachel. 'What she told us before we dropped her at her flat this morning. But it seems likely that she was lying.'

'Well, one thing's certain,' says Simon. 'Howard's not a

rapist. I need to call the office.' He kicks the stool aside and slams out of the room.

Rachel looks at her daughter. 'Are you alright?' she says.

'Why do you assume she's lying?'

'Amber, this is complicated enough and very hard for your father.'

'I get that.' She lowers her voice. 'But, Mum, you know as well as I do Howard is a creepy guy. The way he looks at women is not cool.'

'He's awkward. And shy.'

They're still talking as if he's alive. It hasn't sunk in yet.

'He's creepy,' Amber insists. 'When he talks to you, he looks at your tits.'

'Did you have any idea that something was going on between him and Emma?'

Amber grimaces. 'She wasn't that desperate. Maybe he tricked her into going back to his flat. Then he attacked her and she defended herself.'

'Then why hasn't she said that?'

Amber huffs in frustration. 'I've no idea.'

'When she came round here this morning and she found out I wasn't here, what was her reaction?'

'She was just traumatised. A mess.'

'What if she came intending to tell me what had happened? She'd got herself in some complicated mess with Howard and it had all got out of hand. Tempers flare, good people are capable of doing things they later bitterly regret. She knows I would understand that. But when she found I wasn't here, she just lost her nerve. She was too ashamed to tell you.'

Amber shakes her head. 'I find that hard to believe. But, I suppose it's possible.'

'I'm beginning to think it's likely. And whatever you

think, my one aim here is to get my sister out of a bad situation. You have to trust me on that, Amber. Okay, she annoys me at times. But this is serious and I'm on her side.'

'I know that.'

'Good. Just give your dad a bit of space.'

Amber nods.

'And me a hug.'

Amber smiles as Rachel pulls her child into her arms.

23

Tuesday, 3.55pm

Dean Jessop drives the Aston Martin north through the open Fen country. The landscape is flat to the horizon, criss-crossed with a network of man-made waterways and drainage ditches. The road is straight, the traffic light. He comes up behind a huge grain lorry, pulls out to overtake and puts his foot to the floor.

The Aston roars up the road like a bullet and Dean gives a little whoop. He loves it! The power under the hood. There's nothing to beat it. British made too. One of the few things this bloody country can still do. But Dean's a patriot, always has been. Like his dad, Queen and country. But the poor old Queen's gone, like Kelly. His sister way before her time, though. Last couple of years, he's thought of little else.

Let it go now. It's done. She can rest.

The sat-nav takes him beyond Ely and Downham Market, but after that, he turns to the scrappy piece of paper Liam gave him.

'No sat-nav'll find it,' said his old mate. 'Totally off the grid, I promise you.'

Leaving the main road, he follows Liam's makeshift map. The lanes are straight, mostly running alongside the high earth embankments built to channel and hold back the water. He crosses a rickety wooden bridge. There's a wire fence and tied to it a length of blue rope. It looks random, but Liam put it there to mark the route. Dean smiles to himself; half a mile to go according to the map. He should make it before it gets dark. Headlights across this landscape are too much of a give-away. He doesn't want to attract the attention of some nosey farmworker.

The route narrows to a grassy track and up ahead a small copse of trees nestled below a ten-foot embankment. He sees Liam's brand new X5 and parked up next to it a caravan. Liam's boy Jaden, is sitting in the car. As he draws up, Liam himself steps out of the caravan wreathed in smiles. He raises his hand in salute.

Dean gets out of the Aston.

His friend chuckles. 'What's this? You're too fucking snobby to drive my Toyota?'

'Sorry mate,' says Dean. 'Craig called it a teenage drug dealer's car, and I have to say, he's got a point.'

Liam laughs. 'Well, I hope you're not going to be snotty about your new digs because me and Jaden had a mare of a time towing the bloody thing down here.'

Dean scans the caravan. 'Don't look too shabby.'

'Bastard,' says Liam affectionately. 'It's top of the range.'

Jaden gets out of the X5. He gives Dean a respectful nod. He's a sharp lad. Useful. And so far it's all going to plan.

Liam opens the door to the caravan. 'Wanna check it out?'

Dean follows him inside. It's compact and everything looks brand new.

'Sweet,' says Dean approvingly.

'Got you some groceries. Few beers in the fridge.' He pulls a small packet out of his pocket. 'Also, thought you could do with this. It's good stuff, not rubbish.'

He thinks you're an addict?

Liam seems to read his mind. 'Stressful few days. Getting out and everything. You need to chill. Can't do any harm, can it?' he says.

Dean shrugs. 'I can take it or leave it. But, yeah, why not?'

He takes it. Then smiles and adds, 'I appreciate all you done for me, mate.'

Liam grins. 'Well,' he says. 'It's just payback. You stood up like a man and kept us out of jail. We all owe you a debt.'

'Pity Craig don't seem to agree with you.'

Liam shakes his head. 'He's gone his own way. Reckons he's going to turn himself into a property tycoon. Big ambitions. Good luck to him, I say. Me, I know what I am and what I'm good at.'

'Every man to his trade,' says Dean with a nod.

'Yeah, well stupid government'll never have the balls to legalise drugs, so I'll always be in business.'

Liam opens the fridge and takes out two cans of beer. He hands one to Dean.

'I had lunch with him,' says Dean. 'He don't change. Posh house, posh wife. He's still the lying, conniving little shit he always was. But he gave me a nice car.'

'Make the most of it, I say.' Liam pulls the ring on his can. Beer froths out of the top. 'Cheers,' he says.

Dean pulls the ring on his own can. 'Here's to old mates,'

he says. 'The ones you can always rely on when the chips are down.'

'How long you reckon you're going to be here?' says Liam.

Dean gives him a side-eyed glance. 'Not long,' he says. 'I'm keeping things moving. I don't plan to hang about.'

Liam pulls a scrap of paper from his pocket. 'This is the number of the trawler skipper I told you about. He runs a couple of boats out of Lowestoft. He's reliable.'

Dean takes the paper, stows it in his top pocket. 'How long have you done business with him?'

'Couple of years. I like him because he's not greedy. Does a run a month for us to keep his business going because there's no bloody money in fishing. I've told him to expect your call. And don't worry about the fee, I'll sort that out.'

Dean nods. 'Thanks, mate.'

Liam puts his can down. 'Right, I'm off,' he says. 'Not much of a phone signal here, but, word to the wise, nowadays we don't even use burners. Police have got too clever with all that stuff.'

'I'll send you an email when I'm on the other side of the Channel.'

'Sensible.' Liam pulls him into a rough hug and pats his shoulder. 'And you take care of yourself, Dean. Because I know Craig; he's got some tricks up his sleeve.'

'Don't worry, mate. I know him too.'

Dean watches as Liam and Jaden drive off down the track. Liam's a good bloke, but he's no different to anyone else in the end. He's out for himself. But that's alright. Dean understands the calculation he's making. He hasn't got the balls to move against Craig, but he's smart enough to know that helping Dean will pay off in the long run.

Smiling to himself, Dean steps back into the caravan. Everything's fine. It's all going to plan. And the beauty is his stupid little brother has no idea yet that his business and his life are about to turn to shit.

24

Tuesday, 4.15pm

Rachel peers out at the garden. The sombre November light is fading and it's pouring with rain. Her mood is a combination of frustration and anger. She hates being excluded from the inquiry, but there's nothing she can do except wait. Wait for her colleagues to do their job, wait for Emma to be released on bail.

She began her day in high spirits, about to embark on the first day of her course. She was excited and energised; once this course was under her belt, she'd be all set for promotion to the top ranks of the police service. Then she received Amber's call.

Her daughter can't be blamed. She did the right thing, of course she did. The problem here is Emma. It always is Emma. Rachel has spent her whole life having to rescue her little sister from whatever stupid mess that she's gotten into through her own recklessness. But this affair with Howard, and whatever transpired as a result, plumbs new depths.

She wonders about calling her mother. Jill Harris is not an easy woman to deal with. Fortunately, she moved to Devon, which provides the sort of distance that makes life easier for the whole family. Jill will have to be told eventually, but not today. Rachel decides to park that up for when she's feeling more robust.

She checks the time on her phone. Still nothing from her husband. But he has the distress of colleagues, clients and employees to worry about. He's in shock, and as a result, in no mood to listen to her advice. He stormed out of the house. She presumes he's gone to his office; she hasn't heard from him. In some obscure way, he appears to be blaming her for what's happened. But Rachel interprets this as displaced anger. Once he gets over the shock of it, he'll return to a more reasoned point of view, and they'll be able to discuss it. In the meantime, she decides to let him be.

Amber has retreated to her room, saying she needs to get in touch with clients of Emma's firm. They have several events coming up. Rachel wonders what her daughter intends to tell them. An excuse? A lie? She decides not to ask.

It seems to Rachel that at its heart, the case is simple. Two unhappy and lonely divorcees started a casual affair. The differences between them in terms of character and temperament were legion. Amber was right about one thing: Howard Sampson was far from any woman's dream. So perhaps her sister was keeping the liaison secret out of embarrassment. She was the popular girl who got all the boys, and now she was reduced to this. An awkward, unattractive man like Howard. It was her vanity that made her keep it secret.

Rachel can imagine how it played out. After the event she was running at the hotel, Emma went to her lover's flat. A few drinks; both of them could demolish a bottle of wine each in an evening, no problem. A difference of opinion escalated into a row. Howard wasn't a big bloke, nor was he particularly fit. In a physical fight, Emma could've matched him. There they were in the kitchen, a tussle and she grabbed a knife from the knife block. Perhaps something in her just snapped? After all the rows she'd had with Neil, perhaps she'd just had enough of men. Howard got the payback that should've gone to Neil.

It makes sense, and with the right lawyers to present it, and the right jury, Emma's sentence could be minimised. She could be out in five or six years. But it depends on her coming over as honest and willing to take responsibility for what she's done. Owning up is half the battle. Rachel's task is to help her understand that.

That's the best way to help her.

She's making herself another coffee when she hears her husband's throaty old Boxster pulling up on the drive. She goes to the front door and opens it. As Simon climbs out of his car, he looks pale and drawn.

She smiles. He walks towards her and sighs. 'Sorry I was a bit, y'know…'

Rachel draws him into a hug. 'You've had a terrible shock. It was an understandable reaction.'

'The office staff are in pieces. I've sent everyone home. They just know he's dead. I didn't give any details.'

'Probably for the best.'

'What the hell are we going to do, Rachel?'

She loops her arm through his and leads him into the house. 'Right now, nothing,' she says. 'Hepburn is a good SIO. He'll do his job. Charlotte is an excellent lawyer. She'll do hers.'

'Do you think she did it? I mean, what could've happened? She and Howard had some kind of fight?'

'I don't know. I don't want to believe it. But I didn't even know they were involved. She might be my sister, but she never confides in me.'

'I'm not that surprised. Howard had a real thing about her, y'know.'

Rachel frowns. 'What sort of thing?'

'Well, after Greta divorced him, he got quite down.'

'You never said. But Greta's such a stupid woman. Neurotic as hell.'

'Even though he's quite an introvert, I think he found it lonely living on his own. Howard's a very private bloke. He's never been able to speak about his feelings.'

'You've known him a long time. If he'd talk to anyone, I should think it'd be you. But he is socially awkward. You sure he's not on the spectrum?'

'Maybe. I've just known him so long. He's just... Howard.'

Simon's hand flies to his mouth. 'God, he *was* Howard. I can't believe he's gone.'

Rachel squeezes his arm. 'Come into the kitchen, I'll make you a cup of tea.'

He nods and follows. As she puts the kettle on, he plonks down on a stool. She strokes the few remaining strands of fringe out of his eyes. He's going grey. For so much of their marriage, he's been rock solid and the caregiver. Now it's her turn to look after him.

She kisses him on the forehead.

'I suppose we can't begrudge them,' she says. 'They've both been pretty lonely. How long do you reckon it'd been going on?'

He sighs. 'Not sure. But y'know what Emma's like. Last Christmas, she'd had a bit to drink, she chatted him up.'

'Since last Christmas?'

'I don't know. But I do know he got a bit fixated on her after that. Asked me all sorts of questions.'

'Like what?'

'What sort of flowers did she like?'

'He sent Emma flowers?'

'I think so. Valentine's Day.'

'So she knew he was interested in her?'

'She must've done.'

'Did he ask her out?'

'Not sure. He didn't tell me he did. But y'know that charity thing we did back in the spring, he asked me if she'd be there. Could've started after that.'

'So this could've been going on for months?'

He shrugs. 'You're the detective, not me. Your sister's going through a horrible divorce. She's been pretty miserable. Howard may be a bit gauche, but he's the absolute opposite of Neil.'

Rachel nods. 'I just wish she'd confided in me.'

'Come on, Rachel. She probably thought you'd sneer at her.'

'I don't sneer.'

'Well, maybe not that. But you're always critical of everything she does.'

Why do people keep saying that? It's not true!

'Simon, she does some bloody stupid things. She always has.'

'Whatever. But what the hell happened? They had a fight?'

'It's how a lot of murders happen. Some trivial dispute. Alcohol is often involved. Anger escalates to violence.'

Simon shakes his head. 'I think this whole rape thing is an elaborate lie that she's cooked up, so she can argue she's the victim. I mean, Howard? He was the meekest of men.'

'People contain surprising secrets. They look at porn, they develop obsessions.'

'Oh, come on, I've known the guy since we were twelve years old. Howard was not a rapist. I stand by that. If anything, he was naively romantic. Greta led him a right old dance. And he ended up paying her a small fortune. He was a pushover for any woman.'

She pats his shoulder. 'Okay, don't get upset.'

He shakes his head. 'The whole thing's just a bloody nightmare.'

'You can say that again.'

'I mean, what the hell's her plan? She's going to say Howard kidnapped her and took her to his flat? I've never heard anything so ridiculous.'

'He paid someone to do it? That could be one line of inquiry.'

'Rachel, you need to talk to her, before she drags a good, decent man's name through the mud. Because this isn't fair. He doesn't deserve this. Bad enough that he's dead. Once the bloody media gets hold of this, it'll be a bloody circus. They'll paint him like some pervy rapist. That is not going to be his legacy. It bloody isn't!'

Rachel looks at her husband. The tears are rolling down his cheeks. It's heartbreaking. She's never seen him this distraught.

She draws him into her arms. His head dips and he lays it on her shoulder and sobs.

'Sssh,' she whispers. 'It'll be alright. I promise.'

25

Tuesday, 5pm

DCI Hepburn, hands in pockets, strolls back and forth at the front of the incident room. It's the first full team briefing. Boden watches him from her desk at the back. His casual manner goes some way to covering up the tension in the room. Everyone now knows that the victim, Howard Sampson, was Detective Chief Superintendent Knight's husband's business partner.

Mackie, in typical fashion, had put the matter succinctly. 'She was shagging her brother-in-law's mate. What's so unusual about that?'

'It's unusual if she killed him,' said Chakravorty acerbically.

Hepburn scans the room. 'Okay,' he says. 'This is day one of this inquiry. Let's summarise what we know so far. Jo?'

Boden stands up. 'The victim's identity has been confirmed. His name was Howard Sampson. He was discovered this morning in his kitchen, with his throat slashed. Time of death is yet to be confirmed. PM is scheduled for tomorrow morning. But the preliminary estimate is around midnight.'

'Can we establish yet when Harris either entered or left the flat?' says Hepburn.

Mackie stands up. 'For a posh block of flats, the CCTV is crap, boss. Several cameras not working. A fire escape at the back, which has no coverage. However, we've picked her up boarding a bus at seven twenty am this morning. She travelled to Great Shelford, the location of her sister's house. We haven't actually interviewed her niece yet.'

'Why not?' says Hepburn.

Mackie glances at Boden.

Here we go.

'I wanted to check with you first, sir, before we went knocking on the Detective Chief Super's door,' says Boden. She's damned if the boss is going to land this on her.

Hepburn looks peevish. He sighs. 'Okay, moving on.'

Sod this! He's the SIO.

'Do you want us to make that a priority, sir?' says Boden.

Hepburn glares at her. 'I think how she presented herself and the allegation of the rape to the first person she encountered is very relevant, Sergeant, don't you? Or is that not how they do it in the Met?'

The temperature in the room plummets several degrees. This is a spanking Boden wasn't expecting. He must be feeling the heat. Caught between senior management and his buddy, whose coat tails he's been riding on.

She says nothing.

Hepburn lets his gaze travel round the room. The shuffling and coffee sipping and covert phone checking has stopped. He has everyone's attention.

'Right,' he says. 'I want to see everyone doing their jobs.'

Boden folds her arms. It's all bluster. They're waiting on forensics, the PM and a full account from Emma Harris of what she says happened. Tasks will be allocated. To everyone's relief, the meeting soon breaks up.

Boden and Chakravorty head back to the interview room.

'That was pretty unfair,' says Chakravorty.

Boden shrugs. 'First rule of organisations, Prish. Particularly the police. If you want to rise in the hierarchy, learn to cover your back. Having a record of not getting things wrong is far more important than the things you get right. He's putting it out there that he's not soft-pedalling on this because of Rachel Knight. He doesn't want any finger pointing later.'

Chakravorty considers this. Then she says, 'That's very cynical.'

'Realistic.'

She could add that bitter experience has taught her it doesn't matter how many cases she's solved, the taint of troublemaker continues to dog her career. Don't upset the wrong people.

It's a lesson she's never quite perfected. Being right and doing the right thing is not always an advantage.

Chakravorty glances at her. 'It's still not fair on you.'

Boden sighs. The boss is using her, making an example of her, because he can. And she thought she was making headway here in Cambridge, in this new job; that she was accepted.

Idiot for letting down your guard.

'Don't worry about me, Prish,' she says. 'I can roll with the punches.' She opens the door to the interview room.

Emma Harris is sitting alone, hands folded in her lap, looking forlorn. She glances at Boden.

'My lawyer's told me to say no comment,' she says.

'Okay,' says Boden. She turns to Chakravorty. 'See if you can find her, Prish.'

Chakravorty disappears in search of Charlotte Rogers.

'Want some more tea?' says Boden.

Emma shakes her head. 'How do I make people believe me?' she says.

'Tell the truth.'

'You really think that's enough?'

Course it isn't. But who's going to admit that?

Boden says nothing. She sits down.

Emma wrings her hands. She seems close to tears. 'I can't tell you what I don't know,' she says. 'I had no idea it was Howard's flat. I can't remember what happened. I had no idea there was a dead body. I just ran.'

But where's the CCTV to prove it?

Boden waits. She has a sense they're on the cusp of something here. But it would be wrong of her to probe without the lawyer present. Still, Harris has been cautioned, and it's up to her what she says.

'I know how it looks. I knew him and I was shagging him but keeping it secret. That's what Rachel will think. No one will believe I wasn't involved with him, will they?'

She gives Boden a piteous look. Boden says nothing.

'They won't. Because, yeah, he did send me stuff like flowers. And I've been thinking, well what if he came to the hotel and I can't remember? I mean, I'm not lying, I did black out. But before that?' She gives a weary shake of the head.

An admission or just confusion?

Emma sighs. 'I just can't remember. I'm totally fucked, aren't I?'

The lawyer comes bustling through the door, followed by Chakravorty.

'Apologies,' she says. 'Had to make some calls.'

Everyone takes their seats. Boden reminds Emma that she's still under caution.

Boden pretends to consult her file, then she says, 'Did you ever receive any flowers from Howard?'

Charlotte Rogers scribbles a note on her pad.

Emma's gaze drifts away to the wall, then up to the camera mounted in the corner. She shakes her head, and stares down at her own hands. 'No comment,' she says.

26

Tuesday, 5.45pm

The interview is dragging on. Emma has lost track of how long they've been questioning her. The lawyer scribbles notes, and Emma follows her instructions and replies, 'No comment' to every question. The whole rigmarole is weird, although the lawyer and the two cops seem unfazed. They're used to it, Emma supposes.

The questions started with the flowers.

Why the hell did you say that?

It moved on to why did she have Howard's number in her phone. She has no idea; he must've given it to her at some point. She can't remember when. They also wanted to know when she last saw him, had she visited his flat before, and predictably, were they having a sexual relationship?

She's tempted to speak. But the lawyer's beady eye is on her; her sister's proxy. And she knows what Rachel would say. She's being advised to stay silent for a reason. It's up to the police to prove she did it, and it's stupid to give them any ammunition.

But what if he came to the hotel and you've forgotten?

She catches the younger cop's eye and smiles.

Just a kid doing a job. What's it like for her working for a boss like Rachel? Emma wouldn't fancy it herself. Most of her own youth was spent listening to her mother tell her she should be more like Rachel. This had the opposite effect; everything that Rachel purported to dislike became even more attractive.

Stupid, really. Why did you never just make up your own mind?

She glances at the lawyer, who raises her eyebrows. Have they asked another question?

'No comment,' she says.

The other cop, the DS, is watching her, head tilted to one side. She's the experienced one and thoughtful. She's looking at Emma with a direct, unwavering gaze, but it isn't unsympathetic.

There's a heavy silence in the room.

'Okay,' says the DS. 'I think we'll take a break.'

They all troop out.

This time, instead of leaving Emma alone in the room, she's escorted out by a uniformed officer, who leads her back to the custody suite where they first brought her in. She looks out through the glass double doors; it's dark which surprises her. She's handed over to the custody sergeant, who takes her down a short narrow corridor. The door to a cell stands open.

They're going to lock you in a prison cell!

Emma stops in her tracks. She feels the panic rising inside her, gripping her chest.

No!

The memory erupts. A sharp slap on the legs from her

mother, and being dragged across the garden to the old shed, shoved inside and the door shut on her. It was dark and full of cobwebs and spiders. She sobbed and screamed for ages. Eventually, the door opened and Rachel let her out.

Emma realises the custody sergeant is staring at her. 'Alright?' he says. 'We'll get you a cup of tea.'

Emma looks in the cell. It's white-walled and clean. No sign of any spiders.

She nods and steeling herself, walks into the cell. The door shuts behind her, the lock turns.

How did it come to this?

There's a narrow bunk attached to the wall and on it a folded blanket and a pillow, and in the opposite corner a steel toilet, which smells of disinfectant.

She sits down on the bunk and shivers. Unfolding the blanket, she wraps it round her shoulders.

They're going to leave you here all night.

A hollow despair grips her gut. She wishes she could talk to her sister. But, as the lawyer has explained, that's not about to happen.

She has to stop panicking and get her head straight.

If she can work out what happened, she'll know what to say.

What if this was another one of her blackouts? Not GHB, just booze.

That thought has been edging its way into her mind for several hours, although she doesn't want to go there.

In the last few years, Emma has cut right back on her drinking. But she'll be the first to admit, her twenties were a wild time. She was never much into drugs, a few lines of coke at a party if she was offered. But she's always loved to drink. How else can you have a good time?

When she was twelve, she'd developed a taste for

Bacardi Breezers. She sneaked a few swigs at a family wedding. Rachel was sixteen and allowed the occasional drink. Once, when her sister was going to a party, Emma filched a couple of bottles from her stash. From then on, she'd get hold of alcohol whenever she could. She drank half a bottle of her parent's dry sherry on one occasion, but that was gross.

Booze and blackouts; she does have history.

Admit you have a problem, there's no shame in that.

Rachel has been saying that to her for years and she's been refusing to listen. Her sister's drinking, like everything else about her, is always restrained and under control.

Emma has blacked out several times over the years, woken with a raging hangover in a strange hotel room with no memory of what happened the night before, who she was with or how she got there.

You haven't done it for ages.

But last night? If she'd somehow bumped into Howard, surely she would've remembered? When she's working, she never touches a drop. That was the promise she made to herself. Getting the business back on its feet after the pandemic was tough. Even Rachel couldn't accuse her of being lazy. She worked damned hard.

A key clanks in the lock and the cell door swings open. The lawyer comes in. Her cheeriness depresses Emma.

'Well,' she says. 'I've had a word with the SIO.'

S I what?

Emma can't be bothered to ask.

'He's waiting for forensic reports to come in, then you'll be questioned again.'

'Am I going to be here all night?'

'Looks like it. Are you going to be alright?'

'Do I have a choice?'

The lawyer ignores the question. 'I think our priority is to get you released on bail and out of here.'

Our priority?

Emma decides not to argue. 'I'll be okay,' she says.

The lawyer departs, no doubt to put her feet up and have a stiff drink. Emma wishes she could do the same. The custody sergeant appears with a mug of tea. He holds up a sachet of sugar; Emma shakes her head.

Left alone, she stares at the walls and the mug of tea which he's placed beside her on the end of the bunk.

Even if she gets out on bail, then what? She's still a suspect.

How did you end up in his flat?

She thinks back over the last year and her various encounters with Howard. Is there anything she could've done to make him wish her harm?

The flowers.

She got a very expensive bunch of red roses on Valentine's Day. She knew they were from him. But she never mentioned it and nor did he.

Back in May, he accosted her at a barbecue at her sister's house. He mentioned her ongoing divorce proceedings with Neil. It seemed at the time as if he was trying to commiserate with her. He mentioned his own divorce and offered help if she needed it. She said she didn't.

She can remember the way he looked at her and it made her uncomfortable.

Several weeks after that, he'd phoned her and said that he had a couple of tickets for the opera at Covent Garden. A famous Italian tenor she'd never heard of was performing; he seemed to regard this as a big deal. She said she was busy and hoped he got the message.

Did he get the message?

Is this what happened? Howard felt rejected by her? And he got angry. And what? He cooked up some plan to abduct her?

But he was a weedy physical specimen; thin, round shouldered, gangling. How would he have pulled it off? He could've drugged her with GHB, as Rachel suggested. But getting her out of the hotel and into his car on his own?

Then it occurs to her; what if he had help? What if he joined forces with the other man in her life who thought she should be punished: Neil?

Neil was stoney broke and he hated her. Howard had money and plenty of it. Did they do a deal? And then what? They fell out? Had a fight? And her ex-husband left her there to take the rap.

27

Tuesday, 7pm

Rachel watches her husband pour a large measure of Scotch into Charlotte's glass. Her old friend looks weary. Rachel knows it is out of respect for her that Charlotte is handling the case and the interviews personally. In most circumstances, even a murder case, she'd be working with a younger associate and letting them do the donkey work.

'I am really grateful for this,' says Rachel.

'I'm grateful for this,' says Charlotte with a chuckle as she raises her glass.

'What will happen next?' says Simon.

'If they've got the evidence, they'll go to the CPS and if they agree, charge her.'

'You think they have?' says Rachel.

Charlotte smiles. 'Hepburn's your man, Rachel. You tell me.'

'I haven't called him. It wouldn't be right to put him on

the spot. It's important that we all do the right thing and are seen to do so.'

If her sister is convicted of murder, Rachel knows her behaviour must remain unimpeachable. She needs that distance to salvage her career. No one can be blamed for the actions of dodgy relatives.

She catches Charlotte looking at her. Those pale eyes and the penetrating gaze. The lawyer knows the score.

Sipping her drink, Charlotte says, 'Emma's not a hard-ened criminal. Put her in a cell overnight to soften her up, then confront her with the evidence in the hope of getting an admission. Isn't that what you'd do Rachel?'

'Probably,' says Rachel. 'I only wish I had the chance to talk to her myself.'

As she speaks, she notices her daughter has just come into the room. They haven't spoken since their earlier row.

'Charlotte,' she says. 'This is my daughter, Amber. Amber, Charlotte is representing Emma.'

Amber nods. She has a bullish expression on her face.

'How is Emma?' says Amber.

'Bearing up,' says Charlotte. 'And I must be off.' She drains her glass and stands up.

'When will she be released?' says Amber.

'That rather depends on the forensics,' says Charlotte. 'Do I recall your mother saying you're going to study law?'

Amber glares at Rachel, who says rapidly, 'Amber's having a gap year.'

As Simon escorts Charlotte down the hall to the front door, Amber turns to her mother. 'Isn't she a bit past it?'

'Amber! Sssh! She'll hear you.'

'I'm just saying.'

Simon returns to the room and pours himself a drink. 'Well,' he says with a sigh. 'Once she's been charged, presumably she'll get bail and then you can talk some sense into her, Rachel.'

'What's that supposed to mean?' says Amber.

Rachel can see what's coming, but can do nothing to avert it.

Simon takes a slug of his drink. 'Emma needs to be persuaded to come clean and tell the truth.'

'What makes you think she isn't telling the truth?' says Amber.

'It's clear she and Howard were involved—'

'Dad, you don't know that,' says Amber.

'Then how come she was in his flat and in his bed?'

'She says she was raped. She needed hospital treatment.' Amber is glaring at her father. He drains his glass.

'Amber,' he says. 'Listen to me—'

Rachel steps between them. 'Time out,' she says. 'This doesn't help anyone, including Emma.'

Amber's eyes are flashing. 'How does it help Emma, when you all assume she's a murderer and you've hired some broken-down old lawyer who should've retired years ago—'

'Amber, enough!' says Rachel.

'Why won't you look at this from Emma's point of view?'

'Believe me,' says Rachel. 'I'm trying to.'

'The idea that Emma would've looked twice at a weirdo like Howard—'

Simon slams his glass down. 'That's it Amber, I've heard enough. You're nineteen and you're being naïve. There's absolutely no reason they couldn't have been lovers.'

'Dad, he asked her to go to the opera with him. I mean, why would he think she'd like opera? I mean, yuk! Boring! She said no, and we laughed about it. She didn't want to be too blunt because he was your friend. But, come on, take it from me, he was creepy.'

Rachel sighs. Her husband has a thunderous look on his face. But he turns on his heel and storms out of the room.

Rachel looks at her daughter. 'Well done,' she says sourly. 'He's just lost his best friend, who was found in his kitchen with his throat cut.'

Amber grimaces.

'Yeah, horrific,' says Rachel. 'You know what it looks like when the carotid artery in the neck is severed? What it smells like? The amount of blood. It's not like something you see in the movies.'

Amber's chin is quivering. Tears run down her cheeks. Rachel shakes her head wearily. She moves towards her daughter.

'Come here,' she says, putting her arms round her daughter.

'I'm not trying to upset him,' says Amber. 'It's just he's making all these assumptions.'

'Of course he is,' says Rachel, stroking her daughter's hair. 'We all are. Because we don't have the evidence. He's loyal to Howard and you're loyal to Emma.'

'I don't know what to do, Mum.'

'You say sorry to your dad, which doesn't mean you agree with him, it means you recognise how upset he is.'

Amber nods.

'I'm sorry.'

Rachel kisses her forehead. 'Y'know Amber, one of the things I've learned as a police officer is that good people can sometimes do bad things. A split-second flash of anger can lead to terrible choices.'

'You do think she killed Howard?'

'I honestly don't know. But if she did, because she is a

good person, the weight of guilt and regret is probably suffocating her.'

Amber looks at her. 'But what if he did rape her? Don't you think he deserved it?'

'Do you think he did?'

'I don't know,' says Amber. 'I'll go and talk to Dad.'

'Good idea.'

Rachel watches her daughter disappear through the door. She waits and listens. There's the murmur of voices coming from the kitchen. She's drained and exhausted. She picks up the bottle of Scotch, puts a small measure into a glass and downs it.

28

Tuesday, 7.30pm

It's getting late and there's already been a shift change in the incident room when the preliminary forensic report pops up in Boden's inbox. The lab has been asked to expedite certain tests and they've complied.

Boden scrolls through the initial findings. One of her major concerns has been that there was a considerable amount of blood in the kitchen, but no evidence of it on Emma Harris. CSI searched her flat in the middle of the afternoon. They found the green dress she claims she was wearing, the underwear she stuffed in a bag, and neither of these items had any quantity of blood on them. And the lab report confirms that: the only traces of blood were from the cut to her head.

If she was stark naked when she had her knife fight with Howard Sampson, how and where did she clean herself up? There was no evidence of his blood in either of the two bathrooms in the flat or the toilet.

Boden brings up the photos from the crime scene on her screen. She runs through them and something just doesn't compute.

The victim is wearing boxers. And socks? There are some shards of a broken wine glass. But does it look like the scene of a desperate drunken fight after rough sex? No. And another thing, the murder weapon. The knife block on the kitchen counter has been removed to the lab for further examination. But all the knives were in place. One could've been used, washed, and replaced. Only a detailed examination will reveal if there are any microscopic traces of the victim's blood. But what if the murder weapon wasn't one of these knives? Why would Emma have used something else? What other sort of weapon would have been available and where is it now? To Boden, it's looks increasingly like someone else was there.

Mackie comes across the room towards her. He's demolishing the remains of a baguette-sized sandwich. Mayo runs down his chin.

She looks up at him. 'Chin,' she says.

He wipes it with his fingers, gulps down the rest of his food and says, 'Got something you might like to see.'

Boden follows him to the analysts' corner. On one of the screens there's the frozen image of dark grainy CCTV footage with a time code.

Mackie nods to the analyst, who presses play. The light is grey with a pool of white from an LED streetlamp. A figure crosses the frame, hunched and hurrying. Female. Wearing a dress. A green dress?

'I'd say that's her,' says Mackie. This is 7.15am this morning, two streets away from the flat on the route she would've taken to the bus stop.'

'If it is her, it backs her story about the time she left,' says Boden.

'Looks to me like she's in a hurry and in a panic,' says Mackie.

'Can we marry this up with the bus footage?'

'We've got her getting off another bus. But she would've had to take one bus into town, then another out to Great Shelford.'

'Okay,' says Boden. 'I think we're getting there.'

Getting where is the question. Boden's shift is ending. A rape turned into a murder investigation, so she's done a double. It's time she went home. But she's niggled.

A team briefing is about to start to bring the new shift up to speed. She's trying to decide whether to pick up an Indian or a Chinese on the way home, when Hepburn wanders into the office, hands in trouser pockets, shirt sleeves rolled up, and looking drained.

Boden meets his eye, and he strolls over.

'You off?' he says.

'Yes, sir. After the briefing.'

'I think we'll pick up the interview first thing. A night in the cells'll focus her mind. She'll feel more like talking.'

Boden hesitates.

Keep your mouth shut. He's under pressure and he's already had a pop at her.

She can't help herself. Diplomacy has never been her style. 'If you want my opinion, sir,' she says. 'I think that's a bad tactic in this case.'

'Why?'

'There are too many things here that don't fit the line of inquiry we're following.'

'Like what?'

'The crime scene. Preliminary forensics are saying none

of Sampson's blood is on Harris. Only her own. Two people have sex in a flat, then have a fight, then one of them knifes the other? It just doesn't look like that to me. Besides the blood, the chaos is missing. And no murder weapon.'

He nods. He looks knackered. Is this even going in?

'Plus,' says Boden, 'we've got CCTV, which suggests she left in the morning, as she said. Staying the night in the flat with the body of someone you've just killed? You'd need to be a psychopath to do that.'

Hepburn puffs out his cheeks. 'Why didn't you tell me all this before?'

Sod him!

'I'm telling you now, sir,' says Boden stiffly.

He waves his hand at her irritably. 'Yeah, alright, don't get on your high horse, Jo. It's been a long day.'

Not only for him.

He sighs. 'If I bail Harris now, you know what that'll look like, don't you? It'll look like Rachel's had a word.'

Arse-covering, that's all he's worried about.

'The other way to look at this,' says Boden, 'is the preliminary forensics don't connect Harris with our body. So why keep a rape victim in jail overnight and compound her suffering?'

She watches Hepburn. He rubs his forehead and sighs. His connection with Rachel Knight has robbed him of his impartiality. He's so anxious not to be seen to be favouring the sister of his boss and friend that he's not reading any of this correctly. Add to that the fact the ACC is probably breathing down his neck and has instructed him to keep the inquiry squeaky clean.

Boden watches as he struggles with all this.

'What the hell are we looking at here, then?' he says petulantly. 'If not her, then who? And why?'

'I don't know, boss. We haven't asked the question, was someone else there? But it's day one, and it's going to take time to unravel it. That's why I think we should consider releasing her on bail.'

He inhales, flexes his shoulders. He's decided. 'Right,' he says. 'I'm going to put it to the CPS. See what they say.'

That's another way to pass the buck.

She smiles. She knows what they'll say: not enough evidence to charge.

He gives her a weary smile. 'Thanks, Jo.'

'No problem, boss.'

29

Tuesday, 8.30pm

Emma lets herself into her flat. The lawyer escorted her home in a taxi, which dropped her at the door. Her release came as a surprise; it all happened quickly. She was forking her way through the microwaved meal she'd just been served in her cell, when the custody sergeant, a different one, appeared and said she was being released on police bail.

Once the formalities had been completed, she stepped out into the night. It was raining hard and she and the lawyer scurried to the waiting cab. Not that the lawyer was much of a scurrier; she moved slowly, puffing and cursing under her breath, which smelt of scotch.

Emma didn't understand any of it, but she didn't care. The prospect of spending the night in her own bed was all she was focused on.

As she closes the door of the flat behind her, a wave of relief rushes through her whole body. She wants to cry. But more than that, she wants a drink. She heads into the main room and to the fridge, which is part of the kitchenette.

What's that smell?

It stops her in her tracks. The room is freezing. Everything feels odd and there's an unpleasant chemical odour. Furniture has been moved, the corner of the rug is turned over and the table lamp that sits next to the sofa is on the floor. The place has the appearance of being turned over by a gang of tidy burglars.

The lawyer said they had searched her home, but it's still a shock to Emma. The reality of a bunch of strangers in those little plastic suits they wear, going through all her belongings, feels like yet another violation. She picks up the lamp from the floor, puts it back on the table, plugs it in and turns it on. Its cosy glow usually soothes her. But this evening its light is eerie.

She opens the door to her bedroom and turns on the light. The duvet is folded on the end of the bed with the pillows stacked on top of it, and the mattress askew. The wardrobe door is ajar. She swallows hard and returns to the main room.

In the small kitchen area, the washing up she'd left in the sink is now piled, still unwashed, on the draining board. She opens the food cupboard. Tins and packets have been rearranged. She finds the packet of muesli that was on the table when the police interrupted her breakfast, in the bin with the remaining contents of the packet emptied on top of it.

They searched her muesli?

She opens the fridge. The vodka is still there. She lifts it out, takes a glass from the draining board, rinses it under the tap and pours a hefty measure. She doesn't bother with ice.

The first mouthful sears the back of her throat, but she follows it with a second. Then she plonks down on the sofa.

The police have still got her mobile, and they have given her no indication of when they're likely to return it. But she also has a landline which she seldom uses. The handset is on top of a pile of books in the corner. It rings, startling Emma.

She reaches over and picks it up. No caller display, no indication of who's on the other end of the line.

'Hello,' she says tentatively.

'For goodness sake,' says her mother in a tone of exasperation. 'I've been ringing you all day. Sent five texts. Why haven't you answered me?'

'Umm, I've lost my phone,' says Emma. 'Sorry.'

Technically true.

'Well, it appears your sister has lost her phone too, because she hasn't been picking up either. But I suppose she could be busy on some case.'

'Probably,' says Emma.

She waits. Phone calls from her mother rarely require much input from her. Jill Harris is perfectly capable of monologuing about her own concerns for the best part of an hour. And this is exactly what she does.

She appears to have crossed swords with the secretary of the bowls club and she rants on about his arrogance for the best part of five minutes and the importance of a dress code for players, which she thinks is not being properly enforced.

Emma listens; in some ways, it's a welcome distraction. It's also a reminder that her mother has a talent for attracting conflict.

Rachel's technique is to refuse to listen to her nonsense. On one memorable occasion she turned to Jill and said, 'Mother, if you will insist on being rude and spiteful to people, you can hardly complain when they're rude back.' This had caused a rift between her mother and older sister that lasted the best part of a month. Jill had refused to answer her daughter's calls until she received a written apology. Emma was caught in the middle. In the end, she persuaded her sister to send a text and that was graciously accepted.

Emma was fourteen when her father threw in the towel and left. He remarried, moved to Scotland and died of a heart attack in his late sixties. Jill's opinion, loudly expressed, was that he'd got his just deserts. But those few rackety teenage years Emma spent alone with her mother softened her attitude. She came to see Jill's attacks on the world as a warped attempt at defence.

But Rachel's view was the opposite. She left home at eighteen and rarely went back. After their father died, she became even more alienated. She blocked most of her mother's attempts to make a relationship with Amber on the grounds it would be toxic and she needed to protect her child.

Emma becomes aware that her mother has stopped speaking. It sounds as if she's paused to take a drink. It suddenly strikes her as intensely sad that they're both sitting alone, each in their own small flats, getting quietly intoxicated as the only way they have of coping.

For a split second, Emma considers just blurting it all out: the rape, her arrest, the day she's spent in police custody. Maybe her mother would understand or at least sympathise. Like Rachel, she probably wouldn't believe Emma's account. The difference is she'd be blunt about it, unlike Rachel.

Did you do it?

She'd definitely ask. But would she believe the answer? And what is the answer?

I don't think so, but I can't be sure.

Emma takes another swallow of her drink and says, 'Listen, Mum, sorry I need to go. Someone's at the door. I'm expecting a delivery. Talk soon. Love you.'

She hangs up, goes over to the fridge, takes out the vodka, and empties the remains of the bottle into her glass.

30

Wednesday, 8.15am

Rachel sits drumming her fingers on the steering wheel as she waits for the bin lorry, which is blocking the road in front of her, to make its stately progress down her sister's road. All the faffing about with the recycling that they do nowadays is obviously a good thing, but still annoying.

She'd had a call from Charlotte Rogers just after nine the previous evening, telling her that her sister had been released on police bail. Her first thought was to go round to Emma's flat straight away, but Charlotte discouraged her.

'I would leave her to her own devices,' said Charlotte.

'She's going to need my support.'

'And she'll be more likely to accept it as such tomorrow morning when she's had a night's rest,' said Charlotte archly.

As such?

Rachel couldn't work out what Charlotte was implying, or indeed if she was implying anything. But she was exhausted herself, had consumed a couple of glasses of whiskey, and decided to accept the lawyer's advice.

Finally, the bin lorry pulls over and a man in a yellow high-vis jacket waves her on. Her next problem is to find a parking space in any of the several roads near to her sister's flat.

She achieves this by gazumping an elderly man who has noticed a space, slowed and is hoping to back up. He's retired; he's got all the time in the world. She hasn't. She slips into the space, jumps out, locks the car with the fob and hurries away, ignoring his gestures of exasperation.

Emma's flat is on the ground floor of a large Victorian property, so when the doorbell remains unanswered, Rachel goes through the side gate into the shared garden and hammers on the window of the french doors at the back.

Eventually, her sister emerges from the bedroom and glares through the window at her.

On several occasions, Rachel has suggested she should be given a key for emergencies, but for some reason, Emma has always found an excuse not to.

Emma unlocks the french doors and lets her in.

'You alright?' says Rachel. They rarely hug on meeting; it's never been their way.

'Not really,' her sister replies. She looks pale and smells of alcohol.

They stare at each other awkwardly for a moment.

'Let me make you a coffee,' says Rachel.

'Feel free,' says her sister with a wave of the hand. Emma then disappears back into the bedroom.

Rachel finds a cafetière in the cupboard and a packet of ground coffee, which smells reasonably fresh. She fills the kettle and puts it on, then she glances around. Emma is not the tidiest person in the world, but the place bears all the signs of a CSI search. It's also freezing cold. The wall thermostat says 18C and if the timer is set to click in, it hasn't done so yet.

While the kettle boils, she goes and stands in the bedroom doorway. Emma is in bed with the duvet pulled up and extra cushions all around her, like a little nest.

'Shall I put the heating on?' says Rachel.

'Can if you like,' says Emma. 'Unless you want to get in bed with me.' She gives Rachel a ghostly smile.

Rachel finds the over-ride switch under the wall mounted boiler in a cupboard in the kitchenette. She flicks the switch and it fires up. Then she makes the coffee and rinses two mugs from the stack on the draining board. She searches for milk in the fridge but there isn't any.

With two mugs of steaming coffee, she returns to the bedroom.

'No milk,' she says.

'I drink it black,' says Emma.

'Since when?' says Rachel.

'Since I ran out of milk.' This seems to be some sort of attempt at humour. Rachel puts the coffees on the bedside table and perches on the end of the bed.

She smiles. All the urgency she felt to get here, but now what? She wonders who's the more uncomfortable, her or Emma?

'Mum's on your case,' says Emma. 'She phoned me last night on the landline. She thinks she's being ignored.'

'That's unusually perceptive of her,' says Rachel. 'Did you tell her what's happened to you?'

'What do you think?'

'That'll be a little job for me, then,' says Rachel.

Emma tilts her head and sighs.

'Oh fuck off, Rachel,' she says. 'You sound like this is

something I've concocted just to make your life more difficult.'

The acid sharpness of Emma's tone surprises Rachel. Since her sister has been arrested in connection with a murder, she'd have expected what? Some contrition?

Hold your temper. This can't turn into a row.

'And in case you've forgotten,' Emma adds. 'I was raped. I didn't make that up.'

'I'm not saying you did. No one is.'

They glare at each other. But Rachel can see the tears in her sister's eyes.

'I realise we don't agree about a lot of things,' she says. 'But trust me, Em, all I want to do is help you. That's why I'm here.'

Emma nods and buries her nose in the top of the duvet. Rachel picks up one of the mugs of coffee and offers it to her. 'Drink it while it's hot,' she says. 'It'll warm you up.'

Emma's fingers emerge and she takes the mug.

It seems to Rachel like she's ministering to a sick child. There's something desolate about her sister, hunkered down under the duvet in her freezing flat.

And Rachel gets a sense of what must've happened in that kitchen. A desperate struggle that could've gone either way. Emma must've thought, in that moment, that she was fighting for her life. But then what? Was Emma so shocked and traumatised by her own behaviour that she's blocked it out?

Rachel sips her own coffee. 'I believe that you don't know how it happened,' she says. 'That you can't remember.'

'Do you?' says Emma.

'Yes. Our minds work to protect us.'

'You think I'm just blocking it out?'

'I don't know. It's possible.'

Emma's gaze drifts away towards the window. She seems to consider this.

'And,' says Rachel. 'I can understand why you might want to keep this thing with Howard a secret.'

'There was no thing.'

'Okay, so this was the first time.'

'I woke up, didn't know where I was. I had no idea it was his flat. Why would I? I've never been there.'

Don't get exasperated with her.

'C'mon, you must've known he fancied you. Amber says you and she laughed about it.'

Emma sighs. 'Yeah, but I made it clear to him I wasn't interested.'

In the end, very clear!

'Listen to me, Emma, you've been released on bail. But that doesn't mean this is over, not by any means. They're gathering evidence and you could still be charged.'

'I realise that. The lawyer, Charlotte... whatever, she explained it all to me.'

'Y'know, Charlotte Rogers is one of the best defence briefs for miles around. And I hope you're listening to her advice.'

Emma sighs. 'Yes, I am. And I'm sure she's doing this as a big favour to you. And I'm grateful.' There's a whiny, resentful tone in her voice.

She doesn't sound it. But ignore that.

'You've got to understand how the system works. This is about constructing a viable defence for you. That's what matters here.'

'I've told the truth to everyone who's asked. I woke up in a strange bed in a strange flat. I had no idea how I got there. I realised I'd been raped. I was scared. I got up and I ran. And I took the bus to your house.'

Rachel sighs. 'Okay, so what are we saying here? You blacked out? Which has happened before when you've been drinking, hasn't it?'

'I was working, and I wasn't drinking. That's the last thing I remember.'

'But you're not sure?'

'Not 100 per cent. I woke up with a cracking headache. You said before GHB could cause that. Look, this might sound outlandish, but what if Howard and Neil got together?'

'Got together to do what?'

'To hurt me, to teach me a lesson? I don't know?'

'Why on earth would Howard want to do that?'

There's a look of desperation on Emma's face. 'Okay, look, you're right. He asked me out and I fobbed him off. Perhaps he felt rejected? I mean, come on, he was a weird guy. He knew I was having a nightmare with Neil over the divorce. Somehow, they got together and cooked this up. They slipped something into my drink at the hotel and between them, they kidnapped me. I've been trying to work it out. How did I get from the hotel to that flat? I'm not a lightweight. It would've taken more than one bloke to move me if I was unconscious.'

'It's an interesting theory. But where's the evidence for any of it? And why would they take you to Howard's place?'

'I don't know. You've got detectives. You could find the evidence.'

She's clutching at straws.

'Emma, it doesn't really work like that. Conspiracy theories are all very well on television, but in real life, the truth is much simpler. Anger fuelled by alcohol. People get into fights and they hurt each other. And afterwards they regret it. They can't believe what they've done, they're filled with guilt and regret, and they try to cover it up.'

'And that's what you reckon I'm doing, is it?'

'Is it what you're doing? First, you say you had no idea where you were and you can't remember anything. Now you're saying there was a conspiracy between Howard and your ex-husband to harm you? So which is it?'

'I don't know what happened, so I'm trying to work it out. I know it sounds crazy.'

'Listen to me, Emma, let's be realistic here. If you make a full confession, you'll get a shorter sentence; it's as simple as that. Obviously the sex you had was pretty rough. You've got injuries to prove it and that's been documented.'

'It wasn't rough sex, it was rape.'

'Okay, he raped you. Maybe you went round there just for a drink. You were trying to be nice to him. But he took advantage. You were understandably angry and upset. You'd been drinking. And he'd forced you to do something you didn't want to. So you followed him into the kitchen, a row turned into a fight, and you grabbed a knife.'

'You think that's what happened?'

'Some version of that. But you tell me.'

Tears are welling in Emma's eyes. She clutches the cushion to her more tightly. Rachel reaches out.

Nearly there. She's letting go.

Rachel has seen this moment many times in the interview room. The suspect wants to tell the truth. The burden of lying is weighing on them. They just need a bit of encouragement to help them let go of it.

She squeezes her sister's hand. 'After it happened, you went back to the bedroom and blacked out. When you woke up, it all felt like a nightmare, but your brain had shut down. You'd done something horrible and totally out of character, so you blocked it out. I believe that now, at this moment, you really can't remember. But that's your mind trying to protect you, Emma.'

'Is it?'

'I think so. And the forensic evidence will probably prove that.'

'So I should confess?'

'You'll be in a far stronger position if you do. I'm just trying to help you here. You have to believe that.'

31

Wednesday, 11.55am

By the time Emma arrives at the police station, it's close to midday. Her sister drove her, and the lawyer had been alerted and was waiting for her outside.

Emma had stood under the shower for a long time and what Rachel was saying to her made sense. It was true, she'd had blackouts before and woken up with no memory of the night before. Was this really what happened? Probably.

She hadn't slept. Or perhaps she'd dozed a little. Most of the night, she watched the shadows creep across her bedroom wall and listened to the rain patter on the windows. A sense of desolation had seeped into her whole body. By the time her sister turned up, she was too weary and confused to argue anymore. As she dried herself, Rachel selected a plain jumper and some jeans from her wardrobe and told her she was doing the right thing.

She just needed to make a statement, a full admission of what she'd done, and it would all be over for now. They'd leave her alone. She could get off this rollercoaster and rest. A guilty plea and the case would come to court sooner. Murder carries a mandatory life sentence, but he undoubtedly raped her and that will be taken into consideration, Rachel said.

You'll feel better once it's over.

A uniformed officer escorts her and Charlotte to the interview room.

'You alright with this?' says the lawyer.

Emma nods. She just wants peace.

After a wait of about five minutes, DS Boden enters the room. She's alone. She doesn't sit.

'Good morning,' she says. Then she turns her attention to the lawyer. 'I understand your client wishes to make a statement. However, before she does, there's some evidence we'd like to disclose to you.'

'Okay,' says the lawyer.

Boden sits down across the table from them. 'First,' she says, 'the semen samples taken from you, Emma, at the hospital yesterday morning have been analysed. So have samples obtained from the sheets on the bed in the flat. The DNA in those samples has also been analysed and it does not match the DNA of the victim, Howard Sampson.'

Emma frowns and glances at the lawyer. 'What does that mean?'

The lawyer raises her eyebrows. 'It means that Howard Sampson did not rape you. So what else have you got, Sergeant?'

Boden consults the notes on her tablet. 'The post mortem was carried out this morning on the victim. The pathologist has estimated the time of death to be between 9pm and midnight. We've spoken to Valerie Mitchell, the hotel manager where your event took place. She confirms you were at the venue from mid afternoon and through the evening and still there at 11pm, which is when she handed over to the night manager and left.'

'What does any of this mean?' says Emma.

'Well,' says Boden. 'When you arrived at the flat, it's possible that Howard Sampson had already been murdered and was lying on his kitchen floor. And we do know that whoever raped you in the bedroom, it wasn't him.'

'Do you know who it was?' says the lawyer.

'We've only just got the forensic report on this,' says Boden. 'And we will obviously check the DNA against the database for a match.'

Emma stares at the cop. 'Someone took me there and raped me after he was already dead?'

'Yes, that is a possibility and a line of inquiry we're investigating.'

Emma's head is in a spin. 'I didn't do it?' she says.

'Well,' says Boden. 'the account you gave us matches the evidence. And we'll be looking at this other line of inquiry.'

'Will she remain released on bail?' says the lawyer.

'For the time being,' says Boden.

'I don't understand,' says Emma. 'Who killed him?'

'We don't know.'

'Will you find out who raped me? Do you think it was the same man?'

'That will be part of our ongoing inquiry,' says Boden.

Emma sighs. She should be pleased, but she feels light-headed and slightly nauseous.

You were about to confess to a crime you didn't commit.

'I didn't do it?' she says to no one in particular.

'Come along, my dear,' says the lawyer. 'Let's get you home.'

Emma stands up. She's unsteady on her feet. She looks at the cop.

'Thank you,' she says.

'I'm sorry this has been such a difficult process,' says Boden.

Process? All this cop speak.

'But it's not over, is it? I'm still on bail.'

'Yes, because we can't say for sure that he was dead before you got there. But at present, there's no forensic evidence to connect you with him.'

Emma nods. It's enough. It has to be. She just wants to get out of there and escape and never ever see the inside of a police interview room again.

32

Wednesday, 12.15pm

Rachel is driving home, having dropped her sister outside the station, when she gets Charlotte Rogers' call.

'Forensics have exonerated her,' says Charlotte. 'She's been released.'

'What?' says Rachel.

Has Hepburn lost his nerve?

'Did she make a statement?'

'Rachel, she didn't do it,' says the lawyer. 'I should've thought you'd be pleased.'

'Of course I'm pleased. Obviously. Is she with you? Can I speak to her?'

There's the sound of a hand over the phone. Then Charlotte comes back on the line. 'She doesn't want to talk. She's got a headache. I'm sending her home in a cab.'

'Can you give me some details?'

'No DNA match, time of death is a three-hour window. Most of which she couldn't have been there. So they're looking at other lines of inquiry. Now I've got to dash. I've got a case conference to go to. I'm sure the SIO will be happy to fill you in. Keep me in the loop.'

'Of course,' says Rachel. 'And thank you for doing this, Charlotte. I do appreciate it.'

'I can see that,' says the lawyer drily and hangs up.

No DNA match? Of what, exactly? The body?

This doesn't add up. Howard is dead. If Emma had sex with him and was in his flat, how does the evidence exonerate her?

She pulls off the main road into a side turning and stops. Turning the car around, she heads back into town. There's only one way to get answers.

Fifteen minutes later and she's striding down the corridor to DCI Hepburn's office. She passes several of her junior colleagues on the way and gets some awkward looks, which she ignores.

Hepburn's door is ajar, but she still raps on it smartly. He looks up from his desk.

He jumps to his feet. 'Rachel?' he says. He's a small man, getting dumpy, and she appears to have startled him. 'I was about to call you. It's good news. Your sister's been released. And I want to apologise to you. But I had no choice in the circumstances—'

She scans him. He's worried; he thinks she's going to blame him for the arrest of her sister.

'I know that, Alistair,' she says equably. 'In your shoes, I'd've done the same.'

'Still, it must've been upsetting for you and I'm sorry.'

'Yes, it's been a tough couple of days,' she says. 'So, the evidence doesn't stack up?'

'No. DNA on the semen samples from your sister does not match Howard Sampson. They didn't have sex.'

Why didn't Charlotte say DNA on the semen?

'Also, PM puts the time of death between nine and midnight. She was still at the hotel where she was organising an event until eleven, probably later. We'll be checking that out. And no forensics to link her to the body.'

Rachel frowns. 'But she still woke up in his flat. Was she raped there?'

'Yes, there were also traces of semen on the sheets.'

'Not belonging to Howard?'

'No.'

'Have you got a hit on the database?'

'We're in the process of checking,' says Hepburn.

Rachel knows this is a long shot. Unless the rapist has a record or previous encounters with the police, it's unlikely his DNA will be recorded.

'So you're assuming she was taken there after he was already dead and lying on the kitchen floor?' she says.

Hepburn shrugs. 'Yes. That's what the evidence is pointing to. But I was already unhappy with the situation last night.'

'How?'

'I reviewed the crime scene photos. It just didn't look right to me. Two people who'd supposedly just had sex having a drunken fight? To my mind, there just wasn't enough chaos. Plus, by then we had CCTV of Emma leaving in the morning, as she said. I didn't find it credible that she would've murdered him in that emotionally charged way, then stayed in the flat with the body. I spoke to the CPS last night. The consensus was we should release her on bail.'

Rachel smiles. 'Obviously, a good call. Thank you.'

'I hope Emma understands. We did perhaps jump to conclusions.'

They weren't the only ones.

Hepburn is backtracking at speed. He just wants avoid any comeback.

'DS Boden did the interview with her,' he says. 'Assisted by DC Chakravorty. I thought she'd feel less intimidated by two women. Boden's very experienced; she treated her like a rape victim as much as a murder suspect.'

Rachel pictures DS Boden. The tall girl from the Met with something to prove. And angling for promotion?

'Thank you, Alistair. I appreciate the care you've taken with this, but where do we go from here?'

'I think we're back to looking for a motive both for the murder and the rape. And focusing on the murder, obviously. Who and why?' He hesitates, then adds, 'Have you any idea who might want to kill Howard Sampson?'

Now he's treating you like a bloody witness. That's no good.

Rachel sighs. 'No,' she says. 'I only knew him as a colleague of my husband's.'

Not strictly true.

But the last thing she wants is an excuse for the ACC to refuse to give her job back.

Hepburn nods. 'I was wondering if Simon has any ideas about this? Who would want to kill his business partner?'

'He's upset, obviously. But I know he would want to assist the inquiry in any way. We've talked about it and it makes no sense to him. But send some officers round to do a formal interview. Boden maybe. She's done well with this.'

'Thank you.'

Rachel sighs and says, 'On the subject of the rape, you may care to look at my sister's ex, Neil Bryant. They're in the midst of a divorce and it's become extremely acrimonious. When I talked to Emma, her feeling was if anyone was out to harm her, it could well be him. I don't know how accurate this is, but their relationship has always been stormy. And Neil is a big bloke, certainly capable of physical violence.'

Hepburn is scribbling on his notepad. 'Okay,' he says. 'We'll follow that up.'

Rachel looks at him. He's handled a tricky situation well; he can't be faulted. But where does that leave her? She's still out on a limb, supposedly transferred to other duties. Her next stop is the ACC's office.

Bloody Graham Carter has had his feet under your desk for long enough.

'Have you talked to Graham Carter about any of this?' she says.

'He's been kept up to speed,' says Hepburn.

He must know how hacked off she is about Carter stepping into her shoes. He meets her gaze. Beady-eyed, Hepburn's always been ambitious. But he'll go with the flow.

'Well,' she says, 'if my sister is no longer a suspect in the murder investigation, I don't see why I shouldn't be involved. But I'll speak to the ACC.'

'It would be great to have you back, Rachel. I'd really welcome your input.'

'Thank you,' she says.

33

Wednesday, 1pm

Returning home a second time is bittersweet for Emma. She didn't expect to be back so soon. She gazes around her tiny flat; it's still a mess. Her life is a train wreck. She feels exhausted and shaky.

You nearly ended up confessing to murder. How?

She knew in her heart that she hadn't killed anyone, or at least she thought she did. But she allowed Rachel to persuade her otherwise. Why? It's mad. Why didn't she stick up for herself? She just seemed to lose all volition. It was easier to give in. Or maybe she was just completely knackered? And why would her own sister think her capable of such a brutal act?

She said she was trying to protect you. But was she?

When Rachel gets an idea in her head, it's hard to dislodge it. She insists she's open-minded, but that's not true. Even when they were kids, Rachel always thought she was right. And over the years, people have admired her conviction and her confidence. It's seen as a virtue, which in Emma's view has made her sister worse.

Rachel will argue that she was only trying to help, and in her mind that's probably true.

Emma wanders into the bedroom, dumps her bag and collapses on the bed fully clothed.

The police have returned her phone. It's still sealed in a plastic evidence bag. Emma wonders if they've been through the dating apps as well as her address book and texts. She'd been required to give them the password. But if she hadn't, they'd've cracked it open somehow. How many random strangers have been through her phone, her flat, all the private corners of her life? Recording, analysing, judging. They searched her wardrobe and so they'd have found her two vibrators. They must've all had a good laugh about that.

With the shame of it all swirling round in her head, she falls asleep. When she wakes again, it's dark outside. Her mouth is dry and she has a thumping headache. She goes into the kitchen and fills a glass with water from the tap.

Then she notices that the french windows at the back of the room are not completely shut. She let Rachel in that way this morning. Did she not lock it? She looks around for the key. It's not in the door; it's not anywhere.

She feels uneasy.

Outside, the garden is black and full of the spectral forms of the overgrown shrubs and trees swaying in the wind. The garden is communal to all four flats, but no one can be bothered to take care of it. The couple upstairs keep a mower in the dilapidated shed at the end, which they use occasionally, but it's only so their dog has somewhere to shit.

Since she moved in a few months ago, Emma has confined herself to the small, rectangular patio outside her flat. There's room for a deckchair. For a short period in the late afternoon, the back of the flat gets some sun. She's sat out, but only a couple of times.

The french doors themselves are old and wooden, part of the original features of the once grand Victorian mansion. But the wood has a tendency to swell in damp weather, making the doors difficult to shut. It must be what happened this morning; she let Rachel in, then forgot about them.

She leans her shoulder against one door and gives it a hard shove. With some force, she jams it shut. But the key is still missing. She searches for it. And the chaos left after the police turned the place over doesn't help.

She sifts through the pile of random books, discarded cups and unopened mail on the coffee table. Nothing. Getting down on her hands and knees, she peers under the sofa. A rising sense of tension is building in her.

Where the hell is it?

She pulls the cushions off the sofa and tosses them aside. She finds a battery, a chocolate wrapper, but no key.

Scrambling to her feet, she moves into the kitchen area, but her hands are shaking.

Why isn't the key in the door?

Her anxiety is morphing to full grown panic.

It's him. Still out there. Still after you!

She spins around. He could've been watching the flat? What if she left the door open and he got in?

Neil? It's got to be Neil.

The key is gone because he's sending her a message. He wants to scare her. The police haven't got him. He's still out there.

Her brain is screaming, her hand flies to her mouth and she sobs. Then she notices the doorbell ringing. Should she answer it?

He knows you're here!

The handset to the entry phone is on the kitchen wall.

She picks it up and whispers, 'Hello?'

It crackles, then a reply comes through. 'It's Amber.'

Relief floods her veins. She rushes out of the flat into the communal hallway and opens the main front door.

Her niece is standing there in the drizzling rain, hood up. She smiles. 'Mum said you didn't want visitors. But I thought—'

'Come in! Come in!' exclaims Emma. 'God, you're wet. How did you get here?'

Amber follows her into the flat.

'Bus then walked,' she says. 'I just had to come and make sure you were alright.'

'Yeah, I'm, y'know…actually I'm not alright. Oh Amber, I think someone's been here and it might be him.'

'How do you know?'

'I unlocked the french windows this morning. And I forgot to lock them again. But I would've left the key in the door. And now I can't find it.'

Calm down! You're freaking her out.

'But I'm probably overreacting.'

Amber takes her hand. 'Understandably. But the key must be here somewhere. Let me help you look for it.'

'You're right. I'm being silly. The place is such a mess.'

Amber scans the room and frowns. 'Did they do this when they searched?'

'They had to do their job.'

Taking her jacket off, Amber hangs it on the back of the door and says, 'Why don't you make a cup of tea and I'll look for the key.'

Emma nods. 'I'm sorry,' she says. 'I'm being stupid.'

Amber smiles. 'Put the kettle on,' she says. She begins to search the room systematically.

The pulse is drumming in Emma's veins, but she fills the kettle. She's no longer alone and her gratitude for that is overwhelming. But she can't expose her niece to any risk. He could still be after her.

Neil wouldn't hurt Amber. He's after her.

Amber pulls back the heavy full length drapes that hang either side of the french doors. She squats down and picks something up.

'Is this it?' she says, holding up a key.

Emma laughs, then the tears come.

'Oh my God,' she says. 'I'm such a fool.'

Amber fits the key in the lock and turns it.

'Well,' she says. 'I'm going to help you clear this place up. And I'm going to stay tonight and sleep on the sofa.'

'Oh Amber, you don't have to—'

'Don't you want me to?'

'Of course I'd love you to but—'

'Forget what you think Mum would say,' says Amber. 'And you'd be doing me a favour. Dad's drowning his sorrows in whiskey and that's winding Mum up, so the shit'll probably hit the fan. And I'd rather not be around when it does.'

'Fair enough,' says Emma, beaming. 'We could order a takeaway.'

34

Wednesday, 8pm

Dean waits until after dark before he leaves his Fenland hideaway and drives south towards Bedford. He parks the Aston a few hundred metres down the road from his brother's house in the gateway to a field. The lane is pitch black; there's no street lighting but Dean has got the eyes of a cat. He doesn't need a torch.

He walks down the road, stops in the shadows of the hedge across from the house and watches. The compound is all lit up with fairy lights in the November chill. Cars drive up to the electric gates, the gates open and they sweep in. Craig is having a party. So why hasn't he invited his brother?

After watching guests roll up for five minutes, Dean decides it's time to rectify this omission. He pulls the packet of coke Liam gave him out of his pocket and administers a little pick-me-up. As the drug kicks in, he leans back his head to enjoy the hit.

Yes! Time to rock and roll.

A beamer draws up to the gates, the driver leans out of his window and grins at the intercom. The gates open, the car cruises through, and Dean slips in unseen behind it.

The house is lit up like a fairytale castle. Guests are entering through the front door. A white-coated waiter is stationed just inside with a tray of champagne. But Dean scoots round the side of the house to where a catering truck is parked up. This is obviously a swanky affair, or perhaps Kate wouldn't want to ruin her immaculate nails doing any cooking.

The kitchen door is wide open to let out the heat and Dean can glimpse a couple of chefs and some waiting staff in white aprons, all busily working away. Craig has plenty of security on the perimeter of the property, but this is his weak spot; he hires staff in. He doesn't know who they are, just that they're happy to take his wages.

Dean walks up to the kitchen door, pulling off his hoodie as he steps through it. He's wearing just a T-shirt and jeans. One chef glances at him.

'Sorry I'm late,' says Dean. 'This place is a sod to get to.'

'Agency sent you?' says the chef. 'You done waiting before?'

'Silver service, mate.'

The chef looks at him doubtfully. It must be his catering business, but getting enough staff is a serious problem.

Dean waits. Pans are sizzling on the stove. Steam is rising. Trays of canapés sit on the counter.

'Imran,' the chef shouts. 'Get this guy from the agency some whites.'

A small, bustling waiter appears. He looks Dean up and down. 'Hope we got a size big enough,' he says. 'You got a name?'

'Dean.'

He's soon kitted out with a white shirt and a long apron to cover his jeans. They don't have trousers to fit him and the shirt is too tight. He rolls up his sleeves.

'Grab a tray and follow me,' says Imran. 'And don't eat any of the stuff yourself.'

'Wouldn't dream of it,' says Dean.

He picks up a large oval tray which is loaded with an assortment of fishy smelling finger food.

As they leave the kitchen, Imran says, 'You got fish, I got charcuterie, just in case people ask you.'

No one asks him. No one even looks at him or makes eye contact as he moves through the room with his tray. Hands bob out and grab and stuff. Most people already have a glass in their right hand, so they use their left.

The vast hallway and several rooms off it are ablaze with light and full of chatter. Dean estimates maybe close to a hundred people. Quite a crowd. It must be costing Craig a fair bit to feed and water this lot.

It seems to be a mix of ages. Some youngsters running about. Blokes in DJs, women in fancy floor length numbers. There are a few blokes hanging round the edges on their own, a couple have ear pieces. That'll be the security.

Dean continues on his progress through the rooms. His tray is half empty.

'When you're done,' whispers Imran, 'straight back to the kitchen for another.'

'Understood,' says Dean. Then he notices someone staring right at him.

It's Liam in a monkey suit and a dickey bow. He comes hurrying over.

He stares at Dean in disbelief and whispers, 'Dean? What the fuck?'

'You want a canapé, sir?' says Dean. 'These are the fishy ones. Bit of caviar on the end there.'

'What the hell are you playing at? If he sees you, he'll go ballistic.'

'That's what I'm hoping,' says Dean with a serene smile.

'Are you jacked up?' says Liam.

'Just a bit. That's some good shit you gave me.'

'It was to chill you out.'

'Oh, I'm chilled.'

'Mate, you need to get out of here now. I'm telling you for your own good. Whatever you're planning, this ain't the place. He's got at least five security.'

'What makes you think I'm planning anything?'

Liam stares at him. He looks rattled. Dean pats his arm. 'Calm down,' he says. 'They'll be no come back on you.'

'Perhaps I just don't wanna to see you killed,' Liam hisses under his breath.

But it's too late. Craig is already striding across the room towards them with a thunderous look on his face.

He is so pissed off. Sweet!

'What are you doing here?' he says.

'Checking out your security, mate,' says Dean. 'And I have to say, it's crap. Pretty much any Tom, Dick or Harry could walk in here. And I'm sure you don't want that.'

Craig is trying to get a handle on his temper, but he's still steaming, which amuses Dean.

'And what do you want, Dean?' he spits.

'Well, an invite to this fancy bash would've been nice. Mine got lost in the post, did it?'

'We're having a celebration for Ariella's sixteenth. For family and friends. This is not business.'

'Aren't I family? Wish I'd known it was her birthday. I'd've got her something nice. What does she like, Craig?

Nice dress, pair of shoes? Remember Kelly at sixteen, she was clothes and make-up mad?'

Craig is glaring at him. His stupid suit is too tight across the belly and there's sweat on his upper lip.

He's gone soft. He's losing it.

Dean smiles sadly and puts down his tray. 'But I didn't come here to upset the apple cart,' he says. 'Certainly not on your girl's birthday. Wish her the best from me.'

He's turning away as Kate appears. Hair piled on her head, dress a skintight silver sheath; she looks like a film star, but her face is livid.

Still very shaggable.

Dean grins at her. 'Hello, Kate.'

'What is he doing here? And why is he dressed like that?' Both questions are accusations and directed at her husband.

Craig raises his palm. 'Kate, I'm dealing with it.'

Stupid bitch winds him round her little finger.

Dean grins. 'He's trying to eject me quietly, Kate. Cause he knows if he sets his five goons on me, they'll be quite a scrap.'

Kate ignores him and addresses her husband in a loud whisper. 'I do not want an ex-convict at my daughter's birthday party.'

Dean chuckles. 'Don't you, Kate? Well, where do you think all this comes from, eh? A few canny property deals? I don't think so. You're living the high life here and you're a smart woman, so I'm sure you know what's paying for it.'

She glares at him for a moment, then turns on her amazing heels and walks away.

Dean turns to Craig and shrugs. 'Sorry about that, mate. But I'm just saying.'

Craig shakes his head wearily. 'You just like to stir the shit, don't you? You can't help yourself.'

Two of the suited and booted goons have materialised either side of Craig. Dean looks them up and down. Young and eager, like two frisky attack dogs. But they're still puppies and Dean is confident he could take them both down. But he's made his point.

'Don't want to upset Ariella or Kate,' he says. 'I just popped round to say hello. Had no idea you were having a party.'

Craig heaves a sigh. 'Oh sod it!' he says equably. 'Come with me and let's get a proper drink. If I had any idea you'd want to go to a teenage girl's birthday party, I'd have invited you.'

'Fair enough,' says Dean.

He follows his brother through the throng to the elaborate bar that's been erected next to the swimming pool. Craig has a point. A bunch of silly girls dancing? But he's put down his marker and now Craig knows one thing at least. Ignoring him is not an option.

35

Thursday, 6.45am

For Boden, it's an early start, but she doesn't mind that. Emma Harris is no longer the prime suspect, but that's ramped up the pressure. This may prove to be a long haul, not a quick result, so the team is being expanded.

But the boss had listened to her. Boden went home, had a long soak in the bath and an early night, which she needed.

Mackie picks her up from her flat before first light, with a squad car in tow. Door knocking a suspect hoping to freak them out is best done in the early morning. It's a favourite of Mackie's and he's good at it. Having a fifteen stone rugby player with a shaved head and a chewed ear come stomping into your home at the crack of dawn tends to unnerve most people.

Hepburn's instruction is that Harris's ex should be cautioned and brought in for questioning in connection with the rape. The information, presumably from Rachel Knight, is that he's a big bloke and potentially violent.

The address is in the middle of a row of terraced houses, originally railway cottages, opening directly onto the street. Parking is bumper to bumper on both sides. Mackie stops in the middle of the road; he has little option. The squad car has its blues flashing, so anyone hoping to get by will have to wait.

Boden follows Mackie out of their car. She checks her watch. It's before seven, a damp and dismal November morning. A few curious passersby are on their way to work.

There's a small silver bell on the doorjamb, but for full effect, Mackie ignores this and applies his fist. It's a solid old Victorian door, but the timber still shudders.

A moment passes and a small puzzled woman in a blue nursing assistant's uniform opens the door. She has a piece of half-eaten toast in her hand.

Boden holds her warrant card out. She steps forward and says, 'Mrs Bryant. We're looking for your son, Neil. Can we come in?'

It isn't really a question. Mackie steps into the doorway and Mrs Bryant is forced to move back.

'Oh dear,' she says.

'Where is he?' says Mackie.

She points up the narrow stairway. 'He's in bed, I think. I was just on my way to work.'

Mackie climbs over the racing bike in the hall and thunders up the stairs. Boden gives Mrs Bryant a tepid smile.

The poor woman looks more resigned than anything. 'What's he done?' she says.

'We just need to ask him some questions,' says Boden.

A couple of moments pass and Mackie reappears, propelling a bleary-eyed individual, almost of similar size to himself, in a T-shirt and boxer shorts. Mackie recites the words of the caution to him as he shepherds him down the stairs.

When he gets to the bottom, Neil Bryant towers over both Boden and his mother in the narrow hall. Boden glances at the open door to the front room. 'In there, Mr Bryant,' she says.

He huffs and follows her instructions. 'What's this?' he says sourly. 'Rachel's sent her bully boys round?'

Boden ignores the comment. 'We want to ask you about your movements on Monday night,' she says. 'Where were you?'

He scratches his head. He has a rough thatch of blond hair and a fashionable amount of stubble. In other circumstances, he'd be considered good-looking. Boden can certainly see the appeal.

'Fucked if I know,' he says. 'Went out for a couple of drinks, I think.'

'On your own?' says Boden.

'With some lads I know.'

'And they will confirm that?'

He tilts his head and gives her a side-eyed glance. 'Is this about Emma? Has that bitch accused me of something?'

'Accused you of what, Mr Bryant?' says Boden.

'Her bloody sister came round here and said she'd been raped. So now she's going to try and put me in the frame, is she? That would be bloody typical of Rachel.'

'Did you rape your ex-wife, Neil?' says Boden.

'Oh Neil, surely not,' says the small voice of his mother from the hall.

But he stares straight at Boden. His eyes are baby blue. 'Firstly,' he says, 'she's not my ex-wife, we're still technically married. And secondly...' there's a tremor in his voice. 'I would not do that to her. We've got our differences, no one can deny it. But I've never laid a finger on her. And I wouldn't, not on any woman. And certainly not on her.'

His Adam's apple is bobbing furiously and Boden has the impression he's swallowing his tears.

He still loves her.

He turns round to face his mother, who's standing behind Mackie in the doorway.

'It's a pack of lies, Mum. I swear to you.'

Mrs Bryant is crying. Boden glances at Mackie.

He turns to Neil. 'We're going to need an alibi, sport. And failing that, your phone.'

Neil scratches his head and huffs. 'I was with my mates in that pub down by the river, the one that shows rugby league. We were watching a friendly.'

'Who was playing?' says Mackie.

'Leeds Rhinos versus Wigan Warriors,' says Neil.

'Saw it,' says Mackie. 'Not a bad match.'

Boden's phone rings. It's Chakravorty. She needs to answer it. She gives Mackie a nod and goes out through the hall and into the street.

'Morning, Prish,' she says. 'What's going on?'

'Hepburn had to get the IT guys in. But we're up and running again,' says Chakravorty.

Problems and crashes of the computer system are becoming increasingly frequent. Lack of funding and investment are at the root of it.

'I didn't even know we were offline,' says Boden.

'Well, we're back on,' says Chakravorty. 'And we've got a hit on the DNA database for the rape.'

'Great,' says Boden. 'I'm guessing it's not Neil.'

'Nope. The suspect's DNA is on file because he was released from prison on licence two weeks ago. Served time for drug dealing and GBH. His name's Dean Jessop.'

'Okay,' says Boden. 'I'll go and let Neil Bryant off the hook.'

She's glad about that.

A glimmer of light in a murky world.

She hangs up and returns to the house to find Mackie and Neil engaged in a discussion of the finer points of a try scored by the Wigan player, Bevan French.

36

Thursday, 9.15am

Emma and Amber take a taxi to the hotel to retrieve Emma's car. It drops them at the main entrance.

Emma looks up at the building. She always liked this place, the arched doorway, the smart bay trees on either side. She's run several events here and her clients love it, posh enough for a special do without being intimidating. But now her feelings are more ambiguous.

What the hell happened? Why didn't anyone see?

Amber is watching her with concern. 'Are we going inside?' she says.

Emma shakes her head. 'No, I just want to get the car.'

'What about your backpack?'

Oh shit!

She's forgotten that she needs to collect her backpack, too. It's full of files she needs for the business. But the idea of going inside is filling her with fear. Somewhere in her mind, he's still in there. Lurking, waiting for her. She knows she's being stupid.

The nervousness must show on her face because Amber immediately says, 'Don't worry, I'll get it. You wait in the car.'

'I'm being stupid, aren't I? I'm just a complete basket case.'

"No Emma, you've had a terrible trauma and you need time to recover.'

You'll never recover.

'Thanks,' she says. 'I would rather not go inside right now.'

Another day. Do it another day.

'Wait in the car,' says Amber. 'Have you got the keys?'

Emma reaches in her bag. Yes, it's one thing her scrambled brain has remembered. She clutches them in her fist.

Amber smiles at her, before disappearing into the hotel.

Her niece has been brilliant. Just the fact of having her in the flat last night meant Emma managed to sleep a bit. This morning, Amber was up before Emma was even awake and she hit the washing up. They tidied the main room together and Amber hoovered. By the time they'd finished, the place was feeling like her home again, not somewhere that had been ransacked by an army of cops.

Emma scurries across the car park. Her little old orange Nissan is sitting in the far corner where she left it. Amongst all the high-end four-by-fours and sportscars, it seems forlorn.

She knows she must relax. And breathe. She has to will the craziness in her head to stop. If she's ever to come back to this place, she has to get over this reaction. Raising her chin and pulling back her shoulders, she strolls towards her car.

A few shafts of sunshine are breaking through the grey clouds. It may even turn out to be a half-decent day for November. At least it's dry. She watches a couple drive by in a brand new Range Rover; they park and get out. The man opens the back door and lifts out a baby; it burbles in its car seat. He coos over it. A young couple who seem to have everything. Hard not to be envious.

Emma reaches her own car and fits the key in the lock. She's praying it will start. But in the few months she's had it, it's been pretty reliable.

She opens the driver's door and is about to get in when she notices that the back tyre is flat.

Of course it is!

A wave of desolation sweeps through her. Could her life get anymore difficult? She feels like sobbing.

She stares at the tyre. Flat as a pancake. She used to have a road side assistance policy, but she stopped paying the premium; it was too expensive.

With the key, she unlocks the boot. Under the matt, there's the spare wheel. She could go into the hotel and have a word with the concierge. They might have someone who could change it for her.

You can't go in there. Not yet.

If she was feeling weak and vulnerable before, this somehow makes it ten times worse. Her eyes fill with tears.

You can change a bloody wheel! Get a grip!

Is she going to let this happen? Will she let him reduce her to this? Turn her into a silly, incapable female? Not now. Not again. Not ever.

Anger surges through her. She roots in the back of the car and finds the jack. It's a scissor jack with a hand crank, a bit rusty, but it should work. There's also a wrench wrapped up with it in an old sack. Must've belonged to Neil. She's surprised he hasn't listed it in the items to be returned under the divorce settlement.

Bending down, she uses the end of the crank handle to prize off the hub cap. She applies the wrench to the first wheel nut, but the bloody thing won't budge. She rests back on her heels and sighs.

A voice behind her says, 'Need some help with that?'

She looks up. He towers over her. He doesn't wait for her to answer, he takes the wrench. She stands up and steps back. His sudden appearance has disorientated her. As he squats down beside her car, she gets a whiff of some aftershave or body spray. Pungent and spicy. The smell makes her gag. She coughs to cover it.

He's already loosened two of the wheel nuts. He works quickly. 'They're a bit rusty,' he says.

Stop panicking. He's just a helpful bloke.

'Yeah,' she says. 'She's an old rust bucket but she goes. That's the main thing.' She tries to laugh.

Sounds like a stupid teenage girl.

Then she sees Amber walking towards them and her heart soars. Amber has the backpack, which she dumps beside the car.

'Oh no,' says Amber. 'A flat. That's a bugger.'

The man glances up at them. 'Wheel nuts are all loose. If you lovely ladies have got a jack, I'll finish the job for you.'

Emma can see Amber scanning her. She's aware her chin is trembling. What is it? The smell of that horrible aftershave?

'No need,' says Amber. 'I can take it from here.'

'You sure?' says the bloke, standing up. He's big. He rubs his hands. They're huge and rough.

'Yep,' says Amber. 'My dad does up classic cars; it's his hobby. I've been helping since I was a kid.' She picks up the jack from where Emma left it behind the car. Looking at it, she says, 'I think this is an old one of his. Did Dad give you this, Emma?'

'Yeah, maybe.' She's shaking like a leaf; she can't seem to stop.

The bloke shrugs. He seems put out. 'Girl power, eh?' he says, raising his fist and sneering.

Amber steps in front of him, jack in one hand, crank in the other. 'Thank you for your help,' she says with a smile.

'Any time,' he says. He shoves his hands in his jeans pockets and strides off. He walks with a swagger.

Amber watches him go. She turns to Emma and says, 'You okay?'

Emma puts her face in her hands. 'Oh, this is ridiculous,' she says. 'Some bloke tries to help me and I freak out. What am I going to do?'

'He was a bit of a dick,' says Amber. 'You should've waited for me. I must've spent half my childhood in a freezing garage with Dad.'

Oh course she did. When they trailed dirt in the house, it annoyed Rachel.

'I'd spaced that out,' says Emma.

She lets her gaze follow the man across the car park; he's heading towards his car.

She shakes her head. 'What am I going to do?' she says. 'I can't let every man I meet scare me. He turned me into a nervous wreck in seconds. Just some random guy.'

Amber follows her gaze. 'Look at him with a critical eye,' she says. 'He's all front. Thinks he's the dog's breakfast. Likes to help "ladies" so they can admire his muscles. Just an idiot.'

'He's got a pretty fancy car though,' says Emma. 'What is it?'

'An Aston Martin,' says Amber. 'But I bet you anything, he's clueless about what goes on under the bonnet.'

'I expect you're right,' says Emma with a smile.

37

Thursday, 9.30am

Rachel is irritated and antsy, so she's emptying the fridge and wiping out the interior. They have a cleaning company that comes in twice a week to do all the housework and ironing. But such an amazing place needs work to keep it up to scratch; the demands of her job mean she rarely has time to do this herself. Until now.

She's in a gloomy mood. Emma's release is obviously a good thing. But it's left her out on a limb. Her encounter with the ACC did not go well. Far from letting her get back to her job as head of MIT, he became evasive, suggesting *some well-earned leave.* This was code for he wanted her out of the building and out of the way. She's spent the night brooding about it.

It's so unfair.

But she gets it. He's such a smooth operator; in many ways she admires him. He was marked out as a high flyer as soon as he joined the police. The current Chief Constable became his mentor. But he never spent much time as a detective. Too slow for an ambitious operator like him. Cases are unpredictable. It's easy to get bogged down and you don't always get the result you want, or indeed any result. And the ACC is a results man. Schemes, initiatives that produce data. Data that can be put into reports that prove that the scheme or initiative is working. This is his area of expertise.

He's also media savvy, comfortable on a podium or in front of a camera, the smart and sympathetic face of modern policing. One of his initiatives was to have a bunch of documentary filmmakers trail round the place for a month *to see some real policing.* Every time you walked round a corner, someone stuck a camera in your face. There was nothing real about it. But this is probably why he's expelled her from the office. He's guarding against any media fallout. A murder case to which she has a personal connection would be like throwing meat to a pack of hungry dogs. And Emma hasn't yet been totally exonerated. There's still the question of the time of death and conclusive proof she was brought there after Howard was dead.

Stop brooding, there's nothing you can do.

Simon wanders into the kitchen as she empties her bucket into the sink and peels off her rubber gloves. He's bare-foot, eyes bloodshot, face gaunt. When she came down this morning, she discovered an empty whiskey bottle in the recycling bin.

'What on earth are you doing?' he says peevishly.

'Cleaning the fridge.'

She starts to replace the various items.

He frowns. 'Isn't that's a job for the cleaner?'

She scans him critically. 'You look awful,' she says.

He slumps down on a stool at the counter. 'Don't sound too sympathetic, will you?'

'Simon, if you will drink the best part of a bottle of scotch, you're going to wake up feeling gross.'

She gets a glass and fills it with water from the tap.

'My best friend just died in case you've forgotten.'

If only they could..

She places the water on the counter in front of him. 'And has marinating yourself in alcohol made you feel any better about it?'

He picks up the water, gulps down several mouthfuls, and belches. 'No,' he says. 'Be a good wife and make me some coffee.' He gives her a smile. 'Please.'

She shakes her head and goes over to the coffeemaker.

'Have you any idea who might want to kill Howard?' she says as she slips a pod into the machine.

Simon grimaces and glares at her. 'Course I bloody haven't! Why would you even ask me that?'

Like a petulant teenager. It's the hangover.

'Well, my colleagues are going to ask you; my guess is this morning,' she says.

'Oh, for fuck's sake,' says Simon, putting his face in his hands. 'How should I know? I was his friend, not his bloody keeper. None of it makes any sense to me. Emma was in his flat. Are they sure she had nothing to do with it?'

'Yes. I told you last night. Not his semen. He was probably already dead when she was taken there.'

'Taken? So now we believe her story, that she can't remember anything, and she must've been drugged or whatever.'

Rachel considers her husband.

He's like most people; the discomfort of changing his mind outweighs any evidence to the contrary. Being objective and rational takes time and work, and the ability to resist the pull of your own emotions. Rachel regards it as a mark of intellect, the capacity to respond to changing situations. It's something she feels she's always had.

'It's the most plausible explanation,' she says.

'You've changed your tune,' he says tersely.

That's the point.

Rachel stares at the dark liquid as it gurgles into the mug. She's had a sleepless night to think about every aspect, every permutation of what could've happened, and she's no nearer to a theory of why her sister was taken to Howard's flat and raped after he was dead.

If she hadn't been cut out of the loop by the ACC, she'd be knocking on the pathologist's door this morning and quizzing them about the time of death. Their findings are not always that accurate.

But if Howard didn't rape Emma, then who did? Alistair Hepburn may be a good SIO, but she can't help thinking it would be far better all round if she was back in the office and pushing this along. Even now, they probably know more than they're telling her, which is infuriating.

She hands her husband the mug of coffee.

'Where's Amber this morning?' he says.

Rachel's stomach muscles tightened.

That's another bloody problem.

'Babysitting Emma,' she says. 'She wanted to go over there last night; it seemed like a good idea. She does get on with her better than I do.'

'Everyone gets on with Emma better than you do.'

She glares at her husband. His sarcasm stings. Why's he being so spiteful this morning? Just because he's had a skinful of booze.

Don't lose it.

'What's that supposed to mean?'

'Oh come on Rachel, you know. Your sister rubs you up the wrong way. She always has.'

Count to ten.

Simon sips his coffee and shrugs. 'Just saying.'

Rachel is up to number eight in her head when the doorbell rings.

Her husband gives her a smirk. 'Saved by the bell,' he says.

Rachel turns on her heel and walks out into the hall.

She opens the front door to two of her young officers. Boden and is the other one Chakravorty? Boden has her chin up and out, but the DC looks nervous.

Rachel beams. 'Morning,' she says. At least Alistair is listening to her suggestions, which is something.

'Morning, ma'am,' says Boden.

'Come in,' she says. 'You want to speak to Simon?'

The two officers step into the house.

'If that's convenient,' says Boden.

'Of course. Jo, isn't it?'

'Yes ma'am.'

'And Trisha?'

'Prisha.'

'Prisha Chakravorty, of course. I do know all my officers' names, but it's been a stressful couple of days.'

'It's not a problem, ma'am,' says Prisha. When she speaks, she sounds more confident and older than she looks.

'Okay, well, my husband is going to be a bit scratchy. He's got a stinking hangover because he's terribly upset about Howard and drank a bottle of scotch last night. That's men for you. Different coping mechanisms.'

Boden smiles. Up close, her gaze is rock steady. 'Well, we can always come back later,' she says.

Right attitude, thank heavens.

'No,' says Rachel. 'This inquiry needs to move on. And rapidly.' She beckons them to follow her.

'How's your sister doing?' says Boden.

'My daughter's staying with her to keep an eye on her.'

'That's good,' says Boden.

Rachel shepherds them into the kitchen. Simon looks up from his coffee. He seems cross. She hopes he isn't going to be difficult and show her up.

'DS Boden and DC Chakravorty,' she says. 'This is my husband, Simon Knight.'

But he smiles and gets off his stool.

'Morning,' he says. 'Apologies for the casual attire.' Then he looks at Boden, grins and does a double take. 'We've met,' he says. 'Some drinks party. A leaving do, I think. You'd just transferred from London, and thought Cambridge might be a bit parochial.'

'Well, I got that one wrong, didn't I?' says Boden.

Everyone smiles and relaxes. Rachel's just relieved he's decided to be charming.

'I know it's not normal practice,' she says. 'But since this is my house, let me offer you both a coffee.'

'Thank you, boss,' says Boden. 'We both take it black.'

Boss. She's being friendly. But why wouldn't she be?

'Course you do,' says Rachel. 'First rule of CID. Drink your coffee black.'

'Where shall we do this?' says Simon. 'Sitting at the table?'

Chakravorty gets a tablet out of her bag. Simon pulls out a chair for her at the long dining table.

Boden is about to join them, but Rachel says, 'So, Jo. I have to say, you were very good in the way you handled my sister. It was a complicated situation.'

'Thank you.'

'I did mention Neil Bryant to Alistair—'

'Yes. We eliminated him from the inquiry earlier this morning.'

'Wow. You are moving fast.'

Boden seems to hesitate, then she says, 'I don't know if the DCI's mentioned to you, but we got a hit on the database.'

Trust Emma to have picked up some loser, probably from a dating app.

'Well, that's a stroke of luck,' says Rachel.

'Yeah, DC Mackie's heading a team and they're out looking for him.'

'Excellent. My sister will be relieved. Do we know who he is?'

'Not sure. An ex-con just released from prison. Did time for GBH and drugs. Dean Jessop? I've never heard of him.'

An involuntary shiver goes through Rachel.

Jessop! WTF!

She creases her brow and inhales. 'Well, doesn't ring an immediate bell. But I'll give it some thought.'

Boden is scanning her.

Rachel isn't taking any chances. She smiles and turns away to make the coffee.

How can this be? Dean Jessop?

38

Thursday, 9.45am

Boden sits at the long dining table in the Knights' swanky extended kitchen, sipping her coffee. As soon as she walked through the front door, one thing was clear to her, even on a Detective Super's pay you don't get a house like this. It looks like something out of a design magazine. For this, you need a husband who's minting it.

Simon Knight is a senior partner in a large firm of accountants. They're based in Cambridge but have satellite offices in Bedford and Milton Keynes. Chakravorty has been checking them out. The firm was set up by Knight and Howard Sampson. They've done well; fancy modern offices in the business park, an impressive roster of clients.

The house is detached with a couple of acres of ground. Boden had a quick snoop before they rang the doorbell. There's a large double garage plus additional covered parking. Several vehicles are wrapped in protective covers. According to Hepburn, Simon Knight is a classic car nut, a hobby that can't come cheap. There's an old Porsche Boxster parked on the drive next to the new Jaguar XF she's seen Rachel Knight driving.

At the end of the table, Chakravorty is asking the questions. She has the notes on her tablet and Simon Knight's answers are being recorded. They're going through a fairly standard list: when did he last see or speak to Howard, how did he seem, that sort of thing?

Knight is a complete contrast to his wife; he comes over as easy and open. He doesn't have Rachel's tension or her poise. Everything about him is more ordinary. His fingers are laced and he answers thoughtfully. He's regretful about his failure to spend more time with Howard. He admits he knew Howard was not in a good frame of mind; the divorce from Greta had hit him hard. He should've given his friend more personal support, and it's clear he bitterly regrets this omission. But he has no clue who'd want to harm him. At several points, his eyes become moist.

Boden listens. She doesn't need to be there and didn't expect to be. Chakravorty could've done this with another DC. But Hepburn had called her into his office and asked her to go.

His usual focused and calm facade was showing cracks.

'A slightly delicate situation, Jo,' those were his exact words.

He knows more than he's letting on about Dean Jessop, thought Boden. And so does Knight. She recognised the name and she freaked.

That's when Boden realised she was in murky waters.

According to Hepburn, the Jessops were a two generation, old-school clan of villains. Jimmy Jessop had been a North London drug dealer selling ecstasy round the clubs until he got chased out by younger and harder ethnic gangs. There were several fatal shootings as the Jessops fought a rearguard action, but the CPS couldn't make the charges stick against Jimmy. He moved out to the leafy suburbs and built up a business selling good quality cocaine to commuters.

Dean Jessop is Jimmy's son, a bit of a clone of his dad. He was in trouble even before he left school, became a dealer in his own right, and, Hepburn added casually, back when she was a DI, Rachel Knight might've crossed paths with him.

Then why didn't he just call her and ask her?

Hepburn's reticence made no sense to Boden and it still doesn't. If a violent career criminal has just been released from prison and appears to have attacked Knight's sister, then that looks like some kind of revenge to Boden. And that's serious.

But Hepburn's instructions were to just mention Jessop to Rachel and see how she reacted.

Why?

Boden decided not to ask questions, but to wait and see what happened. She doubts it'll take Mackie long to find Jessop. It was a condition of his release on licence that he was staying in approved premises under the supervision of the probation service. They'll soon pick him up.

As Chakravorty continues with her questions, Rachel Knight is across the other side of the room, busily loading the dishwasher and wiping down the work surfaces. Boden watches her covertly. The tension is zinging off her.

She recognised the name of the rapist, and yet she brushed it off and pretend she didn't know him. But why? It looks like she's been targeted. She must've realised that, and she must be worried.

Boden is not happy. Until Jessop is apprehended, they should take steps to protect both Rachel and her sister. This situation can't be ignored. She gets up from her chair and wanders into the kitchen area.

'Listen, boss,' she says, 'I've been thinking—'

Rachel is wearing yellow rubber gloves, and she raises a preemptive finger. 'You're a smart woman, Jo, but whatever you think you know here, you're probably wrong.'

This feels like a rebuke. Boden is surprised.

'Okay, well, maybe you should speak to DCI Hepburn.'

'I realise that.' Rachel's tone is sharp and dismissive.

Boden shrugs. 'I'm just trying to do my job.'

'I realise that.'

She meets Rachel Knight's gaze. Knight doesn't look frightened, but she does look mightily pissed off.

39

The smell is overwhelming. Pungent, sickly. It's choking the breath out of her. Her lungs are fit to burst. But she's got to keep running. If she can make it to the door. If she can get through the door and get out of there…

Emma wakes with a start. Her pulse is thumping.

It's a dream. Just a bad dream.

She sits up. She's lying on her own bed, in her own flat. This is a relief. But she's fully clothed. She reaches over to the glass of water on the bedside table and takes a sip. Did she sleep in her clothes? What time is it? She's disorientated. No sign of her phone.

Just breathe.

Everything's fine. Light seeps through the curtains. A car passes in the street outside her window. The fog in her brain lifts. Thoughts slot into place.

They came back, and she was so exhausted she had to lie down. But they got her car back. Amber changed the wheel.

Her niece is staying with her. She's not on her own. Amber is here, sleeping on the sofa in the other room. Everything's fine.

As she stands up and her bare feet touch the floorboards, she shivers. The heating in the flat has never been that reliable. The boiler needs replacing, but she hasn't got the money for that. And she needs to get her head together and get back to work, or she won't have the money for anything.

She can't keep crashing out like this. She must get her laptop out and check her emails.

As she opens the bedroom door, a blast of cold air hits her. On the other side of the room, the door to the french windows stands open. And there's no sign of Amber.

Panic seizes Emma. Where's Amber?

He's taken Amber!

The notion jumps into her head. She doesn't need to think; she knows it's true.

She rushes over to the french doors and looks out. The garden is dank, a grey-green mass of overgrown foliage. It provides the perfect cover for someone to hide. But how did he get in?

The key? Where's the key?

The key is in the door, on the inside. Is she going crazy? Did she open it? Did Amber open it?

She steps out into the garden. Her bare feet sink into the wet grass. She opens her mouth and hollers, 'Amber!'

Her voice echoes, cracked and desperate. The backs of the houses opposite stare at her blankly. There's no sign of anyone and no response.

He's got Amber. It's all your fault.

She sinks down on her hands and knees. She must call Rachel, tell her what's happened. But she can't seem to move. Her limbs are like lead.

Then she feels a hand on her back. She jumps and spins round, ready for the attack.

'Emma, Emma, it's okay. It's me. It's okay.' Amber is leaning over her.

Emma rocks back on her heels. 'I thought he'd got you!' she gasps.

Amber squats down next to her. 'I popped to the shop to get some more coffee and something for lunch,' she says. 'You were exhausted when we got back from the hotel. You crashed out so I thought I'd let you sleep.'

None of it makes sense.

'But the door,' says Emma weakly. 'Who opened the door?'

Amber examines the door. 'It was unlocked from the inside,' she says. 'Did you do it?'

Did you? Were you trying to escape?

But the dream has evaporated.

'I don't know,' she says limply.

'Come on,' says Amber cheerfully. 'You can't sit there in the wet grass.' She offers her hand and hauls Emma to her feet.

Emma looks down at her jeans. Soaking; she feels a fool.

'I think I just had a bad dream,' she says.

'Go and change your jeans, and I'll make us some lunch. Fancy some soup?'

Emma nods, like a sick child who's being cosseted. She can't remember her mother ever doing much of that. But Amber is doing it. She's much younger; she shouldn't be the care giver. It's all wrong. But Emma doesn't have the energy to resist.

She lets Amber shepherd her back to the bedroom.

'Can you manage?' says Amber.

'I'll be fine.' She peels off her damp jeans. She's shivering. In the drawer she finds an old snuggly pair of trackie bottoms. She pulls them on.

Amber returns to the main room and she can hear her closing the french windows, shoving the door hard to force it shut. Wood grinds on wood.

Hard to shut, hard to open.

The wooden frame is swollen. How did she even get it open again? She must've. Somehow. Why doesn't she remember?

She returns to the main room. Amber is at the hob, stirring a saucepan of tomato soup.

'You okay?' says Amber.

She nods. But she can tell from her niece's solicitude and tone of voice that she's not okay. Far from it.

'I got some fresh rolls,' says Amber. 'In the hessian bag if you want to get them out.'

Emma walks over to the table. And that's when she sees it. Small and glittery. The light from the window catches it. Placed on the corner of the table. Then she sees the glitter is cellophane. A small, wrapped sweet. She picks it up. A mint humbug?

She turns to Amber. 'That's nice. Did you buy some sweets too?'

'No,' says Amber.

'It's a mint humbug,' says Emma, holding it up.

'I didn't buy it,' says Amber. 'We must've unearthed it this morning when we were cleaning up.'

Did we?

The mint humbug is beige with darker brown stripes, an old-fashioned sort of sweet. She hasn't bought anything like this for years.

The hand cradling the sweet shakes. She glances at the french doors.

He's been here. He left this sweet.

Amber is serving the soup into two bowls.

'Here we go,' she says. 'Nice and—'

'Amber, he's been here! There was no sweet here before.'

'Well, how could he have got in? The key was inside, on the inside of the door.'

'I don't know how!'

'Emma, it's not possible.'

Emma flings the sweet across the room, clutches her arms around her head and collapses on the sofa. 'He was here! I know it!'

Suddenly she can't breathe, her chest tightens with a vice like grip, her lungs can't get enough air. Just like in her dream. It's her heart. She's having a heart attack. She's going to die.

40

Thursday, 11.40am

Dean unwraps another mint humbug. He pops it in his mouth. As a lad, he was never much of a sweet eater. Cans of coke, the other sort, that was his sugar hit. But Kelly loved her sweets and mint humbugs were her favourites. When it was tough at home, he'd nick a bag from the corner shop and give them to her.

He's hunkered down in his surveillance spot in the bushes at the back of the house. But he's thinking about his sister. Of course, all that sugar and chocolate turned into a bit of a problem for her. She got pretty chubby as a teenager which upset her even more. He understood. No point lecturing her on eating right and keeping fit. Sweets were her comforter. She needed them. It was only when she met that junky bastard that she started to use other stuff. When he was in the nick, they used to talk about addictive personalities. And that was Kelly; it wasn't her fault; it was a sickness.

It's different if you can handle it.

He scans the back of the building. The bitch lives in the ground-floor flat, french doors, a gift to any half-decent burglar. He couldn't pick any lock. He hasn't had enough practice. But he managed that one. No problem.

He watched the other girl go out, then he went in. The bitch was asleep. He thought about having another crack at her; it would serve her right. But he decided it was too risky. He settled for spooking her.

About five minutes ago, she came out and she went batshit crazy. Then the other girl came back. He watched with satisfaction. She was freaking out, just like Kelly freaked out in prison. If he keeps pushing her, eventually he'll get her to the edge. Not part of the original plan, but plans can change.

Have a bit of fun? Why not?

Now the other girl has come back, it's time for him to make himself scarce.

The feds will have figured it out by now; when he screwed the bitch, he made sure he left his marker. That was part of the plan. So they'll be looking for him. But they're plods; they'll look in all the wrong places.

He thinks about Craig and the second phase of the operation. It would be foolish to underestimate his brother. And he doesn't. But, right now, he's buzzing. He hasn't felt this good for years.

On top of the world. Invincible.

It's like a when a soldier goes into battle; he's seen plenty of movies about soldiers, and not only fiction. When the operation finally starts, there's a sense of elation. A few nerves, but that gives you the edge. The coke helps, as long as you keep it under control, which he does. He's got a job to do and nothing else matters. Everything else, life's usual crap, all just falls away. He's going to enjoy this, every moment of it, otherwise what's the point?

He gets up, stretches himself and vaults over the wall into the garden behind. He walks down the side path, climbs over the gate, and he's in the street where the Aston is parked.

Getting in, he starts up the engine. It growls to life like a caged bear waking up. And that's him. They caged him, but now he's free. His time has come. He can feel it. Craig would never have the balls to do something like this, which goes to show who's the better man. Now it's time his little brother accepted the fact and stepped aside.

41

Emma can feel Amber's hand on the back of her neck, holding her head down between her legs.

'Breathe, Emma,' she says. 'It's a panic attack, but you'll be okay. Deep breaths.'

The blood is rushing to her head, but she can breathe again. Amber puts a hand on her shoulder and eases her into an upright position.

Her heart thuds. But the attack is passing. She was convinced she was dying; this has never happened to her before.

She meets her niece's worried gaze. 'I think I'm going crazy,' she says.

'I don't know what to think,' says Amber. 'But we should call Mum.'

Emma nods. Amber is a capable young woman, but she's only nineteen, and this is too much of a burden to put on her. They're both out of their depth.

Emma leans back on the sofa and closes her eyes. She's had down times in her life before. But she's always managed to bounce back and crack on. Go out for a drink, forget your troubles. She realises that until now she's never experienced true despair.

Amber disappears into the bedroom to make the call to Rachel. Emma knows why. She's about to tell her mother that Emma has completely lost the plot.

But have you?

Amber returns and says, 'She's coming straight over.'

'Amber, I'm so sorry. I'm losing it, and you shouldn't have to deal with this. It's not fair on you.'

'Sod that,' says Amber. 'I've been thinking. I wiped that table down. It was the last thing I did before we set off for the hotel. We came back and after you fell asleep, I went to the shop. I bought a carton of soup, two rolls and a packet of ground coffee for the cafetière. I took the hessian shopping bag. When I came back, I put it on the table. I took out the soup. And you're right, neither of us put a mint humbug on the corner of that table.'

Is this real?

Amber is pale, but her expression is bullish and deter-mined. In many ways, she is her mother's daughter.

She sits down beside Emma on the sofa, takes her hand and squeezes it. 'The french doors are locked,' she says. 'He can't get in. We just sit tight until Mum gets here.'

They wait in silence for a while. But Emma's mind is drifting. She's lightheaded, in the backwash of too much adrenaline.

Why you? What have you done?

Has she somehow invited this into her life? She thinks about Neil. When they were first together, it was explosive. The sex, then the rows. Her ex may have a hair-trigger temper, but it erupted, then it was gone. The make-up sex was some of the best they had. Neil had a short attention span. He was always on to the next thing. He wouldn't have the patience to stalk her.

She's exhausted. She must stay awake, but her head lolls. Amber strokes her arm.

The ringing doorbell brings Emma sharply back to consciousness.

'It's Mum,' says Amber, getting up.

Is it? How can they be sure?

She hears her sister's voice on the entry phone. Only then can she relax. Amber goes and lets her in.

Rachel strides into the room. Her brow is furrowed, but there's another expression on her face, one that's hard to read. Is she nervous?

'Are you okay?' she says briskly.

'No,' says Emma.

'Well, we've identified your assailant.'

Assailant? Such a weird, impersonal word.

'Can't you say rape, Rachel? What's wrong with saying that?'

'Okay, rapist,' says her sister.

'How did you find him?' says Amber.

'The semen sample has been matched with his DNA on the database.'

Emma struggles to process this. 'You're saying he's been arrested?'

Rachel sighs. 'Not yet. But we're looking for him.'

'Rachel, he was here. When I was asleep and Amber went to the shops. He's still after me.'

Rachel nods. 'Amber told me. And I've passed that on.'

Passed it on?

Emma stares at her sister, but she doesn't know what to say. It's hard not to collapse into a wailing heap.

'Why is he doing this to me?' she whispers.

Rachel puts a hand on her shoulder. 'Listen, Emma,' she says. 'This is a complicated situation—'

'Why didn't you just believe me?' says Emma, fighting back the tears. 'There's nothing complicated about that.'

Her sister steps away and folds her arms. 'It didn't make a lot of sense.'

'But me having a secret affair with Howard, and lying about it, and killing him, that did make sense to you?'

Rachel can't hold her gaze. Dipping her head, she exhales.

She looks ashamed. And she bloody well should!

'At the time… well, there was a certain logic to it,' she says.

'Logic?' says Emma. 'You mean as in Emma is a stupid slag and a liar who has stupid drunken affairs—'

Rachel reaches out to her. She has tears brimming on her lashes. 'Emma, stop, please!'

Emma glares at her. 'You just want to see me fall, don't you? You always have. You hate me.'

'That's not true,' Rachel whispers.

'Isn't it? My whole life I've looked up to you. My clever big sister. But you've only ever looked down at me. Why? I've never understood. As far as you're concerned, I'm always in the wrong.'

Rachel wipes her face with the back of her hand.

'It may sometimes seem—'

'Sometimes? And don't blame Mum. She's a total cow, granted. And she loved to play us off against each other. Still does. But you didn't have to fall for it.'

'I don't know what to say, except I'm sorry.'

'And that's the trouble, isn't it? You get away with it because I always forgive you. I always have. You put me down. Put me in my place. But I still forgive and forget because you're my sister. Because I'm soft, and yeah, I'm stupid.'

Rachel dips her head sorrowfully.

Emma becomes aware of Amber, standing between them, watching with a look of dismay on her face.

'And I'm not trying to take your daughter away from you,' she says. 'I'm just trying to be a good aunt.'

'I know that,' Rachel murmurs.

All the energy and life has drained out of Emma. She didn't realise she was this angry with her sister. It erupted from nowhere. Rachel's lips are tightly pursed.

Emma feels bad. 'Look, I'm sorry,' she says. 'I'm just a mess.'

Now you're backtracking! Don't!

'What are you sorry for?' says Rachel. 'You don't need to apologise.' She hesitates. 'I haven't told you, but it seems likely that you were targeted because of me.'

Emma stares at her. 'What do you mean?'

'This man is a criminal, part of an Organised Crime Gang I've had some dealings with in the past. He recently got out of prison. One theory is this is his attempt at revenge.'

Emma stares at her sister. It takes a moment for this to sink in.

A criminal?

If it was insane before, this is ten times worse. It's as if she's caught in a net. Her limbs are flailing. She can't escape.

'This is because I'm your sister?'

'Probably.'

'How does he even know that?'

Rachel sighs. 'I've no idea.'

'But Rachel, he was here. He's still after me!'

'We've identified him. He'll be arrested. I promise you.'

'Did he kill Howard?'

'I don't know.'

'So what happens now?'

'Well, we will get him, have no doubt about that. But until we do, I'd like you to consider coming to stay with us. That way you'll be secure.' She glances at the french doors. 'There are various ways he could've forced that door. It wouldn't be that hard. The lock is old.'

Emma stares at the beautiful Victorian french windows. One of the flat's original features.

See, you brought it on yourself. Again.

Amber takes Emma's hand. 'It's for the best,' she says. 'And you and I can sit down and sort the business out. Do some online advertising, get some new clients.'

She's trying to make it sound normal.

'Doesn't sound like I've got a choice,' says Emma.

'I hope we can make it as pleasant as possible for you,' says Rachel.

Pleasant?

Emma nods. How many more ways can Rachel find to fuck up her life, she wonders.

42

Having dropped Amber and Emma back at the house, Rachel drives into town. The ACC may want her at arm's length from this inquiry, but she refuses to accept that. She'll find a way round it, unofficially if necessary, and Hepburn's going to help her.

She walks into the incident room, which causes a few heads to turn. DC Mackie is perched on a desk, consuming a double cheeseburger. She's known him since he became a detective; a solid cop. What he lacks in brains, he makes up for in brute force.

'Mackie!' she says from across the room.

He looks like a badger caught in the headlights. He stands up, drops the burger on his desk, and wipes his mouth with his hand.

'Ma'am,' he mumbles through a mouthful of burger.

'Why are you always eating?' she says.

He swallows. 'Always hungry,' he says.

'Did you get Jessop?'

'Well, no, we—'

Shit!

'What do you mean, no?'

'Checked the hostel where he's supposed to be staying. Talked to his probation officer, who was cagey. Basically, he's got no idea where Jessop is.'

This is going from bad to worse.

'You saying he's still out there?'

'Umm, well…'

Rachel shakes her head. It's not Mackie's fault. He's doing what he's told. This is a failure of strategy and leadership.

You need to get back in control.

She notices Jo Boden watching her. Boden's the outsider and therefore a potential ally. Everyone else will err on the side of caution. Hepburn will want to cover his back.

'Sergeant,' she says. 'Would you come with me?'

Boden looks surprised, but follows her out of the room.

'No one's going to find Dean Jessop by just looking under the usual rocks,' she says, as they walk down the corridor to Hepburn's office.

'We have put out a general alert,' says Boden.

'Do we even know what he's driving?'

'No, I don't believe so.'

'My guess would be he'll have borrowed something from his brother, Craig Jessop.'

'Okay,' says Boden. 'We can check that.'

'Have you even discussed Craig Jessop?'

'The SIO mentioned him.'

Mentioned? That's the tactic he's using.

They stop at the office door. Rachel tilts her head and

smiles. 'You've had a bit of a chequered history, Jo. But my guess is that's not your fault and you're a good officer.'

Boden seems taken aback. 'I hope so,' she says.

Will this be enough to get her onside?

Rachel knocks and, without waiting for a response, enters. Hepburn looks up from his laptop. He doesn't seem surprised.

'Why didn't you phone me and tell me?' she says.

He sighs. But before he can reply, she cuts him short.

'Instead, you send the Sergeant here to *mention* it. You think I'm stupid, Alistair.'

'Rachel, I'm sorry—' he has to grace to blush. Boden is watching the exchange, and she's riveted.

Good.

'I want that scum found, Alistair.'

'We're doing our best.'

'No you're not. Because to find him, you've got to go and rattle Craig Jessop's cage. Hard.'

He inhales. 'There's no reason to suppose—'

'They're a family of villains. And Craig will know where Dean is.'

'Craig Jessop is a respectable businessman who's never been in trouble with the law.'

Carter's warned him off.

'And what makes him so respectable nowadays? The Police and Crime Commissioner plays golf with him?'

Carter wants her job. And he's playing politics.

Hepburn puts his face in his hands. 'Rachel, believe me, this is not straightforward. You know the politics of this. You know how it works.'

'I know life was simpler when all you lads just got together, rolled up your trouser legs and joined the Masons. At least the nature of the corruption and the undue influence was obvious.' She glances at Boden, who cracks a smile.

'Rachel, you've got this all wrong.' Hepburn sounds pathetic.

'Have I? Are you saying Craig Jessop didn't pay for the Police and Crime Commissioner's election campaign indirectly. It's an open secret. Does that put him above the law?'

'No, of course, it doesn't.'

'Well, at least we agree on that. But Dean Jessop is still out there and he's stalking my sister.'

'Stalking her?' says Hepburn. 'You sure? We didn't know that.'

He's out of his depth.

'That's why I'm here. To tell you that. Dean Jessop gets out of jail and he's got revenge on his mind. Who's to say Craig isn't facilitating that? That there's not a conspiracy and Craig isn't aiding and abetting his brother's escape.'

Hepburn rubs his face and sighs. 'That could be true,' he says. 'But there's another thing here.'

'What?'

'Did you know that Kelly Jessop committed suicide in prison?'

'Dean's sister?'

'I've been digging through the files. I knew he had to have a motive. She died about two years ago, I discovered.'

Shit! Shit! Shit! Now it makes sense.

Rachel exhales. 'So you think that's why he went after my sister? This is his perverse notion of justice.'

Hepburn gets up, glances at Boden, and hesitates. Then he says, 'This could come back to bite you, to bite us in so many ways, Rachel. Obviously, we'll step up the search.'

She looks at him. They've known each other for years, worked a lot of cases. Hepburn's a straight shooter. Maybe he even regards her as a friend. Is this his idea of loyalty? It looks like he's soft-pedalling, but actually he's on her side, trying to work this out and cover for her.

Stop reacting, start thinking.

'But why target Howard?' she says. 'That's the bit I don't get. Because he's my husband's business partner? Why would Jessop pick on him? Or even know who he is.'

Hepburn shakes his head. 'A random co-incidence? He followed your sister back to Howard Sampson's flat?'

Back to Emma again? She is lying about being involved with Howard.

Boden pipes up. 'Sorry, boss. What about the time of death?'

Hepburn shrugs. 'There's still a window of about half an hour. What makes most sense here is Dean's got a grudge, so he targets Emma, follows her to her boyfriend's, kills him and rapes her.'

Rachel nods. 'You're right. It's the only explanation that makes sense.'

There's a knot in her stomach and it's tightening. It may be her fault Emma was targeted, but Emma got Howard killed. And she's still lying about it.

'How does he know Emma Harris is your sister?' says Boden.

Rachel huffs. 'She's always putting family stuff on Facebook and tagging me. I've asked her not to. I don't think it would be that hard.'

'We will find him,' says Hepburn. 'He's not that clever.'

'What about protection for me and my family?'

'Of course. I'll speak to the ACC about it.'

Rachel turns on her heel. She has to get out of there before she bursts into tears.

This can't all be your fault. It just can't.

As she strides down the corridor, she reflects on Emma's

angry accusations against her, not to mention her pathetic self-pity. This insistence by Emma that she can't remember what happened is all a pretence.

Stop! Just stop! Think about this like any other case.

Cut out the emotions and get back to the facts. Dean Jessop is an unstable villain with a grudge. Looking back, the way Rachel dealt with him at the time was a mistake. But it was just a bad judgement call. None of this explains how Howard ended up getting killed. The only explanation for that is that Jessop followed Emma to his flat. And Emma is still lying about that.

Emma must be made to tell the truth.

For Simon's sake, for all Howard's colleagues and friends, Rachel knows she must persuade her sister to come clean. This is a question of moral culpability. Howard was an innocent victim and collateral damage. If he wasn't involved with Emma, he wouldn't be dead.

His death is down to Emma. She knows this; that's why she's still lying. She can't accept her guilt, so instead she's attacking Rachel.

Why are you surprised? It's how she's always been.

Once Rachel's out of the building and walking towards her car, she allows the tears to come. They'll get Jessop, put him back behind bars, but in terms of her career, she can probably forget promotion to the top job. And there's nothing she can do about it.

43

Emma sits in her sister's palatial kitchen. The floor space of the kitchen diner is larger that her whole flat. When Simon bought the house, he had this added on as an extension. The sliding doors onto the substantial garden are double-glazed and triple locked. She is now cocooned in granite, glass and money.

She sips her camomile tea and looks out of the window. A small suitcase of her snatched possessions is out in the hall. Amber has gone upstairs to make up the guest bedroom for her. Rachel has gone to talk to her colleagues. And no one seems to know where Simon is.

Emma has never felt so alone and beleaguered. Her years with Neil were tumultuous, but, in his way, he supported her. Since they split, Emma's life has been slowly rolling downhill. She has nothing to fall back on. Everything has become fraught and complicated. She's worked harder but become poorer.

The house she and her husband lived in together was one that he built. It wasn't big like this, but it was compact and modern with loads of eco-features. Neil was hot on that. She thinks of the en suite bathroom with the walk-in shower. Neil was an imaginative builder, but a lousy businessman. He did projects he liked for people who couldn't always pay. In the end, he was up to his eyeballs in debt. He declared bankruptcy and it all went under the hammer to pay his creditors. After that, he didn't seem to give a shit about anything, including their marriage. He was both resentful and angry, and in the end, impossible to be with. So she left.

She should've picked a man like Simon, solid and reliable. Her mother had told her as much in her usual blunt way. Just another thing Rachel got right and she got wrong.

As she contemplates the stupid decisions of her life, a ginger cat wanders past the window. Emma wonders who it belongs to. Rachel would never countenance any kind of animal in the house. Amber always wanted a dog. Rachel's view is that they create too much mess and trouble. But this ginger tom is still wandering across her sister's patio as if he owns the place.

This amuses Emma. You can't control cats; they have their own agenda. And you can't control people, although Rachel tries to. Her sister is out there now, trying to *sort this out*. That's what she said as she dropped them off at the house. Tense and wound up, she gunned her fancy car off down the street. But what did that mean? She was going to issue orders. Send officers to arrest this man. But he's like the cat. He has his own set of rules.

She thinks about the mint humbug. Such a random act. Was its purpose to unnerve her? It did, and the realisation he'd been inside her flat frightened her so much she had a panic attack. If his plan was to terrorise her, he's succeeded.

She thinks about this. About being terrified. Even now, in her sister's house, she's jittery. Her nerves are in shreds. And she doesn't know what to expect next. But isn't this the nub of it? Not knowing what's going to happen next.

Her own mind is now doing the job of scaring her. The fear arose from the fact he got into her flat while she was sleeping. He'd raped her once. But this time, he simply left a sweet. If he'd wanted to harm her, he could have. This was about power and making her feel powerless. If he's trying to drive her crazy, he's succeeding. Even once he's been caught, how will she stop feeling like this?

But if she can work that out, then whatever he does is no longer unexpected and she can fight him. She gets up and paces.

Refuse to be powerless, that's the first step.

He killed Howard, kidnapped her, raped her, now he's stalking her. None of this is random; he's working to a plan. Rachel says it's some kind of revenge. Yet it's not a direct attack on Rachel. Why? That's the first question. Why her and not Rachel?

She was just easier to get to?

He must've gone to some lengths to identify her as Rachel's sister. But she's posted plenty of family stuff online. Rachel has always complained. Cop paranoia. So she did it all the more. It wouldn't have been hard to stalk her online and to find her business. She has a web page and has recently started a chatty blog to attract more clients. Does she reveal too much personal stuff? Perhaps.

He kidnapped her from the hotel. Was he working there? Or staying there?

The questions spin in her head.

It hits her like a freight train. The man with the sportscar, the Aston Martin. He appeared from nowhere to help her change the wheel in the hotel car park.

That smell. The spicy body spray. It was him!

This is why it freaked her out. Her nose and brain remembered the smell, even though she was unconscious.

Emma feels a surge of energy and anger. Now she can see his face and the sneer when they refused his help.

How did she even get a flat tyre? He could've easily done it.

Amber returns to the kitchen. 'The room's ready for you,' she says. 'I've put fresh towels in the en suite.'

'The man with the Aston Martin,' says Emma. 'It was him.'

'How do you know?'

'His body spray.'

'How can you be sure?'

'Because it made me gag. The whole experience was just… peculiar.'

'His attitude was odd,' says Amber.

'Amber, the more I think about it, the more I'm sure. We must call Rachel and tell her.'

'Tell Rachel what?' says a weary voice from the hall, as her sister appears in the kitchen doorway. She walks into the room and dumps her bag.

'I think he was staying at the hotel,' says Emma.

'As a guest?' says Rachel. She seems tetchy and disinterested.

'Yes,' says Emma. 'We saw him when we went to pick up my car. I discovered I had a flat, and he came and tried to help us. But he was quite weird and hassley. And he drives an Aston Martin.'

Rachel pulls her laptop out of her briefcase. She opens it

on the kitchen counter. A few keystrokes and she's into some kind of database.

'Take a look at this,' she says. A police mugshot pops up on the screen. 'Is that him?'

Emma peers at the face. The dead eyes, the hint of a sneer; a spasm of dread shoots straight through her.

But Amber is looking over her shoulder. 'Yes, that's him,' she says. 'The man who tried to help us in the hotel car park.'

'Well then,' says Rachel. 'You did encounter Dean Jessop. That's him.'

Emma stares at the mugshot and it gives her an odd sense of clarity. He's no longer a ghost. This is the criminal who targeted her. And he still wants to terrify her. But now she'll see him coming, she'll recognise him and she can defend herself.

44

Thursday, 1.45pm

Since she left London and the Met, Jo Boden has given office
politics in all its forms a wide berth, and she's always avoided
applying for promotion. Once she was ambitious, but she
learned the hard way that ambition can lead down some dark
roads. As an experienced DS, she's a good candidate for
Inspector. But the more she sees of management, the more
reluctant she is to enter the snake pit. Who needs that kind of
stress in their life? Juggling inadequate resources, placating
oversized egos higher up the food chain, making excuses for
inevitable failures, trying to achieve more with less. It's a
daily battle.

Hepburn is the SIO on this case, but he's become curiously passive. Based on her previous experience of him, this
is out of character. His exchange with Rachel Knight, which
she insisted Boden witness, was strange and full of ambiguity.
They're both tied up with the Jessops in ways that are
hampering the inquiry, that's clear. Somewhere in the past,

lines have been crossed and rules broken. And it could've been for good reasons, to nail dangerous villains who otherwise would've walked free.

Yet Rachel Knight seems to be casting her in the role of the clean skin; she's hoping that Boden will do her job. Why? Because she's worried that Alistair Hepburn won't, or can't. That he's being leant on.

He probably is.

After Knight left, Boden wandered back to her desk. There was a lack of urgency in the incident room. Hepburn's attitude has filtered down through the ranks. Three days into a rape and murder inquiry, there was bound to be a hiatus and a slowing of momentum.

Mackie was out *turning over the usual stones* in the expectation that Dean Jessop would pop out. But Knight was probably right about that. And then there was the question of Craig Jessop, a bone of contention between the bosses. Boden decided to do some digging and found plenty of information swilling around the internet about him.

A businessman and philanthropist, well-connected with all the local bigwigs, his wife is his cover; she runs a non-profit that collects food past its sell-by date from supermarkets and distributes it to food banks. And she's also a local councillor. Pretty much everyone who's anyone knows the Jessops. They throw terrific parties.

It was only when Boden dug much deeper that she found a piece by an investigative journalist that presented Craig Jessop as something other than a rough diamond who's risen because of his own efforts as a businessman. It didn't accuse him outright of making money as a drug dealer, because what's also clear is Craig Jessop will sue anyone who he thinks is defaming him. He accepts his family used to be criminals, but insists that's not him. You can't help your relatives; he's another one using that line.

She's going through all this material when her phone rings. An unknown caller, who turns out to be Rachel Knight.

'I've just been talking to my sister,' says Knight. 'She's identified Dean Jessop as the driver of an Aston Martin that was at the Waterside Park Hotel this morning. Check with the DVLA if Craig Jessop owns such a car. I'm guessing he does. Then you can feed it into the ANPR and track Dean.'

'Okay,' says Boden.

'I'm presuming Mackie hasn't found him yet?'

'He's on it. But no.'

'And I'd appreciate it if you'd keep me in the loop,' says Knight, although her voice sounds tentative.

'Of course, boss,' says Boden. She hangs up.

Why not?

Hepburn may be SIO, but if he's checked out, that's not Boden's problem. She'll just do her job. This is a legitimate lead.

She calls Chakravorty over as she clicks through into the DVLA's database. There are several Craig Jessops to scroll through, but only one lives in the area and he owns five vehicles, including an Aston Martin.

Chakravorty beams. They both know they can now track all the routes the vehicle has taken through the National ANPR Data Centre. But Boden will need to get Hepburn to sign off on this.

'I'll talk to the SIO,' she says.

When she enters Hepburn's office, he's sitting behind his desk, staring into space. It looks as if he's been like that for a while. Given that the boss is a roll your sleeves up and get on with it sort of bloke, this is worrying.

He stares at her with a blank expression as she recounts

her phone call with Knight and their discovery that Craig Jessop owns this type of sportscar.

'Good work, Jo,' he says, although there's a lack of conviction in his tone.

'So we can get on it?' she says.

'Absolutely.'

She's half way to the door when he steeples his fingers and says, 'You must've heard the theory, Jo, that in most areas a very small group of people commits the majority of the crime. Often families of villains, like the Jessops. Usually they're both stupid and violent and that's what gets them in the end.'

'I've heard that, boss.'

'Rachel Knight's a smart copper. She knew this and she focused on the Jessops years ago. With some success. But now and then you come across a Craig Jessop, canny as a bloody fox. You know what he was doing in his twenties, when his brother Dean was brawling in pubs and getting nicked? He was buying land. You may say, where did someone like him get the money? And indeed, the National Crime Agency has an open file on him which seeks to answer that question. They've been trying for years, but they can't trace the money from his family's drug dealing enterprise to his many business interests as a developer. Yet logic dictates that one funded the other.'

Boden nods. Why is he telling her this? Some philosophical analysis on where crime ends and business begins? She scans him. He seems stuck. What's stopping him doing his job?

He looks up at her and says, 'Do you believe Emma Harris is lying when she says she wasn't involved in any kind of affair with Howard Sampson?'

'My gut feeling is she's telling the truth,' says Boden.

'That does rather upend our line of inquiry,' says Hepburn.

He asked.

'And,' he adds, 'Rachel seems to buy the idea that her sister would want to cover the affair up and has therefore lied about it.'

'Maybe the DCS's view of her sister is a bit skewed,' says Boden.

'How do you mean?'

Sisters? Don't go there. Why do old wounds still hurt so much?

Boden sighs. 'Took me years to figure I'd read my sister all wrong. Although we were much younger.'

Leave it at that.

Fortunately, Hepburn is following his own train of thought. 'My wife doesn't get on with her sister,' he says. 'Always squabbling as if they were still kids.'

Boden shrugs. 'It's a common thing boss, the love and hate and rivalry between sisters.'

He frowns. 'You think I've let Rachel's bias cloud the issue?'

'I don't know, but let's say we buy Emma Harris's story she wasn't involved in any sort of relationship with him. Then why was Howard killed? Why was she taken to his flat and raped? The time frame the pathologist has given us makes it possible he was dead before she ever got there.'

'That's true. You think why Howard was killed is the key to this? He's not some kind of collateral damage.'

'Yes. If we're keeping an open mind and looking at the two things separately,' says Boden. 'But if we can track this car Dean's driving and catch him, we may get some answers to that.'

Hepburn nods. 'You'd better get on with it,' he says.

She turns to go. But one suspicion continues to niggle. And Hepburn's not going to like it. It'll open a can of worms.

Just go and track the car.

She hesitates then she says, 'I can't help thinking, boss, that we should be looking more closely at Howard Sampson.'

'And?'

'He's an accountant. What if something connected him and Craig Jessop?'

The DCI sighs, but his expression is inscrutable. He gives her a glassy stare. 'What are you implying, Boden? That Rachel Knight's husband's business partner is a money launderer?'

'Just a suggestion, boss.'

'Yeah, well keep it to yourself,' he says briskly. 'And go and find this bloody car.'

'Sir.'

As she walks out into the corridor, she realises what's just happened. She and Hepburn have come to the same conclusion. He's just been using her to check it out. Craig and Howard, there must be a link. And that's the problem he's grappling with. No wonder he seems paralysed. Boden's glad she's not in his shoes.

45

Thursday, 2pm

Dean sits on a lounger beside his brother's pool. It's a miserable day, but the pool house is warm and lit like a little grotto with coloured lights under the palm trees. Must cost Craig a fortune in heating bills. But the bastard can afford it. When this is over, Dean plans to base himself in Spain. He'll have an outdoor pool. The climate out there is much better. He'll build himself a villa, get the old man out there, in his own wing of the house, with a full-time nurse. Dean's got it all worked out in his head. Once he's finished with this.

Craig phoned him and said they needed to talk. But when he arrived, he was told that Craig was *in a meeting*. He doesn't like being kept waiting, and he'll certainly tell his brother that. But he doesn't want it to turn into a row. Not yet. Not until he's ready.

The black girl who served lunch when he came before, brings him a drink. Just a beer. He wants his wits about him. No sign of Kate; she's steering well clear. But after the party, it doesn't surprise him. That was fun. He put her nose completely out of joint.

Another reason to feel good. These bitches need putting in their place.

Eventually Craig appears. He's not happy.

'Alright, mate,' Dean says, raising his bottle in a toast. 'You said you wanted a word. And so here I am.'

Craig puts his hands on his hips and stands over him. Dean grins. Is he trying to be intimidating? He's got a fucking hope. Dean could pick him up and dump him in his own stupid pool.

But Craig must know this. A couple of his young guns have turned up in the doorway, standing with folded arms at a discrete distance but ready to back their boss up.

Craig cricks his neck and sighs. 'I've tried to do right by you, haven't I, Dean?'

'I dunno, have you?' says Dean, taking a swig of beer.

'I think I have. But you still think you can play me for a mug, don't you?'

Dean shrugs, all innocence. 'Mate, I got no idea what you're talking about.'

'You've been a busy boy.'

'Just a few scores to settle. I've been inside a while. You get out, you know how it is.'

'No, I don't. Because I'm not some kind of psycho with a temper I can't control. I haven't been to prison and I don't intend to. And I'm not thick.'

Dean inhales and huffs. 'No need to start slinging personal insults about, mate.'

'Look at you,' says Craig with a sneer. 'All muscles and swagger. Punch your way out of any situation, can't you, Dean?'

'I can take of myself.'

'You reckon. You're a loser, you always have been. Let's be clear, if you weren't my brother, we wouldn't even be having this conversation.'

'Is that a threat, Craig?'

'No, it's a reality check.'

Dean raises his palms. It's tempting to show him who's boss here and now. But if Craig believes he's just a fire-cracker with no patience, well, that's useful.

'If you're upset about the car,' says Dean. 'I had no choice.'

'What d'you mean the car?'

Dean smiles inwardly. That's wrong-footed him.

This is fun.

'What about the car?' says Craig.

'Sorry mate. I had to dump it. You know what the police are like nowadays. All these cameras they got. It was a precaution.'

'Dumped it where?'

'Oh, I dunno. In some drainage dyke up near Ely.'

Craig's face reddens with fury. 'You put a two hundred grand Aston Martin in a fucking drainage dyke!'

This is great. He's losing it.

'Oh, come on, Craig. It's not that big a deal. You can afford it. Let's not fall out over a bloody car.'

Dean scans his brother. Craig is reining himself in, but it's taking him some effort.

Who's the psycho now?

Craig turns away. When he turns back, he has a different expression on his face. Composed and hard.

'You want to go off to Spain and deal a bit of coke to the tourists to feed your own habit? That's fine by me. Good luck to you. But don't come out of jail and start murdering people. Not if that affects my business.'

Score! So the intel he got from Liam was right.

He puts on an innocent face. 'Who have I murdered? And how does it affect your business?'

'Don't play games with me, Dean. Two nights ago. You slashed his throat and raped some woman. His girlfriend?'

'You got this all wrong, Craig. You and the cops. I picked up some slag at the hotel. It was just a bit of fun. Bit of R&R.'

Liam was his wing man. He doesn't know that.

Craig shakes his head. 'An animal like you, you probably believe that.'

'Once I get out to Spain, start earning, I'll pay you back for the car. How's that?'

Craig tilts his head. 'When you planning to leave?'

'Couple of days.'

'Be sure you do.'

Dean stands up. He towers over his podgy little brother. He puts his empty beer bottle on the table.

'Alright, mate,' he says. 'Say goodbye to Kate and the girls for me.'

He walks through the pool house and out into the drizzle. But he doesn't care; he turns up his collar. One of Craig's bodyguards escorts him.

It was an interesting encounter. And the fact Craig wasn't about to accuse him outright of murdering the accountant tells him what he needs to know. Craig just wants him gone.

He's got a hope.

As he walks off, he's feeling the buzz. He's got his brother on the back foot, well and truly. He's winning the game. Liam's waiting for him with the Toyota.

'How did it go?' Liam asks.

'Sweet,' says Dean. 'All going to plan.'

46

Thursday, 3.15pm

Emma can't sit still. Her whole body is a bundle of nerves. She paces from one side of the massive kitchen to the other to relieve the tension. Then she adds a circuit of the dining table, also vast. It seats ten people.

Amber watches her with concern.

'You sure you don't want something to eat?' she says.

Emma shakes her head. If she eats, she'll puke.

Rachel called someone, possibly the girl that came to arrest her, wasn't she called Boden, and told her about the Aston Martin. But now she's gone off on a tangent of her own. She's concerned about her husband. Simon isn't responding to texts or messages. She's on the phone trying to track him down.

Is Simon the sort to despair at the murder of a friend? That seems to be what Rachel is worried about. He strikes Emma as more level-headed than that. But she's not married to him. Perhaps he needs to spend some time alone and process what's happened? She tried saying this to Rachel, but her sister wasn't listening. Her sister's focus has swerved on to Simon, tracking him down and bringing him back under her control. And she's pursuing this goal with vigour.

As usual.

All part of her sister's ongoing mission never to stop but always to push forward and sort things out. It's exhausting to watch.

Emma can sense the bitterness rising inside her. Here she is, trapped in her sister's house, with a police car parked outside, waiting for her *assailant* to be arrested so she can go back to her life.

But Rachel doesn't buy her account of what happened; she's made that clear. She still thinks Emma was involved with Howard. Why? And now she's distant and exuding resentment.

Perfect Rachel can't stand the fact that this is all her fault, not yours.

Emma wishes she was at home. At least there she could have a drink to take the edge off all this. Herb tea doesn't cut it.

The doorbell rings. Amber goes to answer it. Emma can hear her sister on the phone to someone. Then a familiar voice talking to Amber.

Neil?

She rushes out into the hall. He's on the doorstep. Big, sheepish, hands shoved in his jacket pockets.

She wants to fling herself into his arms.

Don't! That'd be really stupid.

He sees her and clears his throat. 'I was just saying to Amber, I've been looking for you. Went to your place. Figured you'd be here.' His jaw is set and his expression is belligerent. 'I heard what happened. And I'm really, y'know… and I came to say…'

She beckons him in. Amber steps back. He comes inside and follows her into the kitchen.

Amber decides to make herself scarce.

He stands and faces her, like a huge nervous bear. 'I had your sister round, and the cops.'

She looks at him, the reality of him; so tough and yet his eyes are soft with sorrow and longing.

'I'm sorry,' she says. 'No one could figure out what had happened, including me.'

He shrugs, but he has tears in his eyes. 'You thought I'd do something like that to you, Em? I mean, really? Tell me his name and I'll go and rip his bloody head off. And sod your sister and her merry band.'

She smiles. Blunt and to the point, one of his better qualities. 'I was just confused,' she says. 'I knew you were angry with me and—'

'I was angry you'd given up on me. I was broke, so you dumped me flat.'

'It wasn't about the money…'

'What then?'

'Neil, you were just… impossible to deal with. Angry with everyone and everything. Especially me.'

'Look, I know I shout a lot, and swear, and I've got a temper.'

'Somewhat.'

He sighs. 'Mum says I need to get a grip. I've probably said some stuff that I shouldn't. And, well, y'know…'

'Yeah, well, we both have.'

'But I'd never harm a hair on your head, you know that.'

He swallows hard. He's almost in tears.

She reaches out and touches his arm. The dam breaks. He sweeps her into a hug.

The relief!

He cradles her and she can feel his tears on her neck. 'I am so sorry,' he mutters. 'I should've been there.'

'We've both made a complete car crash of things,' she says.

'My solicitor said we should come after your business. His idea, not mine.'

'It's okay. That all seems pretty irrelevant now.'

He rocks her gently and for the first time since she woke up in Howard's flat, she can breathe and let go. The relief is overwhelming. He still loves her and she can feel it. She's crying too. He leans her back in his arms, looks at her face, and wipes the tears away with his solid, chunky fingers.

'Sssh, it's okay,' he says. 'It's gonna be okay now.'

There's a discrete cough and they become aware of Rachel standing in the doorway.

She looks them up and down, smiles and says, 'Hello, Neil. Fancy a coffee?'

This is vintage Rachel. Cool and taking charge.

Neil glares at her, then he shrugs and says, 'Cheers, Rachel. Black with two sugars.'

Amber joins them. He smiles at her. 'Alright, Amber?'

'Hey, Neil,' she replies.

There's an awkward silence as the coffee machine gurgles.

Rachel turns to her daughter. 'Darling, can you find some sugar for Neil?'

Amber goes to one of the bank of enormous cupboards and opens it. A tall stack of baskets glide out containing a neat array of dried goods.

'Demerara or regular?' says Amber.

'Just the usual is fine,' says Neil. 'So who is this bastard? You got any ideas?'

Rachel is about to answer him, but Emma jumps in ahead of her. 'He's a criminal and he's been ID'd from his DNA in a semen sample.' She watches his brow darken as he absorbs the implications of that.

She continues. 'His name's Dean Jessop and Rachel has had some dealings with him in the past.'

'Dean fucking Jessop!' says Neil in astonishment.

'You know him?' says Rachel.

Neil huffs, hands on hips; now he has a name, he's fuming. 'Dean fucking Jessop?' he repeats. 'I thought he was in the nick. I've done building work for his brother Craig. So, have you arrested him?'

'Not yet,' says Rachel.

'What d'you mean?' says Neil. 'Not yet?'

'He's driving around in an Aston Martin,' says Emma.

'All the kit you've got nowadays and you bozos can't even find him in a bloody Aston Martin.' He's glowering at Rachel.

'It's not that straight—'

'Bullshit. Have you asked Craig? Cause it sounds like one of his cars. In fact, I'm pretty sure of it.'

'We know that, and—'

'Fine. I'll ask him,' says Neil. Emma watches him. This is her husband; from nought to white hot rage in thirty seconds. But he's defending her; he's on her side without question. And it's so good. He turns to her. 'You coming, babe. Because I'm going to find Dean and rip him limb from limb?'

Rachel steps forward. 'Neil, I really don't think—'

'Fuck off, Rachel,' he says savagely. 'I know what the Jessops are, and how to deal with them. Craig's been running rings round you lot for years. Payoffs and back handers. Wife on the bloody Council. But I know a few things about him you don't.'

Rachel raises her palms.

'Fair enough,' she says with a shrug. 'If you think you can deal with Craig.'

'Oh, trust me, I do.'

'But Emma should stay here.'

Emma looks from her husband to her sister; both pig-headed in their own way.

She shakes her head. 'No Rachel. I'm going with Neil.'

'Don't be ridiculous. You need to—'

'Need to what? You got me into this, but with Neil's help, I'll get myself out of it.'

47

Thursday, 3.45pm

The afternoon light is fast fading. The garden is full of shadows. Rachel sits at the end of the dining table with her phone in front of her. Nervous tension has depleted her energy and brought her to a standstill. She traces the grain of the wood with her index finger. Her coffee is cold. She's alone. The text messages to Simon have all gone unanswered and she's getting frantic.

Could he have done something stupid?

Amber has tried to call him too. Even when he's upset with her, he would always respond to an urgent call from their daughter.

Rachel doesn't want to think the unthinkable. But it needs to be considered. Howard's death has unmoored him in a way she has never seen in all the years of their marriage. And it is only now occurring to her that perhaps he had as close a relationship with his friend as he does with her.

Emma is still refusing to admit the affair, which makes

everything worse. When they discovered it wasn't Howard's semen, Rachel had interrogated Simon. She's asked him who would have wanted to kill Howard and he got upset. And who can blame him? Only when she found out Jessop was the rapist, did it make sense. But Simon was right all along. Howard did nothing wrong, and it happened because of Emma. No wonder he's gone off and is not answering her calls. He's probably getting drunk again.

Please, please, just call!

After more than twenty years of marriage, their lives have settled into predictable patterns. They live in parallel worlds that rarely overlap. They attend each other's social events as required. And Simon has always proved himself to be an asset, doling out free advice on tax and investments to her colleagues. They all like Simon.

The mysteries of numbers and accountancy have never interested her much, but she understands that the amazing success of her husband's business rests on his complementary partnership with Howard.

Simon is outgoing, sociable, clubbable, a golfer; he knows how to keep a diverse clientele happy. Howard was the opposite, the nerd, the backroom boy who came up with new schemes to side-step the tax man and ensure their clients held onto more of their hard-earned cash. A marriage made in heaven. Unlike hers, which was full of wrinkles and compromises.

Now Simon is caught up in a downward spiral of grief. Death is one thing. Always shocking. Murder is a more disturbing experience. It calls all the basic values into question. Shows us what predatory, vicious creatures we are under the veneer. She's used to that, but he isn't.

She keeps going round in a loop in her mind. Okay, this is shocking, but he's never been a depressive type. He bounces back and has an optimistic nature. At times, his blasé attitude can be annoying. So why the hell isn't he answering his phone?

If he's punishing you, you can't blame him.

Rachel's thoughts are in disarray. She has to think about this as a cop. And that leads to the obvious question: has Jessop now targeted her husband? Her sister, now her husband?

The thought sends an icy shudder through her entire body.

What the hell does Jessop want?

Criminals often want revenge. Often they're violent, damaged individuals who blame everyone but themselves for their situation and lash out. Rachel's been threatened before. It comes with the job.

But Dean Jessop is different. He's not just being reactive. The kidnap from the hotel and the rape of Emma, this all took planning. And some help.

But what does he want?

It was back in her days as a DI, she first encountered Dean. She arrested him after a pub brawl; he'd cracked a bloke's skull and glassed him; he was looking at some serious time. But the witnesses were reluctant to testify, and the victim himself didn't want to proceed. The bar was a dive and there was no CCTV. But Rachel twisted Dean's tail. He didn't know the case was full of holes. She promised him a way out in exchange for information about a London gang the Jessops had done business with.

When charges against Dean were dropped, he believed it was down to Rachel. That's when their unconventional arrangement began. There was no way he'd become a proper chis. It all had to remain off the books, or he wouldn't play. He wasn't a grass, he told her. Now and then, when it suited him, he'd help her out.

Rachel knew she was more than bending the rules on handling informants. The results seemed to justify it. She got some high class intel which led to convictions. And her success as a DI meant rapid promotion. She took some serious and violent criminals off the streets, plus quantities of Class A drugs. How can that be wrong?

Then Dean became worried about his junky sister; he was desperate to keep her out of jail. He offered some very useful intel, which led to a significant bust. Rachel told him straight she could do nothing about Kelly, who was caught red-handed dealing. But Dean didn't believe her. He insisted they had a deal.

It doesn't surprise Rachel that Kelly killed herself. She was an addict with mental health problems who probably shouldn't have been in prison. But there was nothing Rachel could've done. It wasn't her case. She had no involvement. Also, she didn't want to expose her relationship with Jessop.

And now he blames you.

This is his beef with Rachel. And he's had a long time to fester about it. In his view, she didn't fulfil her part of the bargain in terms of Kelly.

Is it that simple?

It would fit with the idea of targeting her sister. Was he trying to put her sister in the frame for murder, facing a stretch in jail? That's why he killed Howard. It has to be. He'd been following Emma, so he found out about her affair with Howard. He could've killed Howard either before or after the rape. That was the set up. And if her sister hadn't persisted with her lies, they'd have got to it sooner.

If Emma had just told the truth about her and Howard.

It all keeps going round in her head. She picks up her phone and rings her husband's number again. It goes straight to voice mail. She feels in limbo and powerless.

Neil and Emma have gone off intending to tackle Craig Jessop. It's crazy. But it's also what the police should be doing. It doesn't surprise her that Neil knows Craig. And maybe he'll find out more than the police ever could.

But where's Simon?

Her phone rings and she seizes it.

But it's Boden.

'Jo,' she says. 'What have you got?' She needs to sound professional and in control.

'Possibly not what you want to hear, boss,' says Boden. 'You were right about the car. Craig Jessop does have an Aston Martin. We've tracked its routes over the last couple of days. It didn't take that long. And we've just found it.'

'Where?'

'In a drainage canal on the Fens. We've got a team up there pulling it out. But there doesn't appear to be a driver. We think it was just dumped.'

Of course it was. He's playing cat and mouse with them. Emma, now Simon?

'He just seems to be one step ahead all the time,' says Rachel. 'But thank you for letting me know.'

'No problem. We may get something off the satnav if the water hasn't damaged it.'

'Hopefully,' says Rachel.

She hangs up. She isn't hopeful. It's a bleak wintery afternoon; soon it'll be dark. And a feeling of dread surges through her. She reminds herself that there are two officers in a car sitting outside her front door.

Simon's just in a bar somewhere. This is paranoia.

It feels as if everything is closing in on her. Dean Jessop has got into her head. But surely this has been his intention all along.

48

Emma scans her husband's profile. Even a day ago, to be sitting next to him like this would've seemed impossible. Neil is driving his mum's car. It's small, Korean and egg blue; he has the driver's seat back as far as it'll go, but he's still crammed in.

For the first few miles, they don't speak. Emma suspects he's amazed she's even come with him. She's amazed herself. Their last encounter took place in a solicitor's office and was full of expletives on both sides.

'Do you know where he lives?' says Emma.

'Yep,' he says. 'Out on the Bedford road. I remember when he built the place. In the middle of farmland. Didn't have the correct planning permission. They were going to make him pull it down. But then what do you know? The planning officer changed his mind. He got it redesignated as a farm. The power of money, babe.'

'Doesn't sound as though you like him.'

'I don't. But there's no denying he's smart. His family were villains; made no secret of the fact. But suddenly he's a businessman and buying up every decent bit of development land for miles around. He priced small builders like me out of the market. And we're supposed to believe it's all legitimate. It's drug money. Everyone knows that.'

'But you still think he'll help us?'

'Dean is a major thorn in his side.'

'Yeah, but if we can find out where he is, we should just tell the police.'

'Why?' says Neil. He's still fuming.

'Because I want him to go to jail, not you.'

Neil grins. 'You've changed your tune.'

She smiles back. 'Promise me, Neil.' She hesitates, then adds, 'The thing is, he could've murdered someone too.'

'Who?'

'The bloke who's flat I was in. But it's complicated. I was taken there. I had no idea where I was.'

Neil frowns.

Don't tell him it was Howard. It'll confuse the issue.

'Who was this bloke?' says Neil.

'I've got no idea. I just woke up in a strange place I'd never been before. I was doing an event at the hotel. Dean drugged me, kidnapped me and took me there.'

Only half a lie.

He doesn't reply, just turns his eyes back on the road.

After a couple of moments, he says, 'I'm not scared of Dean Jessop.'

Once they get out of town, it's open countryside for about five miles, until they come to Craig Jessop's so-called farm. To Emma it looks more like an American ranch, with a white picket fence and several horses grazing in a field in front of the sprawling single-storey house.

Neil turns into the gateway. The gate itself is made of thick steel bars, with high brick-built pillars on either side and a video phone entry system on the wall.

Emma glances up at the cameras on top of the gate. 'He doesn't intend to be taken by surprise, does he?' she says.

Neil lowers his window and presses the intercom. 'Neil Bryant,' he says. 'Got a meeting with Craig.'

There's a crackle, then a voice comes through. 'Can't see you in the diary.'

'Look again,' says Neil.

'Sorry, no. What's it concerning?'

'His brother, the rapist.'

Emma watches her husband's expression. It's determined and obdurate. One thing you can say about Neil, he doesn't back down. This has been the problem with the divorce. He doesn't believe in compromise.

The intercom goes silent. A moment passes, then a figure emerges from the outbuilding at the side of the house and walks across the drive towards them.

He's young and wears branded sports gear.

Neil chuckles. 'Look at this joker,' says Neil. 'So called security.'

None of this intimidates him; not the gates, nor the cameras. Emma has always envied that sort of male confidence. But maybe size helps; it's hard for people to make you feel small when you're looking down at them.

The young man stops at the other side of the gate. Neil gets out of the car and goes to face him. They eyeball each other.

'This is private property,' the young man says. 'Mr Jessop doesn't see people without an appointment. You need to leave.'

Neil leans with one hand casually on the gate. 'What are

you? The work experience trainee? Go and tell one of the grownups that Neil Bryant wants to talk to the boss. And the boss is going to want to talk to me if he knows what's good for him.'

The security guard seems uncertain. He turns away and pulls out a phone. Neil smiles at Emma through the windscreen. He seems to be enjoying this.

Several moments pass and another figure emerges, this time from the house. He strolls towards them with more of a confident swagger.

He gets to the gate; Neil has his hands on his hips.

'Alright, Liam,' says Neil.

'What you playing at, Neil?' the other man replies.

'I wanna talk to him,' says Neil. 'And I'm not shifting until I do. And I doubt you and your lad here are gonna make me.'

'Is this about Dean? Cause he's not here and Craig's got no idea where he is.'

'You expect me to believe that?'

'Yeah. Cause it's the truth.'

Neil seizes the bars of the gate and rattles them furiously. 'That fucking piece of jail bait raped my wife. And he'd better hope the cops get him before I do!'

'Thought you was divorced.'

'Separated. But she's still my wife.'

Emma sees Liam glance in her direction. He raises his palms. 'Listen mate, you got my sympathy. Dean's a psycho, always has been. But Craig can't help you with this.'

'Where is Dean?'

'We don't know.'

'You're such a fucking liar.'

Liam shrugs and folds his arms. 'Sit here all night if you like. The answer'll be the same.'

'I might just do that.'

'Don't block the gate.'

Neil gets back in the car and huffs.

Emma watches Liam and the security guard walk away.

'What now?' she says.

'They'll think about it,' says Neil. 'Depends if Craig reckons protecting his brother is worth the aggravation.'

'Thanks for doing this,' says Emma.

'You don't need to thank me.'

Neil folds his arms. An awkward silence descends. Her husband's gung ho attitude has got them there, but now Emma feels ridiculous, sitting at Craig Jessop's gate and begging for an audience.

'You said you've worked for Craig. When?'

'I've been project manager on a couple of sites for him recently. Cash in hand, so it didn't go to the creditors. But he's not much of a builder. He needs people like me, experienced in the building trade, but who are prepared to work for him. I wouldn't unless I had to.'

'Will that sway him?'

'It might.'

They fall silent again.

The afternoon is fading and lights have come on in the house. Emma is chilly. She pulls her jacket around her.

'Cold?' he says solicitously.

She smiles at him. 'I'm okay.'

It's been a while since a man took care of you.

She sighs. 'What happened to us, Neil?'

'Beats me,' he says. 'I've been out with a few women since we split, but none are a patch on you.'

'A ball-breaker, you mean? That's one of the things you've accused me of being.'

He gives her a rueful look. 'I get upset, I say stuff.'

She raises her eyebrows. 'Really? Is that your excuse?'

He frowns. 'Yeah, alright. I know. I just ended up feeling so… powerless. I remember your face when we found out the bank was taking the house. I thought she'll never forgive me.'

'So you never waited to find out whether or not I would? The barriers went up. You hit the bottle and pushed me out.'

'I was just, y'know, ashamed, I suppose. I let you down.'

'The business going bankrupt didn't let me down. That stuff happens. We'd've found a way through together. But you focusing your anger on me. That's what I couldn't deal with.'

'I didn't mean… it just came out that way. I'm sorry.'

He reaches over and takes her hand. 'I wish we could turn back the clock.'

In the gloom, headlights come down the road right at them. A vehicle pulls up and honks.

Neil starts the car and backs it out of the way, so the other vehicle can pull up to the gate. It's a local taxi. The driver speaks into the intercom and the gates open. Emma watches.

It produces an odd feeling. The taxi has legitimate business at this rich man's mansion, but they don't. They're kept waiting at the gate. She finds it annoying. For a moment, she wishes she was her sister, a person with authority who could force them to let her in and give her some answers.

Neil squeezes her hand. 'What do you say?'

She glances at him. 'About what?'

'Can't we just somehow go back to how we were…'

She sighs. 'How we were when, exactly? When you were off doing stuff with your mates every weekend? Or just down the pub midweek to watch the footie? Or Friday night after work, when you needed a quick one to wind down and didn't come home until nine o'clock?'

'I thought we were happy? You went out with your girl-friends.'

'You were happy, Neil. Mates, wife tucked up at home, sex on tap, plenty of beer. I was lonely.'

'I didn't know you felt like that.'

'You did. I told you. For years. You didn't want to listen.'

The taxi is driving up to the house; it stops at the front door. Emma watches the door open. Liam comes out, and he has his arm round the waist of another man, obviously quite drunk, who he shepherds towards the open back door of the taxi.

As they move across the porch, a floodlight comes on, cutting through the encroaching darkness, and Emma does a double-take.

'My God,' she says. 'That looks like Simon.' She peers hard. 'It is. It's Simon. He's completely wasted.'

'What the hell's he doing here?' says Neil.

Emma frowns. 'How does he even know Craig?'

Liam shoves Simon in the back of the taxi and slams the door. As it sets off back towards the gate, Emma jumps out of the car and pulls out her phone. She points it at the house and films the taxi pulling away. It drives towards the gate. The gate opens. And Emma continues to video it. The taxi drives past her and she pans along the side to the passenger slumped in the back seat.

It's her brother-in-law. She's sure of it.

49

Thursday, 5.15pm

Rachel is staring out of the study window at the front of the house when the taxi draws up. It stops behind the squad car. In the pool of light from a streetlamp, she sees Simon half clamber, half tumble out of the back of the back of the cab.

Thank God!

Her heart soars. Then he staggers and nearly topples over. He's drunk. Very drunk.

She rushes to the front door. But by the time she gets out of the house, one officer from the squad car is supporting Simon by the elbow and shepherding him up the drive.

The young PC gives her a bashful look and says, 'I think he's had a few, ma'am.'

She doesn't need telling; he reeks of alcohol. 'Thank you. I can take it from here,' she says, grasping his other arm.

Her husband stops and turns to look at her.

'Sorry,' he mumbles. 'I am sorry. I'm letting you down, aren't I?' His speech is slurred.

'Don't be daft,' she says, squeezing his arm. 'But I've been calling you. Why the hell didn't you answer?'

'Have you?' he says vaguely. 'Sorry.'

'Stop apologising.' She manoeuvres him towards the front door. 'Mind the step.'

He stops and stares down at his feet. He sways, lifting one foot slowly and placing it on the step.

Rachel takes a breath; she's been worried sick about him. He's been out getting pissed. But the relief far outweighs any anger.

'Come on,' she says. 'Lean on me.'

They make it into the hallway just as Amber comes down the stairs.

'Dad, are you alright?' she says.

'I'm a bit… blotto,' he says. 'But listen, I know how lucky I am. And I love you guys. I really do. I really…' He has tears in his eyes.

Rachel can't help smiling. This is her husband, and the booze brings out his true nature. He's always been an amiable drunk. Never offensive, or even aggressive. He tends to just collapse and fall asleep. And in the circumstances, maybe it's just his way of coping.

'We love you, too,' she says. 'But I've been worried.'

Amber takes his other arm. He continues to sway as they zigzag down the hall.

'I love you, Rachel. You are the love of my life. Do you know that? How did a bloke like me get a wife like you, eh? You're a ten.'

'You're not being sexist, are you?' she says, but she enjoys the compliment. She and Amber exchange smiles. 'Let's get you in the kitchen, get some water and paracetamol down you.'

Progress is slow; finally they edge him through the kitchen door.

'I'm not a bad man, am I?' he says, as they lower him onto a chair.

'Course you aren't,' says Rachel, helping him out of his jacket. Amber goes to the sink and pours a glass of water.

She glances at her mother. 'He's completely wasted. Where do you think he's been?'

'Drowning his sorrows at the golf club would be my guess.'

She did phone them. They said they hadn't seen him. But that's not reliable. They say that to all the wives. He could've been in some pub; what matters now is he's home. And more or less in one piece.

Her darker fears are receding. This isn't about the Jessops. He hasn't been targeted.

His head lurches forward, then he starts and lifts it. 'Not a bad man, but a rotten friend. I let him down, y'know, let him down badly.'

Rachel holds the glass for him to drink. 'No, you didn't. What happened to Howard is not your fault.'

Simon's head lolls to the side. 'I'm not so sure about that.'

'Well, we are,' says Rachel.

'I tried to talk him out of it, y'know.'

'Talk him out of what?'

'But when he gets a notion in his head, there's no shifting him.' He grasps Rachel's hand. 'I did try, I promise you. But he wouldn't budge. And that's Howard. Stubborn. You know that, don't you Rachel?'

She glances at her daughter. Amber is frowning anxiously.

'What's he talking about, Mum?' she says.

Yes. What is he talking about?

'It's drunken nonsense,' she says. 'Somehow, we've got to get him upstairs and into bed.'

'Wouldn't it be easier to put him on the sofa in the sitting room?'

'Yeah, you're right. Can you get a duvet off the spare bed? Oh, and a bucket from the laundry room.'

Amber nods and disappears.

Rachel squats down in front of her husband. She takes his face in her hands. 'Listen to me, Simon,' she says. 'Whatever you think you've done, you need to forget about it for now. We'll talk about it later, okay? But Amber's getting upset.'

He beams. 'I love Amber,' he says. 'She's just so beautiful and brilliant. How did the two of us produce her, eh? You ever ask yourself that?'

'Frequently. And that's why we don't want to upset her, do we?'

He gives his head an exaggerated shake. 'I'd do anything for her, y'know. She's the best thing that's ever happened to me.'

Rachel smiles. 'I thought that was marrying me?'

'Two best things. Family is what matters, isn't it? I've always put the two of you first.'

'I know that, my darling. Now you're very drunk, and you need to sleep this off. Let's go into the other room and put you on the sofa.'

With some effort, she gets him to his feet. He's taller than her; he drapes an arm round her neck and she tows him towards the kitchen door.

But Amber is in the hall, clutching a duvet. The front door is open. Emma and Neil are on the doorstep.

Rachel stops in her tracks. Did the bell ring? She didn't hear it.

She manages to contain her irritation. Emma and Neil crowd into the hall, raindrops skidding off their jackets.

'As you can see, Simon's had a skinful,' she says.

'We know,' says Emma. 'We saw him.' Emma is scowling at her, and her tone is unfriendly.

'Where?' says Rachel.

'Coming out of Craig Jessop's house.'

Rachel stares back at her sister. What the hell is she playing at?

More bloody nonsense!

'What are you talking about?'

Emma pulls out her phone. 'I'll show you,' she says.

Simon's eyes are closed and he can hardly stand up. Rachel is struggling to support him. Neil steps forward and grabs him under the arms. 'Where do you want him?' he says.

'In there,' says Rachel, pointing to the sitting room. 'On the sofa.'

Neil more or less carries Simon through the door and Rachel is left facing her sister.

'We were parked outside Craig's,' she says. 'He was refusing to talk to us. And then this is what we saw.'

Emma presses play on her phone and hands it to Rachel. The camera shakes at first. But then it steadies on a taxi at the front of a large house.

Is it even Craig's place?

'How do I know where this is?' she says.

'Just watch,' says Emma.

Amber is beside her, watching too. On the screen the light isn't good. A man comes out of the house and is helped into the back of the taxi.

'This could be anyone,' says Rachel. 'It's too dark to see.'

'Keep watching,' her sister insists.

The sequence continues to play. A taxi drives towards the

camera. There's a large gate with steel bars. It opens and as the taxi passes through, the camera pans across the passenger in the back seat.

Amber glances at her mother. 'It is Dad,' she says.

She's right.

'I'm sure there's an explanation,' says Rachel.

'You never said he knew Craig Jessop,' says Emma.

She never knew.

A maelstrom of thoughts and questions swirl in Rachel's brain. But Simon is in no fit state to provide any answers.

'Listen,' says Rachel. 'Let's not jump to any conclusions here.'

'Oh no, let's not,' says Emma, her voice dripping with sarcasm.

'Emma, please, he'll have an explanation, I'm sure. Perhaps he went there for the same reason as you, to ask Craig where Dean is?'

'Then why is he stinking drunk?' Emma is glaring at her, seething and spiteful. She's never seen her sister like this before. Emma hates confrontation. She usually backs down or evades or lies her way out of sticky situations.

Neil emerges from the sitting room. 'He's out cold,' he says. 'I don't think you'll get much out of him tonight.'

Emma shakes her head wearily. Tears prickle her lashes. 'What the fuck is happening, Rachel? Some criminal has attacked me. Your husband knows his brother. Has clearly been drinking with his brother. When are you going to tell me the truth?'

When is she going to tell the truth?

'I am telling the truth,' says Rachel.

'I don't believe you. What's going on? You're saying this is all because you nicked this guy and he wants revenge?'

'Emma, I can't tell you what I don't know. When Simon

266

sobers up, I'll talk to him. There's nothing more to be done tonight.'

Her sister is staring straight at her, jaw clenched, anger and hatred in her eyes.

'I'm going home,' says Emma.

'Is that a good—'

'I'm going with her,' says Neil. 'She'll be safe with me.'

'Though I doubt you care,' mumbles Emma as she turns towards the front door.

'Don't be silly. Of course I care.' But Emma ignores her. She opens the door and she and Neil walk out into the pouring rain. The door slams behind them.

Rachel looks at her daughter. Amber is scowling, her shoulders hunched. Rachel sighs. 'She's just upset and—'

'Are you surprised?' says Amber tartly. 'I'll get that bucket.'

Rachel watches her walk away. Emma's outburst is one thing, but Amber appears to be judging her too, and that smarts.

She releases her clenched fist and notices her nails have etched four red welts in her palm. In the sitting room, her husband lies flat out on one of the long leather sofas, quietly snoring.

50

Thursday, 6.30pm

Emma is nervous as she opens the door to her flat. It's dark and chilly. She hasn't been back since she left in a panic this morning. The first thing she does, after turning on all the lights, is go to the french doors and check they're locked. Then she looks around; her home still feels violated.

Thank God you're not alone.

Neil rubs his hands and says, 'Think we need to whack the heating on.'

Emma stands in the middle of the room; she's close to tears. Raindrops slide from her coat and puddle on the wooden floor.

'Come here,' he says, drawing her into a hug.

'He was here,' she splutters. 'He just broke in, no problem.'

'Yeah, well, I'm going to take a look at that lock, replace it and add a couple of bolts. You should also consider an alarm system.'

'What's that going to cost?'

'Don't worry. I know a bloke. I'll get you a deal.'

He eases her out of her coat and drapes it over a chair. Then he rubs her upper arms. His big paws and the warmth his body radiates is hugely comforting.

Don't get too comfortable.

She pulls away. 'Let me get the heating on.' She goes to the control panel below the wall-mounted boiler in the kitchen.

It's as well to remember that they split up for a reason. Neil has some major blind spots. Over the years, the heartache he's caused her outweighs the good stuff by some margin. He's an overgrown boy, impulsively generous and loving when it suits him, self-centred and mean when it doesn't.

He's opening the kitchen cupboards. 'Where are the glasses?'

'Top right,' she says, pointing.

They stopped en route for a bottle of red and a Chinese takeaway. The two bags of food are exuding their own warm and aromatic smells.

She gets out plates and cutlery, lifts the foil cartons from the bags and peels back the lids. Neil finds a corkscrew, opens the wine and pours.

So easy to fall into old routines.

He chuckles. 'This is what we used to do most Friday nights,' he says. 'Get a Chinese, curl up on the sofa and watch a film.'

She smiles but says nothing.

Some Friday nights.

It was often the prelude to sex. Friday night after a couple of bottles of wine, Sunday morning if they weren't too hung over; after the first couple of years, that was the shag pattern of their married life.

He hands her a glass of wine and holds his up. 'What shall we drink to?' he says. 'Having another try?' His eyes are twinkling and the pheromones are buzzing.

She raises her glass. 'Not fucking it up,' she says.

Optimism over experience?

Once the food is served, they take their plates over to the sofa and settle, one in either corner.

'This is nice,' he says. 'I've missed this.'

She nods. 'How's your mum?'

He's shovelling forkfuls of chicken chow mein into his mouth. She's forgotten that this is how he eats, like a half-starved hound.

Mouth full of food, he mumbles, 'Yeah, she's fine. But I think I get under her feet a bit.' He swallows and adds, 'So if you're looking for a roommate...'

He thinks riding to her rescue just cancels the rest of it?

Her look must be sceptical because he adds, 'It wasn't all bad, y'know.'

She smiles. 'I know. But I'm feeling quite fragile.'

And the very idea of sex...

'Course you are,' he says. 'I'm just here to help you get through this. No pressure. No expectations.'

'Good.'

They continue to eat in silence. He's soon cleared his plate. He gets up, brings the bottle of wine from the counter and tops up their wine glasses.

'What do you think Simon was doing?' he says.

Careful. He doesn't know about Howard.

'No idea,' she says.

The lie sits between them, and she's beginning to regret it.

She should've told him about Howard and tried to explain. But Neil is volatile and prone to jealousy.

The stress of it is making her queasy.

He sips his wine. 'Well, tell you the truth, I've seen him and Craig Jessop drinking at the golf club. But y'know, that's Jessop's thing. He knows everybody. Always buying rounds.'

'Buying his way in?'

'Yeah, pretty much. Let's face it, you splash enough cash around, most people don't care where it came from. And Craig's a charming bloke, got a lovely wife. He's very subtle in the way he operates. No one sees him as a gangster. And he has distanced himself from all that.'

'Until his brother got out of jail.'

'He's got to be pissed off about that. Dean could really rock the boat for him.'

'So he won't want to see him arrested?'

'More likely the opposite. If his criminal brother goes back to jail, he can wash his hands of him, and carry on pretending to be a solid citizen.'

'But he still won't talk to us.'

'I think he will. We just need to be patient. And persistent.'

'You think that'll work?'

'You know me, Em. Once I get the old bit between my teeth.'

She smiles, although a deep sense of misery is seeping through her.

Why couldn't he be like this before? You have to get raped?

She forks over her food. 'I'm not that hungry,' she says.

'Just try a bit,' he says. He's treating her like an invalid.

Isn't that what you are? A broken creature.

The tears are welling. Her hand trembles and she has to

put down her glass. 'What he did to me,' she says. 'I was unconscious. I was drugged.'

'Perhaps it's better you were.'

'But it's the trickery, too. I've dealt with plenty of leery blokes. He gave me no chance to fight or defend myself. And that's robbed me of my confidence. I feel like he's turned me into a nothing.'

The tears burst out of her. She clasps her hand over her mouth. 'And I'm so angry,' she splutters. 'And I don't know what to do.'

He watches her, a scowl on his face.

But does he understand?

He huffs. 'Craig knows where he is. And he'll tell us. I promise you.'

'I appreciate your support, I do. But I… I can't just—'

'Hey, I'm not stupid. And I'm not trying to take advantage of your vulnerability. Let's get you tucked up in bed. I'll be out here on the sofa, so you can sleep easy.'

'Thank you.'

'It's the least I can do. And if you don't want that, I'll eat it.' He grins and picks up her plate.

'I'm going to take a shower.'

'Fine. I'll just be here.'

She walks into the bedroom and closes the door. Amber was her protector last night. Now it's Neil. But what about tomorrow night, and next week and next month? She'll have to cope on her own eventually. Even when her attacker's back in jail, a paranoid sense of threat lingers because her confidence is shot. How will she ever survive?

It feels impossible.

51

Friday, 8.30am

Rachel leans on the doorjamb, sipping her coffee and staring at her sleeping husband. A leaden morning light slides through the blinds. He's on his back, one arm lolling over the side of the sofa. He's kicked back the duvet and it's half on the floor. A plastic bucket is positioned six inches from his head. The whole room reeks of stale alcohol.

She's had another sleepless night to consider the fact that in three short days her life and career have spiralled out of her control.

Before she going to bed, she tried to speak to her daughter. But Amber was distant and evasive. It seems that both she and Emma are thinking the same thing: that Rachel has some secret insight into what's going on that she's not sharing.

If only that were true.

And one question still hangs in the air. Why did Simon go to Craig Jessop's house? The explanation she offered Emma last night was plausible. But Rachel has a deep visceral fear that it hardly scratches the surface.

In his drunken rant, Simon said *he tried to talk Howard out of it.* Out of what? It sounds ominous. Overnight, a picture has been forming in her mind, and it's not good.

She thinks about Howard. He was always there in the background, ever since she and Simon first met. The nerdy, tongue-tied sidekick. She'd persuaded several girlfriends to go on double dates. But it never worked. There was always something strange about Howard. And it went beyond the social awkwardness of a self-conscious introvert.

Simon's view was that Howard lived on a different planet, but was essentially harmless. He was a numbers geek. Whenever he needed to make a decision about anything, he created a spreadsheet. What was the data telling him? Apparently, he did it when he was trying to decide whether to propose to Greta. Well, that didn't work out well. She was a complete oddball, too.

Over the years, Rachel has rarely asked Simon questions about the actual running of his business. She'd always been too busy with her own job, and running a home and bringing up a child. But what was the balance of power in the Simon and Howard partnership? Simon always did the client-facing stuff; he had to. But when it came to strategy, who was in the driving seat? What if it was Howard? And what if Howard had decided, on the basis of the data, that there was money to be made in doing business with the Jessops?

Simon said he'd tried to talk him out of it. But Howard was stubborn.

Would Howard even have had the moral compass to see that doing business with a man like Craig Jessop was wrong? Probably not. To him, money laundering might even have seemed like an interesting technical challenge. And his spreadsheet would've told him how lucrative it could be.

On the sofa, Simon stretches and grunts. He opens his eyes and scrunches them against the light.

'Oh shit,' he groans.

'Is it bad?' she says.

He peers at her. 'What the hell happened?'

'You tell me.'

He struggles to sit up, rubbing his face with his hands. 'I had a skinful,' he replies.

'Where were you?' she says.

'Just at the golf club. A few of us got together to raise a glass to Howard. I guess it got a bit out of hand.'

'Did you go anywhere else?' she says.

He stands up, cricks his neck and sighs. 'No,' he says. 'I remember them putting me in a cab and sending me home. One reason I never complain about their exorbitant membership fees. God, I need some water.'

He walks towards her. Gives her a peck on the forehead and smiles.

'Sorry,' he says. 'I must stink.'

He heads down the hall towards the kitchen. She follows.

'You were pretty drunk,' she says. 'You sure you didn't go anywhere else? Maybe you can't remember?'

He goes to the sink, turns on the tap, dips his head down, and drinks straight from the gushing stream of water.

She gets a glass from the cupboard and hands it to him. He wipes the water from his face, then fills the glass. He slumps down on a stool at the breakfast counter and gulps half the glass in one go.

'Any chance of a coffee?' he says with his best boyish grin.

'You get drunk, I make coffee. This is becoming a habit.'

He looks remorseful, 'Yeah, and I'm sorry. I know I'm a pain.'

She scans him.

Does he really not remember what he did?

'You sure you didn't go anywhere else?' she says, filling the reservoir on the coffee machine.

He tilts his head and frowns at her. 'Like where?'

'I don't know.'

'What's with the twenty questions? We were drinking in the main bar, about half a dozen of us. I guess it was quite a session. Phil, he's the barman, and he's a good lad. He finally came over and suggested he get me a cab. I'd lost track. It was getting dark. He called the cab, took me out and put me in it.'

'And it brought you straight home?'

He huffs. 'Yes.'

'After you'd arrived, you remember Emma and Neil were here?'

'Yeah, course I remember. It was Neil who lugged me into the sitting room and dumped me on the sofa. So don't tell me those two are back together?' He chuckles. 'That's going to be a nightmare.'

'Simon, they followed you back here from Craig Jessop's house.'

He frowns and shrugs. 'What are you talking about?'

'Don't you remember going there?'

He drains his glass and puts it down with a snap. 'That's complete nonsense. Why the hell would I go there? I hardly know the bloke.'

'You sure?'

Her heart is thumping.

Why is he lying?

He shakes his head wearily. 'Rachel, you're talking a load

of bullshit. I got drunk at the golf club. Phil put me in a cab. It brought me home.'

'They saw you, Simon.'

Shaking his head, avoiding eye contact? Typical signs.

Then he forces himself to meet her gaze directly. 'They're lying,' he says emphatically. 'Bloody Emma, y'know what she's like.'

'She videoed you. At Craig Jessop's house, being put into the back of a taxi.'

'That's not possible. I have never been to bloody Craig Jessop's house, Rachel.'

You've spent your career in interview rooms watching people do this. Doesn't he realise that?

She has a sick feeling in her stomach.

'Simon, she showed me the video on her phone.'

He bats this away angrily with his hand. 'Well, it's some kind of bloody camera trick.'

'I don't think so.'

'Are you really going to believe some nonsense of Emma's? I'm telling you, I've never been to Jessop's place, not sober, not drunk.'

Offer him a way out.

'You sure you weren't so drunk you just didn't know?'

'Yes. For chrissake, you're prepared to take your bloody sister's word over mine. That lying cow was screwing my best friend, and she got him killed as a result. I just don't understand where you're coming from here, Rachel.'

'The evidence would suggest—'

He's sweating. Tears are welling in his eyes. But his jaw is rigid with fury.

'Fuck the bloody evidence! I'm your husband, and I'm telling you the truth. And I expect you to believe me.'

He's standing right in front of her, dishevelled and belligerent.

'Simon,' she says, her voice quivering.

'Don't bloody Simon me,' he replies, placing his hand on his hips.

'Just tell me the truth,' she whispers.

'I have,' he says. 'And if you can't see that, you're not much of a bloody detective, are you? Now I'm going to take a shower.'

He stalks out of the room.

Rachel has to swallow down her own tears. What's he doing? Protecting Howard? Because Howard was money laundering for Craig Jessop.

How can he lie to you like this?

She thinks about the video on Emma's phone. It certainly looked like him. Amber thought so too. But perhaps it wasn't Jessop's house?

Where was it then? She wants to believe him. She wants it desperately.

But she needs to calm down and think this through. He's upset, and he's trying to protect the reputation and memory of his oldest friend. He'll come clean, eventually. At least to her.

And that's what matters.

52

Friday, 9.15am

It's a damp morning and Emma turns on the wipers to clear the fine drizzly mist from the windscreen of her car. She and Neil are in the little orange Nissan and back outside Craig Jessop's impenetrable gates.

Emma slept soundly as soon as her head hit the pillow. It was pure exhaustion, but she was grateful. Now she's feeling more robust. They're on a mission, her and Neil. If she can be the catalyst for Dean Jessop's arrest and return to prison, that might go some way to restoring her dignity. But what if she has to confront him face to face? That still feels like a bridge too far.

But now you've got Neil.

Last night, she couldn't eat. She was sick with stress and fatigue. But this morning she's tucking into the bacon rolls they've bought. A hot coffee sits on the dash, steaming up the inside of the window. Emma wipes it with her hand.

Neil is watching her with a wistful smile. 'You're beginning to look a bit more like your normal self,' he says.

'Better watch out then,' she quips.

He grins. 'Yeah.' He reaches over and squeezes her hand.
Be careful.

Trusting her husband again will take time. Trusting any
man. And then there's her sister.

One step at a time.

They continue to eat in companionable silence. But
Emma wishes they had more of a plan.

When they arrived, Neil had pressed the intercom again,
announced his presence and demanded to see Craig. He got
told politely Craig wasn't available, which made him sound
like the CEO of some important organisation, not a two-bit
gangster. Neil replied he wasn't going away. It was a
stand-off.

'He'll get fed-up in the end,' Neil insisted.

Emma wasn't so sure.

Once the coffees are drunk and the bacon rolls eaten, Neil
gathers up the packaging and the empty cups, rolls it all up
into a ball, gets out of the car and lobs it over the gate. It
lands on the wet drive.

As he does this, the front door opens. Kate Jessop comes
scurrying out. She glares in Neil's direction, pulls up her rain
hood and trots towards the white Land Rover Evoque parked
at the side of the house.

Neil jumps back into the passenger seat of the Nissan.
'I've got an idea,' he says. 'Let's follow his missus.'

'Is that a good idea?' says Emma.

Neil shrugs. 'Who knows? But I can guarantee you, it'll
piss him off.'

There's no time to discuss the strategy further because the
gate opens, the Evoque runs over the litter on the drive and an

irritated Kate glances at them as she pulls out of the gateway, turns left and guns the car up the road towards Cambridge.

'Okay, why not?' says Emma, pulling out after her. 'Let's hope we can keep up.'

The rain, the crawling morning rush hour into town and the sheer weight of traffic are on their side, and they manage to stay a couple of cars behind the Evoque into the centre of Cambridge. But it turns right and heads out of town on the Cowley Road. Emma puts her foot down to keep up. Her little Nissan wheezes and strains. Then Kate Jessop runs a red-light, and she's away. Emma slaps the steering wheel and curses.

'It was a good idea while it lasted,' says Neil.

'Let's carry on. Maybe we can see where she's gone.'

They have nothing to lose. About a mile on, set back from the road on the left, a line of small industrial units sit behind a row of trees. It looks like the entrance to an industrial estate. Parked in the service road next to the units, there's a white Evoque.

Emma grins. 'We may've just got lucky.' She turns off the road. Stalking Kate Jessop is ridiculous, and will probably get them nowhere, but the chase is energising.

She parks across the road from the Evoque. No sign of Jessop. But a faded board on the wall of the building informs them that this is the distribution centre for St Barnabas's Trust Food Bank.

Bingo.

'This must be where she does her good works to help whitewash her old man's reputation,' says Neil.

They get out of the Nissan and head inside.

The interior warehouse space contains lines of pallets stacked with cans or bags or boxes of everything from toma-toes to rice and pasta. Jessop herself is standing next to an open fridge of milk, talking to a small, stout lady, wearing a clerical collar.

As soon as she sees them, Kate Jessop's brow darkens and she strides towards them.

'What the hell is this about?' she snaps. 'You've been parked outside my house, now you've followed me here. What are you? Press?'

'Didn't your husband tell you?' says Emma. 'We're looking for Dean.'

Her jaw slackens. 'Dean?'

'Your husband's brother,' Neil adds. 'We want him. The police want him. He's a suspect in a murder investigation. And he drugged and raped this lady here. My wife.'

Kate's jaw slackens even more. Her eyes dart around, checking who's listening. Then her flickering gaze comes to rest on Emma.

'I… why on earth would I know where he is?' She's flustered.

'You probably don't,' says Emma. 'But we think Craig might. But he won't speak to us.'

Emma meets her gaze.

Kate shakes her head nervously. 'Craig has nothing to do with him, I can assure you. And if Dean has done you some harm, you have my sympathy. But…'

'You've got an Aston Martin, haven't you?' says Emma.

'My husband has several cars…'

'Dean's been driving around in it. He attacked me, and he's been stalking me.'

'Look, I don't know how you think I can help you.' Her expression has gone from irritation to panic.

'We just want a face to face with Craig,' says Neil. 'Then we're gone. We're out of your hair.'

Kate raises her palms defensively. 'Dean's a thug. But we

have nothing to do with him. It's not Craig's fault his brother is a criminal. My husband's never broken the law.'

Neil chuckles. 'Come on Kate, does anyone believe that? The Jessops are villains.'

'That is completely slanderous. And if you repeat it, my husband will sue you.'

'Yeah, I know,' says Neil amiably. 'And he'll pay his lawyers out of one of his many offshore accounts where he keeps his drugs money.'

Emma puts a restraining hand on Neil's arm. She turns to Kate and says, 'I'm not attacking your husband's reputation. I'm just asking for your help. One woman to another. Dean drugged me, raped me, left me in a flat with the body of a man he'd murdered.'

Kate stares at her for a moment. She pulls out her phone. 'I'll call my husband,' she says. 'If he talks to you, will you leave us alone?'

'If he tells us what we want to know,' says Emma.

As the phone is ringing, she walks away from them into a corner.

The vicar approaches, wreathed in smiles. 'Are you friends or colleagues of Mrs Jessop?' she says. 'Her patronage has absolutely transformed the fortunes of our small organisation. We can help so many more people now.'

Emma gives her a tepid smile. 'We're looking for her help, too.'

'I'm sure you'll get it. She's a generous soul.'

She can afford to be.

Ten metres away, Kate is walking in a small circle as she speaks on the phone. They can't hear what she's saying. A moment later, she hangs up and walks back towards them.

She glances at Neil. 'You know the golf club?'

Neil nods.

'Craig will be in the bar at eleven.'

'Thank you,' says Emma.

Kate gives her a curt nod. 'Whatever his family background, my husband does not support or condone Dean's actions,' she says. 'He doesn't know where Dean is, but he's happy to tell you that in person if it will help you.'

'I'm grateful,' says Emma.

'If it's any consolation,' says Kate. 'I think Dean should be in jail too.'

As they walk away, Neil pats her arm. 'Well done,' he says. 'Now we'll get some answers.'

Emma knows she should be pleased. But she has a curiously hollow feeling in the pit of her stomach.

53

Friday, 9.30am

Boden sits back and watches her young colleague conduct the interview with the manager of the Waterside Park Hotel. In her view, this should've been done at the outset of the inquiry. But the discovery of Howard Sampson's body sent them off at a tangent, and Emma Harris went from victim to potential murder suspect.

Now they're playing catch up. This investigation is like an iceberg with the inquiry only looking at what's on the surface.

Nightmare.

No sooner did they find out that their prime suspect was driving around in an Aston Martin than the vehicle was found dumped in a drainage ditch on the Fens.

Boden wanted to knock on Craig Jessop's door, tell him about his car and question him. But Hepburn vetoed it. A call was made to let him know his car had been recovered;

predictably he said it had been stolen. They'd missed a trick in Boden's opinion.

Hepburn's reluctance to confront Craig Jessop suggests he has some powerful friends, with the Police and Crime Commissioner top of the list. Boden knows she needs to keep her head down, but the stench of corruption is strong and hard to ignore.

Focus on the task.

The Waterside Park Hotel is where Emma Harris was running an event when she was targeted and kidnapped. It's on the outskirts of Cambridge, an old Georgian mansion, modernised and extended, four AA stars and various other upmarket listings. Room rates start at £150 a night.

The manager, Valerie Mitchell, is in her forties, an energetic and capable woman, sharp suit, perfect grooming, who is falling over herself to be helpful.

Why? Boden suspects a combination of guilt and fear for the hotel's smart reputation. A waiter has just brought in a tray of coffee: silver pot, fine china cups.

As Mitchell pours, she says, 'I just feel so awful. I've worked with Emma on several occasions. She's such a lovely woman, and a brilliant events planner. If I'd stayed just a half hour longer…'

'But your shift was over?' says Chakravorty.

'In this job, we don't exactly work shifts. It depends on the workload. Like everywhere in the hospitality sector, we're desperately short of staff.' She frowns and hesitates.

Here it comes, thinks Boden. The thing that's worrying her.

'As I say, we've had staffing problems. And getting night managers has been a particular issue. We use a recruitment agency. They have an excellent reputation. But since Emma told me what happened, I've been trying to get in touch with Jaden.'

'Who's Jaden?' says Chakravorty.

'Jaden was the night manager. I handed over to him about eleven on Monday. He hasn't been with us long. But I've tried to get in touch with him. Left messages. I've asked the agency to contact him. But we've not had a response.'

'Has he been into work since that evening?' says Chakravorty.

'No,' says the manager with a sigh. 'I'm afraid to say no one's seen him. And he had a shift scheduled for last night, but he didn't turn up.'

'What's his full name?' says Chakravorty.

'Jaden Smith.'

'Like the American rapper?' says Chakravorty. 'The actor Will Smith's son?'

Val Mitchell exhales and her whole body seems to deflate. 'Oh dear,' she says. 'You think maybe that's not his name?'

'We'll check it out,' says Boden. 'And we'll speak to the recruitment agency.'

The manager looks like she's about to go into a tail spin. Boden reads this as an honest woman, genuinely shocked and upset, rather than anything suspicious.

'The agency is supposed to check references and… oh my God.' Val Mitchell puts her face in her hands.

'Let's move on,' says Boden gently. 'We want to show you a picture. This man may have been staying here as a guest.'

Chakravorty pulls up a mugshot of Dean Jessop on her tablet. 'Take your time,' she says.

But Mitchell is flustered. 'I feel like this is our fault,' she says. 'I don't know what I'm going to say to Emma. And the idea that someone working here isn't safe…'

'Val, listen to me,' says Boden. 'No one's blaming you, but we need as much information as you can give us. Okay?'

'Sorry,' the manager replies. She peers at the mugshot, but her expression remains blank. 'We have a lot of guests,' she says. 'Plus non-residents who use our restaurant and bar.'

Boden looks at Chakravorty. This is like wading through treacle.

'This one may have been driving an Aston Martin,' says Boden.

'Oh, well we keep a log of guest's registration numbers,' says Mitchell. 'For car park security, obviously.'

Boden smiles. Chakravorty provides the registration number of the Aston, and it takes Mitchell a couple of minutes to find it on her laptop.

'The guest's name is Liam Smith.' She gives Boden a tepid smile. 'That seems a bit of a co-incidence, doesn't it?'

'What else can you tell us about Mr Smith?' says Boden. The manager returns to her laptop. She pulls up several files.

'Stayed two nights. Booked a suite. Paid with a company Amex card.'

Boden scans her. Val Mitchell is so desperate to be helpful that this is where they might come up with a breakthrough.

'The payment details of that would be very useful,' says Boden. She wonders if Mitchell is going to baulk. It's confidential information and her company's policy will be to refuse it without a warrant.

Mitchell gives a diffident shake of the head. 'Well, you are the police,' she says. 'And this is important.'

'Thank you,' says Boden.

By the time they get back to their car, Chakravorty has received an email with all the card details. She forwards them to an analyst in the incident room.

They sit in the car and wait.

Boden lets her gaze rest on a row of evergreen cypresses that divide the car park from what was once the mansion's formal garden. An upmarket hotel, but with enough comings and goings for no one to notice unusual activity. They need to trawl through all the CCTV too, but Boden suspects it won't reveal much.

She sighs. 'This was quite a set up to trap Emma Harris. But why? Dean was in jail two weeks ago. How could he have done all this on his own?'

'He couldn't,' says Chakravorty.

'So who's helped him, and why?'

'Has to be his brother,' says Chakravorty. 'Why won't the boss let us question him?'

'Another interesting question,' says Boden.

Chakravorty's phone chirrups. She answers.

'Yeah.' She listens for a minute, says thanks and hangs up. 'Bank card is a small UK company with a holding company offshore.'

'There's a surprise,' says Boden. 'But the puzzle here is what it's always been. Why were these two things, the rape and the murder, carried out together?'

'To make it look like Howard Sampson's murder is collateral damage for a rape,' says Chakravorty.

'Yes,' says Boden. 'But why?'

Chakravorty shrugs. 'So we're not looking for a motive for his murder?'

'Exactly. And for that to work, Emma Harris had to be involved with Howard.'

'But she swears she wasn't. I thought you believed her.'

'Follow the evidence,' says Boden.

'So she must be lying?' says Chakravorty.

'Looks like that doesn't it?,' says Boden. 'But let's suppose she isn't. However, Dean Jessop and whoever helped him set this up thought she was. And why would they think that? Because it's the information they were given.'

'And where did they get that information?' says Chakravorty.

'Only Dean can answer that. But I doubt Mackie will find him. I suspect he's long gone.'

'So the why remains a random question we can't answer,' says Chakravorty.

'But we should keep asking it,' says Boden.

And the person she wants to ask is Craig Jessop, but she doubts she'll be allowed to do that.

54

Friday, 10.30am

Rachel couldn't face breakfast. The row with her husband remains raw and unresolved, and it feels as if the tectonic plates underpinning their marriage have shifted.

Why is he sticking to the lie?

As a couple, it's usually Simon who extends the olive branch. But that's not what happened this morning. Once he'd showered and come downstairs, Amber was in the kitchen and Rachel had no chance to speak to him alone. His manner was distant, bordering on curt. He apologised for being drunk, said he was late for a meeting at the office and he was gone.

Mother and daughter watched him disappear out of the door. Amber was uncomfortable. She was not used to seeing conflict between her parents.

So Alistair Hepburn's phone call, asking to meet, came as a relief to Rachel.

As she enters the coffee shop, he's already seated in a

corner. It all feels quite covert. His phone call was ambiguous. Just that they needed to talk, somewhere well away from the office. He didn't want to come to the house.

She approaches the table. 'Morning, Alistair.'

He stands up. 'Rachel. What can I get you?'

She sits down. 'Oh, I'm fine. I didn't come to drink coffee.' She's not sure why she has come.

He sits down too and exhales. 'No, well...'

A reluctance to make eye contact?

She decides to take the bull by the horns.

'Okay,' she says. 'Let's be upfront. I used Dean Jessop as an informant, but I avoided all the proper procedures. It's all going to come out, I know that. I'll have to answer to the Independent Office for Police Conduct. But I won't involve you. I take full responsibility. I'll make the argument that I had no choice. They may buy it; probably not. I'll be disciplined.'

After that, her career will limp along and promotion to the most senior ranks will be blocked.

Best to be honest, at least with yourself.

There it is, the unvarnished truth. On the table. He gives her an uneasy smile.

'You've always taken care of your officers, Rachel. I know that and I appreciate it. But loyalty works both ways.'

She smiles back. She's reading nervousness and some hesitancy.

'Why are we here, Alistair? It's not just about that, is it?' she says.

He's smart. Of course not.

'No.' He gets a laptop out of his bag and opens it. 'We've done a forensic analysis of Howard Sampson's phone. There are a lot of texts between him and Simon.'

Rachel shrugs. 'That's to be expected. They were colleagues and partners.'

'In this thread, the question is who are they talking about? I was hoping you might shed some light.'

She scans him. 'Why are you asking me?'

'Because I'm hoping you'll give me a straight answer.'

Has he figured Howard was connected to Craig Jessop?

'Why don't you just ask my husband?' she says. 'I'm sure he'll be happy to help.'

He frowns and sighs. But Rachel's streets ahead of him. This is about motive. He's looking for a motive for Howard Sampson's murder, and he thinks he's found it.

You've got no choice.

'Let's just do it,' she says.

He brings up a document on the screen and turns the laptop round for her to see.

A transcript of the exchange of texts has been created. She skims through it:

Simon: Sorry mate, but we have to be pragmatic.

Howard: I'm concerned about the business.

Simon: Me too. Bottom line, we need big bucks clients like this.

Howard: I disagree.

Simon: So what we going to do? Start making staff redundant?

Howard: It won't come to that.

Simon: It will.

Rachel gets to the end. She has a queasy sensation in her stomach. Her thoughts are reeling. But the best form of defence is attack and she goes for it.

'For chrissake, Alistair. What are you playing at? You want to know who they're talking about here, then ask

Simon, properly and formally. Because my husband has done nothing wrong.'

You hope. He says we need clients like this, so he's only thinking about it.

'No one's saying he has, Rachel. But I just thought you might—'

'No. I have no idea who they're talking about. It could be anybody.'

He can't prove it's Craig Jessop or he wouldn't be doing this.

She glares at him. He sighs.

'I'm sorry,' he says. 'I was hoping you'd take this in the spirit it was intended. I want to help you and Simon.'

What total bullshit!

Rachel stands up. 'Thank you for the thought, Alistair. But I can't answer your question. And the ACC made it pretty clear to me I should stay out of this inquiry. That's what I intend to do.'

She walks out of the coffee shop with all the dignity and strength she can muster.

Be cool. Don't look back.

Once she's out on the pavement, she stops. She needs a moment to steady herself.

Why was Howard killed? It looks like she's got her answer. Her husband was the one in favour of doing business with Craig Jessop. Howard was the one blocking it. And that may well be what got him killed.

How can Simon have been so naïve?

He couldn't have known what Jessop was planning. Howard was his best friend. But afterwards, he put two and two together. That's why he went to Jessop's house and came home so drunk.

55

Friday, 11am

It's a while since Emma's been to the golf club. This is how the membership talk about it, it's just *the* golf club. And in Emma's opinion, it trades outrageously on its supposed exclusivity and social snobbery. The reality is the greens are okay; no true golfer would consider them to be championship quality. It has a small sweaty gym and a middling spa.

But the centrepiece is the bar and restaurant. This pulls in the punters and makes the real money. The food isn't fancy. It's standard bistro fare, with plenty of stodgy puddings to soak up the booze. Emma has always reckoned that close to half the membership, most of whom are male, would keel over with a heart attack if they ever tried to play a full round of golf. It's the venue locally where money comes to be seen, to do business and pretend they're wealthier and more successful than they are. This is why Neil loves it and scrimps on everything else to pay the ridiculous membership fee.

He walks into the bar with a swagger, as if he's coming home. Emma follows. The last time she was here, she got quite drunk, which she'd rather forget.

Craig Jessop is propping up the bar, literally. His elbow rests on it next to a bottle of beer. He's wearing a Ralph Lauren polo shirt and tapered pants, which do little to disguise his paunch. But he's chatting to two other men and they look as if they've actually been playing.

As they approach, Craig breaks off his conversation and steps forward. He offers Neil his hand to shake.

'Mate,' he says with an exaggerated frown. 'This has all been a big misunderstanding. No one told me you wanted to speak to me.' He laughs. 'But then, you know Liam. He knows how busy I am. He was probably trying to protect me.'

So busy he can spend the morning playing golf?

'Probably,' says Neil. 'But we're here now.'

Craig meets Emma's gaze and a pained expression crosses his features. He reaches out a hand towards her. 'Oh Emma,' he says. 'I'm speechless. I'm just so ashamed that I'm even related to this piece of shit. Cause that's what Dean is, no question.'

There's an earnestness in his expression as he squeezes her hand in both of his. 'When Kate told me what happened to you…' He shakes his head and sighs.

'This is the first you've heard of it?' says Neil.

'Absolutely,' says Craig. 'And I can promise you this. We are gonna do something about this.'

'Do you know where Dean is?' says Neil.

'No. He and I don't get along. Never have. We chose very different paths in life. But y'know, I want to do all I can to help, because, after Kate called me, I made a few calls of my own. And I gather that bastard is also suspected of killing your boyfriend, Emma?'

What? Not this again.

Neil shoots her a puzzled frown.

'Howard Sampson was not my boyfriend,' she says emphatically.

'Oh,' says Craig. 'I have some pretty good contacts with the police. That's what they told me. But, y'know, we all call it different things, don't we? You were seeing him and they reckon Dean followed you to his flat, knifed him and attacked you.'

Emma looks into his eyes; iron grey and hard as nails.

So this is how he's going to play it.

'I wasn't seeing him,' she says. 'Howard was my brother-in-law's business partner. Simon Knight? He came to see you, didn't he?'

Craig nods earnestly but ignores the question. 'We're acquainted. So you're saying you and Howard weren't involved? How did this end up happening in his flat, then?'

'I don't know,' says Emma. 'I'd never been there before.'

Craig shrugs. Then he glances at Neil and raises his eyebrows.

It's that look.

Emma's seen it plenty of times before. The look that passes between men when they're cutting you out of the equation. It says: *do we believe this silly bitch?*

Neil shuffles uncomfortably and stares at his feet.

Is he really buying this shit?

Emma can feel the rage surging up through her, and it's hard to contain.

She glares at Craig. 'You say you don't know where Dean is, and you expect us to believe that?'

He raises his palms. 'Okay, I can see you're upset. And it's understandable—'

Here comes the crazy woman card.

'You think we're all stupid, don't you?' She raises her voice and flings her arm wide. 'Half the people in this bar know what you are, Craig. Your family are the biggest villains round here. You made your money as a drug dealer. All the cash you splash in here, all your wife's good works, will never whitewash that.'

Neil is pulling at her sleeve. 'Em, let's not make a scene. Not here.'

He's changed his tune.

'Make a scene? Isn't that what we came to do? To get some bloody answers.'

Craig is watching her with a smug smile. The public accusation hasn't even ruffled his feathers. He knows he's winning because she's lost it. People are looking away; ignoring the outburst.

Just another crazy woman. He's got you.

She folds her arms to calm herself. 'Okay,' she says. 'You want to prove who you are and what you stand for? Turn Dean in.'

'Believe me,' he says sadly. 'If I could, I would. Y'know, Emma, I feel for you and for Howard. He was a decent bloke, I hear. And he certainly didn't deserve to get caught up in the middle of this.'

There's the sting.

'But in the middle of what? What is this? Are you saying Howard died because of me?' she says.

Craig shrugs again. 'Dean is a law to himself. He's violent and unpredictable. I don't know why he targeted you and followed you.'

'He didn't follow me.'

Craig shakes his head wearily. 'How else did he end up killing Howard? It makes no sense to me. Perhaps the police will sort it out. Your sister's a senior officer, isn't she? I'm sure she'll get to the bottom of this.'

He smiles, but the eyes that zone in on her are chilly and merciless. It's a stalemate.

Neil is shuffling from foot to foot. She can feel his embarrassment. All his promises to get some answers from Craig were hot air.

She turns around and stalks out of the bar. There's a ripple of chatter as she goes.

She can hear her ex-husband apologising for her to Craig.

When push comes to shove, he just wants to be one of lads. No change there.

Neil catches up with her in the car park. She rounds on her heel to face him.

'What the hell was that about?' she says. 'I thought you were going to help me. Stand up for me.'

'Emma, you put me in an impossible position. You never told me you were involved with this bloke. I'm walking in there to defend my wife. But you'd already moved on, hadn't you? We aren't even divorced and you'd got yourself a new boyfriend. And you lied to me about it. That makes me look like a right fool, doesn't it?'

'It's not true about me and Howard.'

He huffs. 'Then why is everyone saying that? Craig says that's what the police think.'

'Craig says? How about this, Neil? Craig's lying and I'm telling the truth.'

'Well, you weren't before, were you? You said you didn't know the bloke who was killed.'

'Yeah, you're right. I should've explained it all to you. But I had no idea I was in Howard's flat. I only found out it was him from the police.'

He's not listening.

She can tell from the pouty expression. This is the other side of Neil, the childishness and the jealousy.

'Now I get why you don't want us to get back together,' he says. 'You've moved on. You've been using me. I just wish you'd been honest with me.'

'So, is this your logic?' she says. 'Because you think I was involved in a relationship with another man, when I get raped, you don't want to help me?'

'It's not as simple as that. It's a trust thing. I think you owe me an explanation.'

'An explanation about what?'

'Why Howard? I've met him. I mean, really? He was a weird guy. What was it about? The money? It has to be. I was broke. But he could give you all the stuff I couldn't?'

Emma watches him. He's off on a complete jag of his own. She's frustrated and sad.

He staring at her like a petulant teen.

It's all about him. Maybe it always was.

'You know what, Neil,' she says. 'You can go fuck yourself. Because I don't need your protection.'

She strides off, gets into the little Nissan and starts it up. Neil stands in the centre of the car park, hands on his hips, walking in a circle.

What will he do now? Go back inside and have a drink, probably.

She drives straight passed him towards the exit. She stood up for herself and that feels good. Turning out on to the main road, she heads back into town, adrenaline still pumping. The high lasts for about five minutes, and as it subsides, it's replaced with a creeping paranoia.

She's back on her own. And Dean Jessop is still out there.

56

Rachel's brain is jangling with a mixture of foreboding and fury. The main offices of Lucas, Sampson and Knight are in the Cambridge business park. They've been there two years. The lease is expensive, but Simon's mantra has always been the right brand image attracts the right clients.

Rachel wonders what the hell he thinks the right brand image is if he reckons working for Craig Jessop is a good idea.

If Howard was blocking it, he hasn't crossed the line. Not yet.

She waits in the spacious reception area. It's tasteful; low leather couches, copies of the Financial Times plus an array of periodicals in a fan on the glass coffee table, and, in one corner, an enormous portrait of Howard, set on an easel and surrounded by floral tributes.

The receptionist puts down her phone, smiles and says, 'Mrs Knight, you can go up.'

Rachel thanks her and heads for the sweeping glass stairway that leads up to the mezzanine level. She's never considered the cost of running this place before; her assumption was that as a successful business, they had it covered. But perhaps not?

Her husband has the large corner office at the end of the corridor. As she approaches it, he opens the plate glass door and beckons her in.

Simon looks awful. Like a man who's been on a bender and is waiting for the paracetamol to kick in.

'I'm sorry about this morning,' he says. 'I left a bit abruptly. You're entitled to be annoyed.'

His shoulders are hunched, his eyes bleary and red-rimmed; all his normal confidence and charm have vanished. A man in trouble, but the question is, how much trouble? They're in uncharted waters here, and she's not sure how to react.

Just cut to the chase.

'Why did you think I wouldn't find out?' she says.

'Find out what?' he replies.

'Simon, you need to be honest with me.'

He retreats behind his desk and slumps into the chair. Swivelling it, he forces a smile. 'What makes you think I'm not?' he says.

Her heart goes out to him. She can't help it. She can see the burden he's carrying and the weight of it; even if it is the product of his own stupidity.

Perching in the client chair opposite him, she says, 'Alistair Hepburn has just shown me a transcript of an exchange of texts between you and Howard. From it, I'm deducing that you wanted to take on Craig Jessop as a client, but Howard was blocking it. Correct?'

He purses his lips and shakes his head. Is he close to

tears? 'You're such a fucking smart arse, aren't you?' he says. 'And the gang all sticks together, don't they? Brotherhood of cops.'

Attack is the best form of defence.

She sighs. 'I'm not the enemy. I'm your wife.'

'I don't discuss every business decision with you. That would be absurd.'

'But you wanted to take on Jessop as a client, didn't you? Even though you told me earlier you didn't know him and had never been to his house.'

She watches him struggle. This is how suspects behave. Evasion then aggression as they cling on to their lies.

But this is your husband.

It's heart-wrenching. She waits; she can feel her pulse thrumming. Let the silence do its work. That's the technique.

He pinches his brow between his fingers. 'Okay,' he says. 'I admit, I did go to see him. I was upset about Howard and I wanted to find out if he knew where Dean was hiding out. Since your lot, with all your high tech gizmos, have failed to track him down. We had a few drinks and talked about Howard. He told me Dean's a complete psycho and, apparently he blames you lot for their sister's suicide. So he went after your sister. Howard was just in the way.'

'And you believe that?'

He juts his chin. 'Yes, I do.'

'The fact Howard was stopping Craig Jessop from getting what he wanted, that's irrelevant, is it?'

She can see him grappling with this. He's in denial.

'Look,' he says. 'Craig's a businessman. And he holds the biggest portfolio of development land in the county. He could do a lot of good.'

'How did he get the money to buy all that land?'

'I don't know, Rachel. And frankly, I don't care. He's

probably not squeaky clean. But let's be honest, who is? This is how the world works. Capitalism; there are no rules. That's the bottom line.'

'I think you'll find there are some rules.'

'And smart people find loopholes round them. Tax avoidance, tax evasion, it's all semantics. We exploit gaps in the regulations. That's what our clients expect.'

'And what about money laundering, which is definitely against the law? Was that Howard's objection? Was he worried you'd end up sailing too close to the wind?'

'Howard was just being Howard, obsessing over the details.'

'What if getting in Craig's way got him killed?'

Simon puts his face in his hands. 'No! That's rubbish. It was just a bad co-incidence?' He seems determined to cling to this idea.

'Because of Howard and Emma?'

'Yes. Dean followed Emma to Howard's flat.'

'Is that what Craig's saying? How do the Jessops even know about Emma?'

Simon's gaze slides away towards the window.

He's talked about her.

Her heart sinks.

'Simon?' she says.

'I don't know.' He's being evasive. 'Maybe Craig saw them together at the golf club. Neil's a member. She hangs out in the bar. I've seen her there.'

Rachel shakes her head. She doesn't know what to say or do. She feels numb.

Does he even believe what he's saying?

'You told Craig Jessop that Howard had a thing about my sister, didn't you?' she says.

Simon turns on her. 'Your sister,' he says, 'is a slag. She's one of these women who hangs out in bars, drinks too much and goes home with whoever's interested. She's divorcing one husband and she's looking for the next. It's common knowledge. I know of at least a couple of blokes, both married, that she's slept with.'

Rachel stares back at him; she won't be deflected. 'But you told Craig that Howard was after her, didn't you?'

He shrugs this off. 'Perhaps I mentioned it. I can't remember.'

He gave Craig the key to set this whole thing up.

Her stomach is knotted with tension. She turns to leave.

'Don't you judge me, Rachel,' he snaps. 'You need to be honest. You like the money, the big house, the nice designer outfits. It's not exactly what you could afford on a copper's pay, is it? So don't be a hypocrite.'

Is this the man you married?

'I've never put pressure on you to make money,' she says.

'Really? Isn't that why you married me?'

'No.'

How can he even think that?

'I remember what your mum said to me when we got engaged. The old bitch took me aside and she said, well Simon…' he imitates her mother's affected tones. 'I was hoping for something better, so you'd better make some money if you want to hold on to her.'

His face is twisted with pain.

Is this his excuse?

How did he become this man? And why didn't she notice? They're trapped in a nightmare. She walks towards the door. 'I need time to think. I'll see you at home tonight,' she says over her shoulder.

'This isn't my fault, y'know.' His voice is cracking. 'I didn't get Howard killed.'

'Simon,' she says. 'You take on Craig Jessop as a client, I will divorce you. That's my bottom line. I will not be compromised by you.'

'What right have you got to be so bloody righteous?' he says tearfully.

She knows the answer.

No right at all. Dean targeted Emma because of you.

But she says nothing, and without a backward glance, she opens the door and walks out into the corridor. The adrenaline carries her down the glass stairway and across the reception area. By the time she gets to the car park, the panic is surging up through her and her knees are shaking. Their marriage, their life together, feels like a house of cards. And it's collapsing.

57

Friday, 12.15pm

After she leaves the golf club, Emma drives around aimlessly for a while. On the move, she's safe. The Nissan is like a little capsule. He can't get to her if she keeps moving.

But how long can that work?

It's a ridiculous strategy, but she doesn't know what else to do. And her phone keeps ringing. Missed calls from her sister, which she ignores.

She ends up on the A14, driving eastwards. She's not sure why. It's always a busy road. Traffic is heavy, streams of container lorries heading for the port of Felixstowe. She slots herself in behind a slow-moving cavalcade of trucks. The enormous high-sided lorries hem her in, but she feels curiously protected. It gives her a chance to settle her chaotic thoughts. She's been ricocheting from one thing to the next. What she needs is space to review her situation.

What possessed you to think Neil would protect you?

Predictably, her ex's attempt to rescue her went pear-shaped. Why did she ever accept his help? She should've known better. His petty jealousy was a feature of their relationship, fuelled by the fear that in the end she'd go off with another bloke. He read her behaviour accordingly. And in his mind, it was all about money and his ability to provide it. The fact she'd always worked and had her own business made no difference. In fact, he seemed to regard that as an affront.

How did she end up marrying such a neanderthal?

He was hot? The sex was good?

Perhaps it's hard-wired in women's brains; the male as predator, but also the male as protector. Because of one, you need the other. She hates the notion. She's always refused to be that sort of stupid, dependent woman, hasn't she? Yet she let him muscle in and take charge, and when he did, it was a relief.

You need a man to survive. Isn't that what it comes down to?

Does she believe that? Surely her problem is she keeps picking the wrong ones. Bad choices, the wrong path, mistake after mistake.

Inherent stupidity.

That's the only explanation. And she doesn't learn from her mistakes, which is why she trusted Neil. Again.

Her sister, of course, has always been the smart one.

Must be genetic.

Somewhere just beyond Newmarket, a new idea creeps into her head. When you examine it objectively, what has she got to lose?

She takes the slip road, loops round the junction and heads back in the direction of Cambridge. A plan is forming in her mind. Craig Jessop was lying, that's obvious. But he's a slimeball who wants to look respectable. That's his weak spot. Neil was right about that.

Let's see how he likes being stalked.

He assumes now she'll give up and slink away. Well, he's wrong about that. Everywhere he goes, she'll be there. Maybe he'll even call the police, although she doubts it. She'll use social media, post her story on Facebook.

As she heads back, all sorts of ideas bounce around in her brain. Most of them are mad. Some are outright impossible. But it's energising. Being on the move helps. She won't be beaten by this. The Jessops won't win.

Face the fear. It's the only way.

The fuel gauge is in the red, so she pulls into a service station. The forecourt is busy; she has to queue. But the proximity of other people buoys her spirits even more. It's just an ordinary day. No one is paying any attention to her. There's certainly no sign of him. Just parents who've collected their kids from school, an elderly man who's struggling with the pump, a young couple having an argument. No one's on her tail.

She fills up and buys chocolate and a disgusting energy drink in the shop.

As she gets back into the car, she checks the texts on her phone. Three from Rachel:

Please call me back x

We need to talk x

I'm sorry. I should've believed you. This is all my fault x

She stares at the phone. Even her sister seems to be coming around. But she decides not to phone her back. Yet again, she'll end up dancing to Rachel's tune. She's done that too many times in her life.

By mid afternoon she's driving past Craig Jessop's mansion. The electronic gates are firmly shut. He's insulated by his wealth; at least he thinks he is.

About a hundred metres from the entrance, there's a lane.

She turns into it. On the right is a field of rough grass with a rusty, five-bar gate that doesn't look as if it's been opened for a while. But there's enough space between gate and roadway for her to park the little Nissan.

It's out of sight of Jessop's house, but she can see his gate through the gaps in the hedgerow.

Now what?

The sky is heavy with low, rain-bearing clouds and the light is fading. On the way here, she had a plan. But her brain can't quite seem to grasp it. It's slithered away. Her mood has flipped again. She's feeling less bolshy. Now she's on her own, the idea of just plonking herself outside his gate is less appealing. She doesn't know what to do.

Stalk him? How?

There's that sensation in the pit of her stomach, almost like a pain. It's tension and fear.

Maybe she'll just watch for a while. It's better to be discreet for now. She unwraps one of the chocolate bars and takes a bite.

This rollercoaster of emotions is exhausting. Since she woke up on Tuesday morning with no clue where she was and what had happened to her, her thoughts just seem to fly from one extreme to another.

Some kind of shock?

She considers calling Rachel. But running to her sister is just another kind of defeat. An admission that she's the useless one. When has she ever felt that Rachel was truly on her side?

The absurdity of it all doesn't escape her. Hiding in her car, in the hope of what?

She starts to cry. It's just self-pity and that's something she hates. Her entire childhood, her mother would moan about everything small or large. It's no wonder her father retreated into himself. She wishes she'd talked to him more, got his side of the story. But it's too late; he's been dead for years.

Now here she is, past forty, childless, soon to be divorced, a victim, sitting in a clapped out old car. Her mother's words have turned into a prophecy: *the way you carry on, it's as if you want to fail at everything.*

Her mother's right. She must give off a vibe: failure and desperation. It explains the way she gets treated.

58

Friday, 4pm

Craig Jessop is having a bloody awful day. His back is twinging again, probably due to stress, and his morning round of golf with the deputy chair of the planning committee cost him two hundred quid. The snakey old bugger was over the moon at beating him, so it wasn't all bad. It will pay off eventually in terms of goodwill and favours. But Craig hates to lose. At anything.

To top that, Kate got arsey about Dean. Neil Bryant, a stupid builder he uses occasionally, chased her down to the food bank and Bryant's slag of a wife laid a guilt trip on her. Craig ended up having to talk to them just to calm Kate down. This rankled. Kate rarely involves herself in his business; she knows to leave well alone. That's how their marriage works.

He sneaked a double cheeseburger for lunch without telling her. This made him feel better, but didn't solve the underlying problem: Dean.

Letting his brother continue to run around loose is causing way too much aggravation. It's time the whole matter was done and dusted. He called Liam and told him to bring Dean in.

Craig takes the meeting in his study, which is in a separate wing of the house. This is business, and Dean needs to know that. Also, the girls will be home from school soon and he doesn't want Dean getting anywhere near them.

When Dean walks in, he's jittery; coked up as usual. He walks in circles round the room, like a caged beast, which is basically what he is.

Craig is sitting behind his enormous oak desk; he laces his fingers and smiles. 'I think it's about time we sorted a few things out, don't you?' he says.

'I got no problem with that,' says Dean. 'If you're still narked about the car, you can take it out of my end of the business.'

Craig smiles to himself. This is the moment he's been waiting for. And planning. He glances at Liam. Poker-faced. Not a hint.

'What business would that be?' he says.

Dean flings his arms wide. 'C'mon, I'm talking about the firm. You've kept the seat warm while I've been away. But I'm back now. And there need to be some changes.'

'What did you have in mind?' says Craig.

Dean chuckles, as if it should be obvious.

'Everything you got here, little brother, is because of me and the old man. We built this business. We put you in this swanky house. Without us, none of this exists.'

'I appreciate that, mate. And believe me, I'm grateful. You gave me a start. Let's call it the seed capital. That's why I'm happy to bankroll you going to Spain.'

'Oh, I'm not going to Spain. Not yet. First up, I'm taking back what's mine.'

'How?' says Craig, with a look of mild curiosity.

Dean grins. 'I think you'll find that me and Liam here are more than a match for those schoolboys you've got lurking in the hall out there.'

This is always the good part when you go in for the kill.

Craig sighs. 'Mate,' he says. 'I think you'll find Liam's got more sense than to back you. And those schoolboys'll shoot you before you can even throw a punch.'

Gotcha.

Dean hurls a dismayed glance at Liam, who gives him a regretful grin.

'Sorry Dean,' Liam says. 'Times have changed, y'know.'

Dean's face reddens with fury. His eyes are glassy with the drugs, which Liam has been feeding him. 'What? You lying piece of shit—'

Craig raises his hand. 'Now let's be sensible here,' he says. 'You're my brother. So I want to help you. And to be fair, you've been very useful.'

Dean is glaring at him. Craig can see the anger and confusion; he's trying to work out what's just happened, and he's about to erupt.

But Liam sees it too, and he's quicker. He grabs Dean and forces him onto his knees with an armlock. The lads who've been waiting in the hall pile in. There's a brief struggle from Dean, but he's quickly subdued and placed in a chair. Liam pulls his arms behind him and secures his wrists with plastic cable ties. Trapped in the chair, Dean is fuming.

Tears of frustration in his eyes? What a moron?

Craig stands up. He slots his hands in his pockets and walks round the desk to face his brother.

'Let me explain this to you, Dean,' he says. 'With Liam's help, I set you up. I know you wanted payback for Kelly.'

'She was our sister.'

He's close to blubbing.

'Yeah, and as I told you before, I tried to help her. But in the end, everyone makes their own choices.'

'Why wouldn't you take her kids?'

'You're kidding. You haven't seen them lately. They're feral. And don't give me any bullshit about family. I know about family. I'm the one with a wife and kids. You're just a psycho who can't make a relationship with any woman.'

Dean's face is twisted with rage and hatred, as he struggles to free himself from the chair.

'This is all just your bullshit,' he says. 'You haven't got the balls to stand up, man to man.'

Craig shakes his head wearily. He taps his temple with his finger. 'Brains, Dean. I'm not going to have a fist fight with a dinosaur like you. Why would I? It proves nothing.'

'You might've taken me by surprise,' says Dean. 'Because I trusted this backstabbing piece of shit.' He glares at Liam. 'But how have you set me up? It's all just bullshit.'

'Then let me spell it out for you,' says Craig. 'We needed a little job doing. And a mug to do it. So we let you believe the accountant worked for us.'

Deans huffs. 'Now you gonna pretend he didn't, I suppose?'

Craig laughs. 'Who told you, Dean? I think you'll find it was Liam. You were just too anxious to prove what a hard man you are and to piss me off, weren't you? So you knifed him.'

Dean splutters. 'I'll fucking knife you too.'

Now the penny's dropped.

'I'm sure you would if you could. No one's denying

you're a useful thug, which is what we needed you for. To remove a little problem for us. Namely, the accountant. Now have you got it?'

'Fuck you!' spits Dean.

'Look,' says Craig. 'You carried out the hit for us, and you got the payback you wanted for Kelly. Let's call it two birds with one stone, eh? Now it's time for you to rein in that temper of yours and be smart.'

'You should listen to him, Dean,' says Liam. 'He is trying to help you. You don't wanna go back to jail. You won't survive.'

'You think you can play me?' Dean is still steaming. 'Make a fool of me.' His face is all scrunched up like a toddler having a tantrum.

Craig sighs. He and Liam exchange glances.

'Mate, you was always easy meat,' says Craig. 'Bit of a hot head, not too bright. You're a born loser, which is why you went to jail. The old man told me years ago, way before his stroke, that it'd be me taking over the business.'

'That's a fucking lie,' splutters Dean.

Craig pats him on the shoulder. 'It's over. But you're still my brother, and I made the old man a promise that you'd be taken care of. So here's the deal. You sod off to Spain. You can have a nice life peddling a bit of coke to the tourists. I've got contacts who'll set you up. But you don't come back here. Not ever. Got it?'

'I should rip your fucking head off.'

'But you won't. Don't make me do something I don't want to. For once in your life, Dean, choose the smart option, eh?'

Dean's body is still twitching with fury.

Craig turns to Liam. 'Give him time to calm down.

Couple of drinks maybe. Then once it's dark, take him to the boat. After that, it's up to him.'

Liam nods.

Craig walks out of the room and back towards the main part of the house. He sees his eldest daughter, Ariella, dancing round the kitchen and his heart soars. It reminds him of what matters; the future, not the past. This is his family now, the one that matters.

59

Emma has watched several vehicles arrive; the Evoque that belongs to Kate, a transit van, a black Toyota. But from her vantage point, it's hard to see more than the driver.

She's freezing. She rubs her hands together. The blow heater in the little car only works when the engine is running. It's dark, pitch black across the fields with pools of light along the road in front of the Jessop's house. There the lights are twinkling and inviting. She can see why Neil thinks everything is about money and how much you've got.

He's probably right.

The chocolate is all gone. She feels sour and defeated. Maybe she should just go home and get drunk. She can't sit here all night.

Her mind is drifting. She's never had that ruthless edge, the determination to stick to your guns. Unlike Rachel. She's a waverer who prefers not to upset people. Not that she's all meek and mild. She speaks her mind, loudly sometimes, but then she always ends up having to backtrack. She flips between extremes. What she lacks is composure and a cool head.

That's why your life has turned to shit.

And she's had enough. She starts the engine and turns on the heater. After a couple of minutes, the interior of the car warms up. She moves out of her hideaway and into the narrow country lane. She's about to turn onto the main road and head back into town, when the gates of Jessop's mansion roll open. The black Toyota 4x4 emerges.

Emma is positioned on the other side of the road, about to pull out. She stares at it. The driver is the bloke who Neil spoke to at the gate. The passenger seat is empty, but there are two figures in the back.

The Toyota pulls out and drives right past her. And that's when she sees him. In the back seat, staring out of the window in her direction.

Dean Jessop!

For a split second, their eyes meet. Does he recognise her? He doesn't appear to. His expression is blank.

Some feeling inside, pure rage perhaps, surges to the surface, and the impulse is too strong to ignore.

This is your chance. Go for it!

She hits the gas, pulling out behind the Toyota and narrowly missing a van coming the other way. It honks at her. The Toyota is speeding up, but she puts her foot flat to the floor.

Her heart is thumping in her chest. Now she is the pursuer. But what the hell does she do next?

Just keep up!

The road snakes round the northern outskirts of the city; it becomes residential, so there's a thirty mile an hour speed limit, which makes it easy to cruise along behind the Toyota. They draw up to a set of traffic lights and stop, bringing Emma close enough to read the Toyota's registration number.

Grabbing her phone, she taps the number into a text. Her fingers are cold and stiff. She blows on them, glances at the number again to check it and sends it to her sister. The traffic signal turns green. The Toyota accelerates off the lights and Emma has trouble keeping up. Another vehicle from the inside lane gets between them. But Emma still has them in her sights. She fumbles in her bag for the earpiece of her hands-free and slots it in her ear.

She presses the call button and rings Rachel's number. After a couple of seconds, her sister picks up.

'Emma,' she says. 'I'm so glad you—'

'Listen, Rachel! I've just sent you a text. Registration of a black Toyota. Dean Jessop is in the back.'

'My god, are you sure?'

'I'm following them. I saw them come out of Craig Jessop's place.'

'Whereabouts are you?'

'Heading towards the A14, I think. And I'm worried I'm going to lose them.'

'Okay, don't do anything risky. I'll deal with this. I'm going to hang up.'

The phone goes dead.

Can you trust Rachel?

The question slithers into her mind and out again. But her sister is a cop, and this man killed Howard, didn't he? Of course Rachel will do something.

The slip road onto the A14 has a slow moving queue. Emma is now three cars behind the Toyota. Once they're on the dual carriageway, they'll get in the outside lane and they'll be away. She hasn't a hope in hell of keeping up. The Nissan just doesn't have the speed.

She slaps the steering wheel in frustration.

60

Friday, 5.45pm

Rachel stands in the middle of the kitchen, phone in hand.
When it rang, she was making a side salad. She's attempting
to restore some semblance of order into their lives by
making a family meal. This is for their daughter's sake. But
Amber is not there. It's her and Simon, and he's staring
at her.

He's only just arrived home with his tail between his legs
like a whipped dog. He offered her a bunch of wilting, frost-
ravaged roses. Breath smelling of whiskey, he embarked on a
fulsome apology. It was the shock of Howard's death. Things
had got out of hand. She must realise that he'd never do
anything to undermine her career. He's always supported her.
Always will.

She felt oddly detached. Watching him deploy all his
charisma gave her a desolate feeling. She was wondering how
much you really know anyone, even after twenty years of
marriage.

'Who was that?' he says. 'Bloody Emma? Don't you think you should ignore her? She's caused enough trouble.'

She's caused enough trouble?

She scans him. There's a jitteriness about him. Guilt and booze? Is he still going to insist Emma is to blame for Howard's death?

'She's chasing Dean Jessop,' she says. 'She's sent me his vehicle registration number.'

His eyes flood with panic. 'What? She's deranged. You realise that, don't you?'

Rachel can imagine her sister in that clapped out old car of hers, racing after the Jessops. The other side of reckless is fearless; and Emma is certainly that. It makes Rachel smile inwardly.

She looks at her husband. He's twitchy and nervous.

He knows something.

She ignores him. She scrolls down to find Boden's number and rings it.

'What are you doing?' says Simon.

'I'm alerting DS Boden, so we can get an armed response team after Jessop.'

'Rachel, listen to me.' The desperation in his voice is palpable. 'Just let this go, then our lives can go back to normal. Sometimes it's best to look the other way. You understand what I'm saying?'

Rachel stares at him in disbelief. 'No, I don't. He killed Howard. Don't you want him arrested?'

'I know, but… well, nothing's going to bring Howard back, is it?'

He wants Jessop to get away.

She turns on her heel and walks out of the kitchen. Half way down the hall, Boden answers.

'Jo,' she says. 'I'm sending you the reg of a black Toyota.

323

Probably headed for the A14. Dean Jessop is in it. Witness has confirmed it.'

'Okay, boss' says Boden. 'We're on it.'

Rachel hangs up. As she forwards her sister's text, she notices Simon standing in the kitchen doorway.

How can you live half your life with someone, and yet still not really know them?

He opens his mouth to speak.

'Don't say anything,' she says. 'I'm not sure I want to listen to you right now.'

'Rachel, I'm trying to protect you. Protect us. Our family.'

'Why? Has Craig Jessop threatened you?'

'No. But I know how important your career is and—'

'Don't play that card. This is not about me.'

'Yeah, but it's not as simple as that, is it? For better or worse?' He's frowning.

What's he admitting to here? It hits her in a flash.

It's obvious.

Alistair Hepburn has figured it out. That's why he tried to talk to her.

She shakes her head. 'I'm an idiot, aren't I? It's not that you were considering taking on Craig Jessop as a client, is it? You're already working for him, aren't you? That's what Howard objected to. I'm married to a money launderer and a criminal.'

'Rachel, I'm not a criminal. I'm just an accountant. This is a very grey area, and I assure you no one can prove—'

The National Crime Agency'll be all over this.

'Shut up, Simon! Did you know he was going to have Howard killed?'

'Course I didn't. Don't be ridiculous. Look, Howard was being difficult. The idea was to shake him up a bit.'

'What do you mean?'

'He'd had this thing about Emma for months.'

'What are you saying? The idea was he would be accused of raping Emma?'

He's visibly shaking. 'Well, yeah. Sort of, I suppose.'

Thank god Amber isn't hearing this.

'You suppose? You conspired with Craig Jessop to facilitate the rape of my sister?'

'No course I didn't. They didn't tell me what they were planning. I didn't know Dean was getting out of prison. I knew nothing about him, I swear. The idea was to put a bit of pressure on Howard and make him realise…' He has tears in his eyes. 'Rachel, I realise I've probably been a bit naïve. But please.'

She looks at him. The man she fell in love with, the father of her child.

Naïve?

She's certainly guilty of that herself.

'Is that what you call it?' she says.

'Howard was supposed to get a bit of fright, that's all. They'd take Emma to his flat—'

'Who would?'

'I've no idea. Craig didn't say.'

'And Emma? What about Emma?'

'Oh, come on, Rachel. Since when have you given two hoots about her? She's the bane of your life. What do you care what happens to her?'

The tears well up. She has to fight them. 'You're disgusting,' she says.

61

Friday, 6pm

Dean is zoned out. He's coming down from the coke. He's taken quite a lot; he wanted to be sharp for his meeting with Craig. But it turned into a shitshow. And it was all because of Liam.

Sold out by your best mate.

Part of him still can't believe it. Why would Liam do this to him? The pain of it gnaws at his guts.

Loser, Craig said. Is that what they all think?

Liam is driving. One of Craig's boys is sitting next to him. He's in the back; his hands still bound with the plastic cable ties.

It's dark outside and they're headed up to the coast. A boat has been arranged. It'll dump him in Holland. But then he's on his own. When Liam handed him the backpack, his expression was blank and cold, like he didn't give a shit.

Did he ever?

'Some cash and a train ticket down to Spain,' he said.

'Why would you do this to me?' Dean replied. He didn't get an answer.

He stares out of the window at the blackness pitted with cold lights. Coming down can be bad; he knows this from past experience. He feels like shit. The nightmare is just beginning. His thoughts jangle.

Loser, Craig said. What if it's true?

He glances at Craig's boy. He's cocky and full of himself. Dean used to be like that. Take on anyone. But since he went away, most of the time, he's needed a little something to give him a boost.

Drugs are a mug's game. You sell 'em to mugs. You use 'em, you're the mug.

He knows it. But when you get banged up twenty-three hours out of twenty-four, it gets harder to remember that. And prison gear is cut with all kinds of crap. At least the stuff Liam got him was pure. Best he's had for years.

He doesn't want to ask, but he's getting desperate.

'Hey, mate,' he says. 'You got any more gear? I could do with a little something.'

Liam meets his eye in the rearview mirror. 'No,' he says.

Don't beg.

'Aww, c'mon. Just a little help to get me through.'

'If I had some, I'd give it to you. But I haven't.'

He's lying.

'When did you become such a bastard?' says Dean.

Liam tuts. 'This is a business. You take everything too personally. You always have. It's always about you, how stuff makes you feel. That's your weakness, Dean. It makes you a liability. I'm sorry for how things have turned out. I really am, but it is what it is.'

Dean clenches his fists. He can't listen to that crap. His thoughts are spiralling downwards. He's losing it.

Hold it together. Don't let them see.

Suddenly the Toyota speeds up. Liam pulls out into the fast lane.

'We might have a problem,' he says. 'About a quarter of a mile back, blue lights coming up fast.'

'Could be an ambulance,' says the boy.

'Could be,' says Liam.

An overwhelming fear surges up from Dean's gut. He cranes his neck round and peers over his shoulder. 'Two vehicles,' he says. 'Could be X5s.'

'Shit!' says Liam.

'We don't know they're after us,' says the boy.

Dean gives a hollow laugh. 'Where d'you get him from?' The boy scowls.

'We can't outrun them,' says Liam.

'You haven't even tried,' says Dean.

'Sorry, mate,' says Liam. 'It's you they're after.'

'What you gonna do then?'

'They come up on us, I'll pull over.'

'Fuck me, Liam. They'll just send me back to jail.'

Dean's chest tightens. A sense of panic and despair grips him.

Back inside! No way!

'There's nothing I can do,' says Liam. 'They're Armed Response Vehicles. No way I can outrun them. Stupid to try.'

'Then pull off at this next exit and let me out. Let me make a run for it. At least I got a fighting chance.'

'Na, Craig wouldn't be happy about that. They'll shoot you.'

'They couldn't hit a fucking barn door. You owe me, Liam. You fucking owe me!'

Liam sighs. The blue lights are getting closer. Liam makes a snap decision. He swerves from the outside lane and cuts across and up the slip road towards an elevated round-about with a bridge spanning the road.

'Take the ties off,' he says to the boy.

The boy looks sceptical.

'C'mon c'mon,' shouts Dean.

The boy pulls out a knife and cuts the cable ties binding his wrists, just as Liam pulls up on the roundabout.

'I'm sorry, mate,' says Liam. 'I wish we'd got you away.'

'Whatever,' says Dean. He jumps out of the back of the Toyota.

The roundabout spans both lanes of the dual carriageway. Two X5s are hammering up the slip road towards them with a marked police vehicle, blues flashing, bringing up the rear.

Dean smiles to himself. They've sent an armed response team to bring him in. The real deal. That's what they think they need to take him down.

Too fucking right.

But they'll never get him. He grabs the top railing of the bridge with his left hand and vaults over it and up into the air.

'Free as a bird, Kel!' he screams.

62

Friday, 6.15pm

Boden is in the marked police car, driven by Mackie. As soon as she told the DCI about her phone call from Rachel Knight, he contacted the duty firearms commander and briefed him. The Toyota popped up on the ANPR system and they were able to track the vehicle.

The firearms commander despatched two armed response vehicles to pursue Jessop. Getting a traffic car in place behind the ARVs was problematic because of the fast moving situation. So Mackie and Boden became their back-up.

They caught up with the Toyota just north of Cambridge at Junction 35 on the A14. The vehicle must've spotted them because it turned off the main road. But then it stopped unexpectedly on the roundabout.

Comms were buzzing. Boden was on the phone to Hepburn, who was in the control room with the firearms commander running the op.

An IC1 male got out the back of the Toyota. It looked like he was going to make a run for it.

No one expected what happened next. He vaulted over the railing, launching himself like a skydiver into the stream of traffic still thundering under the bridge. Did he shout something?

'Bloody hell, he's jumped,' exclaims Mackie.

There's a squeal of tyres as a huge container lorry brakes and jackknifes across the carriageway. A thud, as a van piles into the side of it, followed by several cars.

Boden and Mackie's car is stationary on the slip road behind the ARVs.

She gasps with horror. 'Oh, my god! We should've closed the road.'

Hepburn's voice booms from her phone. 'What the hell's happening?'

'He's thrown himself off the bridge into a stream of traffic,' says Boden.

She jumps out of the car. It's hard to even see in the dark and the smoke and mayhem, but still more vehicles are slamming into the back of the pile-up with the sickening crunch of buckling metal and smashing glass.

'We've got an almighty pile-up, boss.'

'I can hear it. Where are the bloody traffic officers?'

'Not caught up yet. We've got to do something.'

She dives back into the car. 'Turn round!' she shouts at Mackie. 'We've got to get down there and across the road to stop this.'

'You got it, Skip!'

Mackie hits the gas, wrenches the wheel around, and with blue lights flashing and siren wailing, they head back down the slip road into the face of the oncoming traffic. Mackie swerves to avoid several vehicles coming straight at them.

Then with a screaming handbrake turn, he pulls the car across the road and stops dead.

The oncoming cars brake, tyres screech, but they manage to stop. Soon the traffic is stationary and backing up. People are putting on their hazard lights.

Boden's heart is drumming fit to burst, but they've prevented any more vehicles hitting the back of the pile-up.

'Shit,' says Mackie. 'That was hairy.'

'Are you alright?' shouts Hepburn.

Boden takes a deep breath. 'Yep. Think we've got it under control, boss.'

Mackie smiles at her; she shakes her head.

Crazy, or what?

63

Friday, 6.30pm

Rachel takes Alistair Hepburn's call alone in the study. Dean Jessop leapt to his death in front of a container lorry, causing a seven-vehicle pile-up on the A14.

Emma was chasing them!

'My sister was following,' Rachel says. 'I don't know how far behind. Could she have been caught up in the crash?'

'It's chaos at the scene,' says Hepburn. 'We don't know yet if there are other fatalities besides Jessop. A major incident has been declared. I'll try to find out about Emma.'

Rachel hangs up the phone. She feels numb. She calls her sister's number; it goes straight to voice mail.

Amber walks into the room. She has a pained expression on her face. 'Are you and Dad all right?' she says.

'No, not really,' says Rachel.

Will they ever be all right again? Doubtful.

'Can I do anything to help?' says Amber. The earnestness in her daughter's face tears at Rachel's heartstrings.

'You were quite right about Emma,' she says. 'We should've simply believed her. That should've been our starting point.'

And now she could be hurt or dead.

'I know,' says Amber.

It should've been the inquiry's starting point too. But maybe Rachel's input had skewed it.

'The man who attacked her and who probably killed Howard was chased by armed police and committed suicide,' she says.

'Oh, my god!' says Amber.

'He jumped in front of a container lorry; the result was a seven-vehicle pile-up. And... it's possible Emma was caught up in the crash, too.'

Was Simon right? You should've just let him go.

Amber is staring at her open-mouthed, but Rachel is immobilised. Her legs seem to give way and she collapses onto a chair. Everything seems to be tumbling in on her.

For the last half hour, she's been agonising over what to say to her sister. How can she explain that her husband's desire to please a wealthy client, whose potentially criminal business he should've never accepted, has led to this cata-logue of tragedies? But underneath it all lurks her resentment and distrust of Emma.

Are you going to admit that? If it's not too late.

'Mum,' says Amber, sharply. And Rachel becomes aware that her phone is vibrating on the desk.

She grabs it. 'Emma?'

'Did you get him?' her sister says.

A cascade of relief floods through Rachel.

'Are you alright?' she says. 'Where are you?'

'Stuck in traffic,' says Emma. 'I kept on their tail to the A14. But I couldn't keep up. I saw the cops come past me.

Now it's just all gridlocked. Someone in front of me was saying a big accident. I don't know how long I'll be here. Nothing's moving.'

Rachel can feel the tears running down her cheeks.

'I'm glad you're alright,' she says.

'I'm assuming he got away.'

'No,' says Rachel. 'He's dead.'

'Oh.' A moment of silence. 'How?'

'It's complicated. But I'll explain when I see you. The main thing is, it's over. He can't hurt you anymore.'

Emma doesn't reply. Rachel suspects her sister is crying too.

'Well,' says Rachel awkwardly. 'Come round. I can fill in the details.'

The details!

'I dunno…'

'Please,' says Rachel. 'We'll have a drink. Possibly more than one. I think you probably need it.'

'I'll see, once I get out of this jam,' says Emma.

'Okay then,' says Rachel. She's damned if she'll beg.

64

Friday, 8.15pm

Boden and Mackie stand in front of DCI Hepburn's desk.

'Firearms commander is talking to the IOPC,' says Hepburn. 'They'll be an investigation. It's a police contact death, so that's standard.'

The adrenaline rush of the chase followed by the inevitable comedown has left Boden limp and enervated.

'We had no clue he was going to jump until he did,' she says.

Hepburn shrugs. He looks bone weary, too. 'No fatalities in the crash, that's something. You did well, both of you. Saved lives. Well done.'

'Scott did the driving,' says Boden. 'I was just a passenger.'

'Credit where it's due, boss,' says Mackie. 'It was Jo's call.'

Hepburn nods. 'The press'll still have a field day. Irresponsible chase. Putting the public at risk.'

Boden scans him and the back of her neck prickles. She knows what's coming. It's obvious from his whole demeanour.

Ask him anyway.

'Where do we go next with the murder inquiry, boss?' she says.

'Our prime suspect's dead. We're not looking for anyone else for Sampson's murder, so it's a bit of a dead end,' says Hepburn.

'What about Craig Jessop?'

Hepburn sighs. 'Let's not get ahead of ourselves, Jo. The two others in the car with Dean have been interviewed. Their story is he was depressed, so they were taking him out to cheer him up. They deny aiding and abetting an offender. Swear they had no idea he was wanted. It's all a pack of lies, but I don't know how we'd prove it. Or connect it to Craig Jessop.'

You knew he's do this!

But Boden is feeling surly. She's just spent an hour at the scene of the accident, helping with first aid until enough paramedics arrived to take over. She's exhausted and sickened.

'So we did all this for nothing?' she says.

The DCI shifts in his chair. 'I wouldn't call dealing with Dean Jessop nothing,' he says.

'But are we assuming he acted alone?'

Hepburn fixes her with a chilly stare. 'You're a good officer, Jo,' he says. 'But you need to learn to quit while you're ahead.'

Keep your mouth shut.

She can't. 'Dean's dead. Closing the file makes it easier for everyone, I guess. Including his brother.'

Hepburn glares at her. 'You forget yourself, Sergeant. This is not your call. But you've had a very stressful few hours, so we'll leave it at that.' He turns to Mackie. 'Take your colleague down the pub, Scott. A successful operation, they'll be drinks for the whole team on me.'

A successful operation? Who's he kidding?

Mackie nods. 'Thanks, boss.' He tugs at Boden's sleeve. 'C'mon, Jo.'

She dips her head to contain her frustration and follows Mackie.

As they walk back into the main office, Chakravorty greets them. She'd remained there to help track the Toyota.

'You all right,' she says.

Boden looks at her hands. Traces of dried blood, and it's not hers. She sighs. 'I suppose I should've expected that,' she says.

'Get real, Skip,' says Mackie. 'What can he do?'

'The Toyota was seen leaving Craig Jessop's house,' she says.

'All that proves is he visited his brother,' says Mackie.

Boden sighs. 'This case stinks to high heaven. Someone wants us to see Howard Sampson's death as collateral damage to a rape. But is it? We know Dean had help to kidnap Emma Harris from the hotel. And Hepburn's just going to shut it down.'

'But we also know why, don't we?' says Mackie.

'Do we?' says Chakravorty.

Mackie gives Boden a knowing look. 'She's such a sweet innocent, isn't she?' he says.

Long may it last, thinks Boden.

'Less of the sweet,' says Chakravorty, belligerently.

'It's politics, Prish,' says Boden. 'If Craig Jessop wanted Howard Sampson dead, then you have to ask why, don't you? And that's a can of worms the DCI is not prepared to open.'

'Because of Rachel Knight?' says Prish.

'He must suspect her old man's involved in this, but he's not going to be the one to wield the knife,' says Mackie.

'Do you think it'll ever come out?' says Prish.

'Who knows?' says Boden. 'But Hepburn's decided it's not going to be him.'

'Out of loyalty?' says Prish.

'Or self interest,' says Boden. 'Depends on your point of view. Come on, let's go and get this drink.'

65

Friday, 10pm

It was Emma's plan to go home, maybe get a takeaway en route, open a bottle of wine and watch trash TV. But curiosity gets the better of her. She tries to get Dean Jessop out of her mind, all the Jessops in their fuck-you mansion, but she keeps wondering how he died.

Did the cops shoot him? She needs to know.

Still, as she rings her sister's doorbell, she wonders if this is a good idea. The last thing she needs is Rachel being sanctimonious. Or worse, walking in on a cosy family scene.

Amber opens the door. Her niece has tears in her eyes. She envelopes Emma in a hug.

'Oh Emma,' she splutters.

It was worth coming just for this.

Rachel is hovering in the hallway behind her. No sign of Simon.

As Amber releases her, she faces her sister. Rachel looks uncharacteristically nervous.

'Are you okay?' she says.

This is awkward.

'I will be,' says Emma. 'When I get that drink you promised me.'

Rachel takes her arm. 'Come on then,' she says, and leads her into the kitchen.

On the counter there's a bowl of salad, a cheeseboard, some charcuterie and a sourdough loaf.

'We didn't know what time you might get here,' says her sister, by way of explanation.

'You shouldn't have gone to any trouble,' says Emma.

All this politeness. We're like strangers.

Amber gets a bottle of Chablis from the fridge. 'This is the one you like, isn't it?' she says.

Emma nods and watches her niece open the bottle and pour.

'So did they shoot him?' says Emma abruptly.

'No,' says Rachel. 'He was chased and cornered. He jumped from a bridge across the A14 in front of a container lorry. The lorry tried to swerve, and there were a number of casualties in the resulting multi-vehicle crash.'

Emma is silent as this sinks in.

A chain of events you set off.

'We were worried you might've ended up in the pile-up too,' says Amber.

'My God,' says Emma. 'If I hadn't given you the registration number... I was just so determined to get him.'

'They'll be an inquiry. They probably should've closed the road before moving in on him.'

'So one of your officers'll carry the can.'

'Not necessarily.'

Emma accepts a glass of wine from Amber and sips it.

She doesn't know what to say.

'Don't feel bad,' says Rachel. 'No one was killed apart from Jessop.'

How can she not?

'You're more used to this kind of stuff than me,' she says.

'You don't get used to it,' says Rachel. 'You just learn to not to show your feelings.'

Emma looks at the food on the counter. All she's eaten since breakfast is a couple of chocolate bars. She's beyond hunger. But this will do her more good than a Chinese takeaway. And it's a distraction.

'Can I help myself?' she says.

'Of course,' says Rachel. She goes to the cupboard and gets out some plates. As Emma takes some salad, Rachel cuts slices of sourdough on the breadboard. Amber scoots around in the background, getting salad dressing from the fridge and some butter.

On the surface, it's such a normal scene, the sort of thing that they've done many times before. Except everything is different. And there's a tension in the air you could cut with a knife.

'Where's Simon?' says Emma.

Rachel glances at her daughter, then she says, 'Simon's gone to stay in a hotel.'

This doesn't make sense to Emma.

'Oh,' she says. 'Why?'

'We're having some time apart,' says Rachel. 'We've both got a lot of thinking to do.'

Emma glances at Amber, who's busily spreading butter on a slice of bread.

'You mean you're splitting up?'

Amber puts down her knife and hurries out of the room.

Rachel sighs. 'Obviously, this is difficult for Amber. She really loves her dad.'

'And you don't?' says Emma.

Rachel takes a moment to consider her words. 'I'd always assumed we shared the same values,' she says. 'Turns out I was wrong.'

'What d'you mean, values?' says Emma.

'Simon may have been laundering drug money for Craig Jessop. It involves moving money between untraceable offshore accounts. He's being very cagey about it, and all he's prepared to say is that I shouldn't worry, because no one will ever prove it.'

'Shit,' says Emma.

'I think Howard was against this and that brought him into conflict with Craig Jessop.'

It takes Emma a moment to process this. What is Rachel actually saying?

'Is that why… Howard was murdered?'

'I'm guessing there was some kind of set up,' says Rachel. 'Howard was murdered. You were raped to cover it up. So no-one would suspect the real reason for Howard's murder and point the finger at Craig. But with Dean dead, I doubt it'll ever be proved.'

'But—'

'Why you?' says Rachel. 'Because you're my sister, and Dean Jessop had a grudge against me. And also because Simon let the Jessops know Howard was interested in you.'

Emma struggles to get her head round this.

'It was never really about me?' she says.

'No. You are a completely innocent victim.'

'But you were convinced that I was having an affair with Howard, and I'd got him killed.'

'Emma, I don't even know what to say to you. I couldn't be more sorry.'

'Will anyone go down for this?'

'Most conspiracies are notoriously hard to prove.'

'So Simon's safe?' says Emma. It's hard to keep the bitterness out of her voice.

'If you think I'm going to protect him…'

'What are you going to do?'

'I'm leaving the police.'

'Why?'

Rachel gives a cynical laugh. 'You're asking me why?' she says. 'How can I carry on? I'm not fit to do the job. What kind of detective am I that I didn't see what was going on under my nose?'

'Did Simon know what they were going to do to Howard?'

'I doubt it. He was genuinely upset. But after the event, he soon figured it out. I'd like to think he just got in over his head.'

Emma takes a large mouthful of wine. She knows she could easily down the whole glassful in one.

'Can you ever forgive me for not believing you?' says Rachel.

Can you?

'Would you, if it was the other way round?' says Emma.

Rachel dips her head. 'I hope I would.'

Emma considers this is. Does it matter what Rachel would do?

No. This is about who you are.

'Well, I'll think about it,' she says.

'That's all I ask. Thank you.'

She can see Rachel swallowing down the tears as she tries to cling on to her dignity.

You know what that feels like.

'Are you going to divorce him?' she says.

'Probably,' says Rachel. 'I'm still in shock. How could he

feel that any of this was okay, Emma? Part of me just can't believe it.'

Rachel has tears in her eyes.

'What are you going to tell Mum?' says Emma.

'As little as possible.'

Emma sighs. She looks across the kitchen to the windows and the dark garden beyond. Putting her glass down, she says, 'I'm going home.'

'If that's what you want. Amber would love you to stay.'

Emma chuckles inwardly.

Typical Rachel. She can't help herself.

'I'll call you,' she says.

Rachel follows her out into the hall. Emma wonders if her sister will ever get over this, if either of them will.

'Don't make a snap decision about the job,' she says.

'Why not?'

Emma shrugs. 'You're good at what you do. Don't let Simon rob you of that.'

66

Saturday, a week later.

Emma drives her little Nissan into the car park at the Waterside Park Hotel. She parks it near the entrance next to a sleek Maserati. The little car is still wheezing and juddering, but it goes, and Emma has changed her attitude to it. It could be argued that it saved her from driving into the back of that terrible crash. She's still trying not to think about that.

Or him.

For most of the last week, she's been ignoring phone calls. She's stayed at home, although she called in a locksmith to put bolts on her french doors. Most of her bruises have faded; the cut on her head is healing.

Towards the end of the week, she received an email from Val Mitchell inviting her in for a chat.

She hesitated at first. But now here she is. She's ironed her silk shirt and polished her shoes. Approaching the door to the hotel, she has a fluttery feeling in the pit of her stomach.

You can do this.

A man coming out of the hotel steps back and holds the door open for her. She thanks him politely. And she's inside.

Val is by the concierge desk and she's been on the look-out. She moves forward to greet Emma.

Please please, don't say are you alright?

Emma's fed up with being asked. Most people don't really want to know the answer.

But Val smiles and says, 'You're right on time. Thank you for coming.'

They head down the wood panelled corridor towards the manager's office.

'I've been giving this some thought,' says Val. 'We're planning to hold a wedding fayre in the ballroom in the spring. I think we can fit in up to fifty exhibitors. We've already had quite a lot of interest. But we need an organiser to run it. It's quite a big project. But I immediately thought of you.'

'Oh,' says Emma, taken aback.

Val smiles. 'And before you ask,' she says. 'This has nothing to do with what happened. I was planning to ask you before that. I need someone with your experience and networking skills. Would you be interested?'

'A wedding fayre?' says Emma. 'Sounds exciting.'

'Yes,' says Val. 'And lucrative. For both of us. I talked to the regional manager about this and we both agree, you're perfect for the job.'

Back in the saddle?

'So what do you say?'

Emma smiles. She takes a deep breath. 'I say great. Yes. Let's go for it.'

LEAVE A REVIEW

If you feel like writing a review, I'd be most grateful. The choice of books out there is vast. Reviews do help readers discover one of my books for the first time.

Scan QR code to review See Me Fall

A MESSAGE FROM SUSAN

Thank you for choosing to read *See Me Fall*. If you enjoyed it and would like to keep up to date with my latest book releases and news, please use the address below.

susanwilkins.co.uk/sign-up/

*Your email address will never be shared, and you can unsubscribe at any time.

Scan QR code to go to Susan's sign up page

Do get in touch and let me know what you thought of *See Me Fall*. I love hearing from readers. You can message me at susanwilkins.co.uk/contact/

Scan QR Code to go to Susan's contact page

BOOKS BY SUSAN

The Informant

The Mourner

The Killer

It Should Have Been Me

Buried Deep

Close To The Bone

The Shout + The Right Side Of The Line (Free when you sign up to Susan's newsletter)

A Killer's Heart

She's Gone

Her Perfect Husband

Lie Deny Repeat

See Me Fall

BOOKS CONT.

facebook.com/susanwilkinsauthor

twitter.com/SusanWilkins32

instagram.com/susan_wilkins32

ACKNOWLEDGEMENTS

Huge thanks to Colin James and Graham Bartlett for their expert advice on how the police would proceed. Some things have been altered slightly in the interests of drama.

In my career as an author, I've received the help and support of too many people to mention. The community of crime writers is friendly, welcoming, and nowadays global. Learning from those who have gone before is essential for any writer.

Big thanks to my Reading Team for their diligence and valuable feedback.

Thanks also to Jenny Kenyon for her unwavering support.

Last, but not least, thanks to Laura Wilkinson for her sharp editorial eye on the manuscript and her many suggestions for improvements.

But getting the books out into the world would be impossible without my partner in crime, Sue Kenyon. I just write the books. She does everything else.

Published by Herkimer Limited in 2023
Summit House
170 Finchley Road
London NW3 6BP

Scan QR code to go to susanwilkins.co.uk

ISBN 978-1-7392493-1-1